SECOND
TIME AROUND

Larry Signy

First paperback edition

ISBNs:
978-1-80541-537-4 (paperback)
978-1-80541-538-1 (hardcover)
978-1-80541-536-7 (eBook)

SECOND TIME AROUND

To June—you never lose it.

Some of the events in this story are based on fact, others aren't.

Which is which? Just guess (if you can be bothered) and weave your own thoughts and ideas, as I did. I just hope my imagination fuses together as a whole.

This is not the story of any living person or persons. It is the story of Rose and Billy, two "ordinary" people who are very much deeply in love with each other.

I hope you can enjoy their happinesses—while they last.

Introduction

It was a sunny but cold early winter's Thursday morning when Billy Saunders was admitted to Peace Hall Care Home. He had been in a nearby hospital for three weeks before being put on a stretcher and moved on a fifteen-minute journey from there to the home in the back of an ambulance, then taken in a wheelchair into the home pushed by a Thai carer with a nurse holding his hand. He sat in the chair looking blank and not really understanding what was going on.

Billy was suffering from advancing mid-term Alzheimer's, a form of dementia that was slowly eating away at his brain.

Because of the disease he did not know his wife was already a resident of Peace Hall and was living in the next room.

Chapter 1

It was just another Saturday night at the dance club. A very normal Saturday night in June in a very ordinary dance hall in a London suburb after a hot summer's day.

The dance was held in a large disused barn-like building in the centre of a growing clump of factories and warehouses; its walls hastily lined with a silvery glitter paper, with a few gold stars tacked on haphazardly.

The club was dark apart from the flashing spotlights blazing reflections on and off the walls and onto a large glitter ball hung from the ceiling over the dance floor, rotating slowly and strobing lances of light over the couples below it; the coloured baffles giving a near-hypnotic haze to it all. It was a popular and fashionable venue for everyone, who invariably (and mistakenly) thought it romantic and "really living".

A small group of semi-professional musicians sat on a low dais at one end, most of them wannabes who could just about put out the popular dance songs of the day for the crowds of young people lined up on opposite sides of the dance floor. As they ranged raggedy through the hit songs of the day, a few couples shuffled round holding each other in alternate bright lighting or near pitch darkness, but in the main, the line of boys stood at right angles to the band along one side of the building, ogling the matching line of girls opposite them, too shy to cross over and talk to them. Between sets, a few did take up the dares of their friends to cross over and ask someone for a dance.

Except for the couples who went regularly for a weekly night out, the club was mainly a place where young men and girls went to pick up or be picked up by someone of the opposite sex.

As a few managed it and the couples started to build up on the wooden dance floor, a small group of girls crossed over and tried to sell raffle tickets for some charity or other. One of them approached a small gang of young men-boys. For one of the girls in the group, it was her first time at the dance and she had been persuaded by a girl friend to go that night because it sounded different and more exciting compared to their usual Saturday night cinema. She was young and although she knew the actual facts and details was still inexperienced, artless and completely unsophisticated. She thought it a good opportunity to sell the tickets.

"Hello, would you like to buy…" she began as she reached the boys, and most of the lads looked away. All except one.

He was wearing the double-breasted suit, dark grey with a faint stripe, and the blue tie he wore for work, while she was in her favoured wide swirling dirndl dress with short sleeves revealing healthy-looking forearms and a narrow-belted waist with a tight bodice over her small well-shaped breasts.

Light was reflecting from the slow turning glitter ball hanging from the ceiling, but it was not enough to let her see his face, so she hardly noticed whether he was handsome or not as he turned to face her after she had tapped him on the shoulder.

"I'm selling raffle tickets for—"

Unlike her, he saw her pretty innocent face, and without artifice or knowing why, he instinctively cut her short and said the first thing that came to mind. "I'm sorry, but I haven't got any money on me," he said. He never knew what made him say it or go on. "But I'll tell you what. Give me your phone number and I'll call to buy one tomorrow."

In all innocence, the girl naively gave him her number, and reached in a sling bag to get a pencil, so he could jot it down on a battered cigarette packet he took from his jacket pocket.

As he gave the pencil back, he told her, "I'm Billy."

She smiled shyly. "Rose."

He gave her a cheeky grin back and watched her as she walked away to sell her tickets to another nearby group, absent-mindedly putting the cigarette packet back in his jacket pocket. She had a very feminine walk, her steps measured and her arms held slightly away from her body.

Billy's eyes followed the girl as she rejoined her friends and, although he couldn't know it, his life suddenly took on a mirror image of that large circulating glass ball above them sending slivers of light flashing down on the dancers. It would spin in continually changing flashes of excitement for the rest of his life.

"You've scored there," said one of his friends, and then they both looked for other girls to approach, both knowing that they would not have the courage to do anything if they did spot one.

It was just another normal Saturday night at the dance hall.But it was the day that Billy Saunders and Eliza Rose Baker first set eyes on each other.

Chapter 2

Eliza Rose had been given her first name by overenthusiastic parents after the Bernard Shaw character in *Pygmalion,* and her second after a well-known musical hall singer of the day. She hated Eliza, and especially when it was cut to Liza or Liz and used Rose instead. She knew that was a Latin name meaning joy, and that gave her pleasure, but even then, she disliked it when people called her Rosie.

She had a jaw-dropping prettiness, with well-balanced features, not yet old enough to be beautiful but with prominent high cheekbones, a deep forehead, and brunette hair cut in a rather long bob that lay behind her ears and bounced on her shoulders.

She had very fair, almost translucent skin, and her eyes were green with very fine, light eyebrows above each. Her slim figure made her seem taller than she was—in fact, in her usual mid-heel court shoes she was exactly the same height as Billy—and her smallish bust gave her a very feminine almost boyish look. She was well spoken, with a well-modulated voice.

People often told her how beautiful she was, but Rose herself never thought of herself that way. She was just... well, just Rose. She had no conceit or vanity at all.

Her upbringing had been normal for girls of her time. She learnt to cook and sew from her mother, studied obediently (and willingly) at school, and talked adolescent romantic dreams with her several girl friends.

There was nothing particularly special about her young life, although she did, rarely, "rebel" against the conventions of the day: playing football with the boys in the school playground, once deliberately using the word "bloody" in front of her father (and being roundly told off for using such foul language), and once even trying to smoke, although she threw the cigarette away after three puffs feeling giddy, nauseous and with an unladylike urge to spit. It was a normal, sedate, fairly naive, sheltered, happy-on-the-whole upbringing.

Rose was intelligent and self-contained, and was a good pupil both at primary level and in the more senior secondary schooling—not naturally clever but always willing to apply herself, concentrate and work very hard. As a result, she was always in the top group and did well, and even later when she went to the technical college where she was now.

She was completely different to Billy, who had actually been named Phillip William. That could have been shortened to Phil or Will, but Billy always seemed more appropriate and a better fit for his ever-cheery personality. His accent was not quite Cockney, but with a twang that-was undoubtedly that of a definite Londoner.

At school, mind, he had sometimes been referred to as Silly Billy despite his natural intelligence, but a few playground scraps soon rid him of that childish sobriquet, and as he grew up even his parents ignored the names they had given him and called him Billy. It suited him far better—he was just Billy, a youthful never serious young man-boy.

In appearance, he had grown to a slightly better than medium height, his body filling out manfully, topped with an open face highlighted by hazel coloured eyes under an intelligent forehead, and with a mop of thick jet black hair with a side parting Brylcreemed slickly back and a curled quiff from left to right that continually fell over his eyes despite the gel he applied every morning.

He had a darker, almost Mediterranean skin that looked permanently tanned, and he usually had a smile on his lips and in his eyes, and he was always ready with a jokey answer to even the most serious question.

Unlike Rose, Billy did not like school and was a bit of a dissenter—always involved somehow with any prank or misdemeanour that was going on, often as its instigator and leader. He was naturally anti-authority and hated the thought of conformity, and his teachers disliked him because he was cheeky and always questioned not only their control but often their knowledge. He usually got himself out of trouble with a natural charm, although his path to the headmaster's office for further punishment was a well-trodden one.

On the day after the dance, Billy felt listless and moped moodily around at home in his shirt sleeves, an unformed thought at the back of his mind that the girl he had met at the dance was rather nice. There was the same carnal desirethat all young men carry with them, and he was desperate to find a girl, simply because none of his friends had one, and he wanted to be able to boast. But something nagged at his subconscious that there was more to it than that.

Rose, meanwhile, was also thinking about that "rather nice boy" she'd met on Saturday night. She remembered that she had given him her phone number, and she hoped he would call. She told her best friend Mary Ecclestone about it on Sunday afternoon.

"I can't get him out of my mind," she said. "I don't know what it is about him, but I feel all tingly when I think about him."

Mary, who couldn't remember Billy, smiled. "It sounds like true love," she replied. "Better start thinking of your wedding dress."

Rose giggled, and for the next hour they played a dream game, both suggesting ideas for dresses—both for Rose as a bride and Mary as bridesmaid—multi-tier wedding cakes (Mary's fourteen-layered cake with pink icing was the most outlandish) and a champagne reception. Rose only stopped the make-believe when Mary started talking of the honeymoon and the first night.It was all very schoolgirlish, and they sniggered a lot.

But that night, Rose dreamt about it in frightening clarity.

Then, on Monday, Billy did phone.But it wasn't until he dressed in his work suit that he found the crumpled cigarette packet in his jacket pocket. There were no cigarettes in it, and he was about to throw it away when he looked at it and suddenly had a very clear picture of the girl who had given him her telephone number. She had been very pretty.

He thought about it during the day, and after work, around half past five that evening, he phoned Eliza Rose as promised. She was not back from college when he called, and her mother told Billy she had an evening shorthand class and would not be home for some time.

Billy took a chance. "Can you tell her Billy will meet her by the telephone boxes outside the underground station at seven tomorrow night?" he said, explaining that he had promised to buy a raffle ticket from her.

The girl's mother said she would pass the message on, but unfortunately, she was severely hard of hearing, and when Rose came home (Eliza as her mother still called her) the message was confused. She was going out with a boy called Willie at the time—a name that always made her giggle—and she could not really be sure if she was going to meet Willie or Billy, the boy she had met on Saturday.

Billy arrived at the meeting place early, having carefully pressed his normal regulation grey flannel trousers (with turn ups), brushed his "best" light blue sports jacket, and selected a plain dark blue tie in accordance with then current convention, and hoping that the girl would be there. He had given himself a second-of-the-day splash of deodorant, with his hair Brylcreemed and parted in an immaculate straight line on the left side.

Eliza Rose did arrive, dead on time, expecting to see her current date, Willie. She was surprised, but somehow a little more pleased, when it turned out to be Billy, the boy from the dance. She was, in fact, delighted and her smile seemed to light up her whole body.

Billy looked at her as she approached, again taking in her youthful beauty and, in particular, her laughing eyes. She had put on a minimum of make-up, just a little lipstick and eye shadow, and her hair lay neatly in a shoulder-length bob with a more casual parting on the right than Billy's. She was wearing a plain white blouse with three-quarter-length sleeves and a dark blue knee-length skirt, and he thought she was the most beautiful girl in the world. As it turned out, that feeling was to stay with him all his life.

Rose saw Billy and was thankful that he was as good-looking as she remembered, and when they met, she instantly noted the sweet masculine smell of his deodorant, which lingered in her nostrils. She rather hoped it would not drown out her own perfume "borrowed" from her mother's bedroom dresser.

They said formal hellos, and Billy immediately realised that Eliza Rose's quiet and seemingly shy appearance covered several layers of her personality, and he somehow felt from the start that she would open up to him like an exquisitely beautiful deep red rose after which she was named.

She looked younger than her seventeen years, and he knew instantly that he could like her, although like all boys his age, it had been a subliminal carnal instinct that had made him reply as he did when she approached him in the dance hall.

For her part, Rose realised that Billy was more than quite good-looking, not in a conventional film star way, but with a mischievous look and features that made him seem interesting.

After a moment or two of embarrassed silence, he asked what she wanted to do.

"Oh, anything. I'll leave it to you," she said.

"There's a new Fred Astaire movie at the Rialto..." He used movie rather than film as he thought it sounded more sophisticated. "I'd quite like to see it. Would you?" He paused, and before she could answer added, "If you haven't seen it, of course."

Rose had actually seen it the previous week, but readily agreed and she said she would love to go, and they set off towards the cinema. Both were quiet as they walked away from the busy station area, but Billy's mind was trying to work out things to say. For some reason he was tongue-tied, and his normal gift of the gab was absent.It took about ten very awkward minutes before they arrived at the cinema.

Billy made a point of buying two of the most expensive seats, thinking that he would probably have to do without lunch at the end of the week, and they were shown to the back row by an understanding usherette, shining her torch obviously across the other couples entwined along the row.

The musical was lively, full of good songs, good singers, good dances and good dancers, and although she had seen it before, Rose enjoyed it again. When it finished, Billy suggested going for a coffee at a small cafe nearby, and they walked there quietly.

After they had ordered two cappuccinos, Billy tugged at his tie. "I *hate* wearing them," he told her. "Do you... would you mind if I took it off?"

"Of course not," she replied.

He tore off the tie and shoved it awkwardly in his jacket pocket, with Rose reaching across as he did so to straighten up the corner of a shirt lapel that had turned up at the edge.

The two coffees arrived, and they sat and sipped them, enthusiastically discussing the film they had seen.

Rose laughed and smiled a lot, and Billy was delighted that she shared his rather off-beat humour, although hewas much quieter than usual throughout the whole evening—his usual exuberant nature and one-liner quips blunted as he became tongue-tied, partly because of his inexperience with girls and partly because he didn't want to say anything that would go down badly with Rose.

For her part, Rose found that, although Billywas quite reticent over-all, there was something about him that appealed to her. She realised almost instinctively that there was an inherent shyness, and she liked it.

After about three-quarters of an hour of bumbling along, Billy noticed that Rose had taken a couple of surreptitious looks at her slim wristwatch, so he suggested they leave the cafe. He walked her home slowly, leaving her at the end of her cul-de-sac road.

"I hope we can meet again," he said, almost formally.

"Oh, I'd like that," she replied rather too quickly. "Give me a call."

She walked down the road, and Billy watched her until she got to her front gate, where she turned and waved happily at him. Then she went to the front door and disappeared from view.

Once she had gone, he walked away, and seeing a bus at the stop just down the road, he ran forward and boarded it just as it set off again, in a hurry to get to Il Ristorante Italiano, a small trattoria fairly near the railway station where he and his friends always met to wind up the day. It was one of the many new Italian-style coffee bars that were springing up in London in the early 1950s.

They had been meeting there every evening for about eighteen months, getting together around 10 after their various evening exertions and sitting over cooling cappuccinos until it closed, talking of nothing but mistakenly thinking the late night was a sign of youthful Bohemian rebellion.

They were not big spenders, but the proprietor, known to the boys as Guiseppe although his real name was Gaetano, liked them in their corner because they gave a young, vibrant mood to his cafe. They were well behaved and rarely rowdy, and on the few occasions they were, they quietened down when he asked. It was their headquarters, where they talked over the events of their days and evenings to a backing of popular music playing non-stop from a bulky radio set behind the counter. Giuseppe, a rather rotund man with pure white wavy hair and a round face constantly lit up by smiling lips and eyes, was almost a cartoon replica of a genial Italian, and he would carefully adjust the sound to match the varying mood in the restaurant.

When Billy walked in, the others were already there: his best friend John (Jonno) Frost, Frank Pierce, Ging(er) Bennett and Terry Fox. With Billy, they called themselves the Five Caballeros, a play on words on a current Walt Disney animated film *The Three Caballeros*.

They were a disparate group really, but in their separate ways alike in that they were all as light-hearted as all young men in their early twenties, craving fun without responsibility and the adventures of life without ever achieving them. Billy was the joker in the pack, always ready with a quip or a smart put-down.

They would meet up after their various evening activities to sit drinking their cappuccino coffees, usually until around one in the morning, idly taking the rise out of each other, talking about girls, discussing football, talking about girls, complaining about some perceived ill that had befallen one of them, talking about girls, lusting after

Hollywood film stars and talking about girls. It was normal behaviour for boys leaving adolescence; it was growing up.

Like Billy, Jonno had his dark hair sleeked back with Brylcreem, but he had no parting or quiff. He was medium height, with broad rugby-player shoulders and thin-rimmed glasses, and was the quietest one of the quintet, as opposed to Frank, who was loud, brash and pushy. Frank was almost six feet tall and carried his blond-haired head high and bent slightly backwards, almost as if he was looking down his aquiline nose. Terry was a handsome lad, slightly the oldest—by about five months—and thought of himself as the brains of the gang, and the last of the group, Ging, was fairly nondescript, average in every way and with the remains of adolescent acne still on his cheeks and chin.

They were sitting at a table immediately to the left of the door, but they ignored Billy and carried on talking as he walked in. It was left to cafe proprietor Giuseppe to greet him.

"Hello, Billy," he called. "Cappuccino?"

Billy nodded and Giuseppe said he'd bring it to the table.

Billy joined the group, and Terry moved out of the way to make room for him.

"A perfect gentleman," said Billy.

"Nobody's perfect," replied Terry.

"Yeah, they are," butted in Ging. "But a gentleman's only someone who rests on his elbows when he's at it." He leered, and the others sniggered.

Billy sat as the coffee arrived.

"How did it go?" Frank asked him. "Does she?"

"She's not that kind of girl," replied Billy.

"Drop her then and get someone who's useful," said Frank.

"Oh, shut up. She's a nice girl."

"Nice girls are called mothers," said Terry.

"What you need is a girl who's happy to drop her knickers," persisted Frank.

"Or doesn't wear any..."

"Did you try?" said Frank.

"Nah, not Mr Innocent," said Ging. "He can hardly raise a smile." With his appearance, Ging was the last one who should have commented. He did not look at all like someone a young girl would date.

"You lot are obsexed with sess," replied Billy, hoping to shut them up but using a phrase they often joked between them to try to lighten his irritation.

"There, but for the grace of God, goes God," cut in Terry.

Frank was lasciviously determined to carry on his theme. "Was it easy to undo her blouse?" he asked.

Billy wished they would all shut up. He had often joined in similar conversations, but this felt different for some reason. He wished the others would change the subject.

"About that last question, don't you mean getting a grip?" said Terry, with a huge leer.

"Oh, shut up, all of you," said Billy sourly. "Just give over. I'm going to get a brioche. Anyone else want one?"

"Blimey, that's what nice girls get you to do: spend your money," quipped Terry.

Billy got up and walked to the counter. It was just the group's normal banter, but this time he was annoyed with his friends. He just wanted to think of Rose as the sweet innocent girl he had been with earlier in the evening.

When he got back to the table, the conversation had drifted to other inconsequential things, although Ging continued to try to bring it back to his crude and laddish ideas of what he would do to any girl unlucky enough to be alone with him. The others ignored him, and after a while the chatter switched to football.

Billy sat on the edges of the talk for about three-quarters of an hour before getting up and saying his farewells. "I'm tired," he said, but the others didn't take any notice, so he just got up and left, not saying a word to the boys but throwing a casual "s'long" to Giuseppe.

Billy went home in a reflective mood, and once he was in bed, he tried to recall the events with Rose during the evening. He wondered if he should have tried the things the boys had suggested. Would Rose have been offended or, as he hadn't tried anything, would she think him too inexperienced?

As he drifted into deep, unthinking sleep, his thoughts turned to recollections of her pretty face as she tried to sell him the raffle ticket.

He never did buy the ticket but that was the start of Billy and Rose's lifelong romance.

Chapter 3

Billy woke early next morning, his mind active and the previous night's thought of the girl at the dance still at the front of his mind. She was pretty, and as he washed and shaved, he smiled at the mental image of her.

The idea stayed with him as he dressed, and he wondered if she would go out with him again. What would she say if he asked for a second date? Would she think he was being "a bit forward" or would she laugh at him for having been so dull?

As he put on his shoes, he began to like the idea of Rose as his girl-friend—his first girlfriend.

He dragged his way through a whole, dreary workday, and when he got home, he found her note and rang the number she had given him. Rose's mother answered the phone and told him Rose was out for the evening, and Billy was disappointed. He had built himself up for the moment—now he had been knocked flat.

He had nothing planned for the evening but didn't want to stay indoors, so he went out and unusually went to the cinema on his own: two films and a news bulletin. After watching the main feature halfway through a second time, he left to go and meet his tight-knit group of friends as usual in Giuseppe's small trattoria on the high street.

They had been friends for many years and rarely quarrelled seriously. Giuseppe regarded them all almost as his own sons, beaming benevolently at their sarcastic banter and mickey-taking.

They were talking aimlessly as Billy walked in, but Jonno looked up.

"Yo, Billy, how's it going?" he called as Billy walked towards the counter. "Where you been?"

"Fine, just been to the flicks," replied Billy, talking loudly over the noise of the espresso machine. "Tried for another date with that girl from the dance, but she wasn't available..."

Giuseppe smiled a fatherly smile. "I bring your cappuccino across," he said, and Billy nodded and turned back to the friends' table.

"Hey, Romeo. She playing hard to get?" asked Ging. "Just get her knickers off and give her one to show you're the boss."

Billy glared at him. "Oh, shut up," he said.

"Where's your sense of humour?"

"He left'it at home." They were only in their twenties on the outside.

Billy sat down, and Terry jumped in. "What was the film?" he asked, and as none of them had seen the film he mentioned, the five friends got on with their usual aimless evening chatter.

They had been discussing women's underwear, a favourite topic for Ging.

"Back to those knickers and things. Does it matter as long as they cover the... er, can I call that area the matter in hand?" Ging was saying, determined to keep what he called an erotic topic.

"Suppose it's a question of money," replied Frank. "Surely the small frippery ones cost less probably pro rata."

"Pro rata?" asked Ging.

"Anything to do with pros."

"Pros?" asked Terry innocently.

"Yes, ladies of the street."

"It's been a business doing pleasure with you," said Billy, quickly joining.

"Stupid yob," replied Ging.

Jonno laughed. "What do they call a friend of a yob then?" he asked.

"Bloody unlucky," quipped Billy without a pause.

It was the usual inconsequential banter of young men as they passed into adulthood (or adultery as Billy often put it). In their own limited, unworldly way, they thought they were being clever.

Around half past midnight, Giuseppe was showing signs that he was ready to close up, so the Caballeros decided to call it a night. Most of them were busy for the rest of the week, so they made arrangements to meet on the following Saturday evening and went their separate ways home, Ging and Frank walking off together laughing.

The week dragged on, and Billy forced himself not to call Rose again because he didn't want to seem too keen. But he thought of her a lot.

Finally, Saturday came, and after going to watch a local football match with Frank, Billy met his friends and they went off to the dance club as usual.

After getting there, they stood to one side as always, eyeing the girls on the opposite side of the dance floor, but Billy kept his eyes on the entrance door until, after what seemed to him to be an endless age, Rose came in with her friend Mary, a short not quite plump brunette with a somewhat saucy grin.

Billy couldn't take his eyes off Rose, and eventually moved away from Jonno, Terry and Frank and crossed the room to ask her for a dance. She accepted and they moved to the edges of the floor and held each other loosely as they shuffled to the music.

As they danced, the lights dimmed even further and the sextet on the stand broke into a slow romantic version of a current pop song. Couples held each, by the waist, round the shoulders, any way they felt, and swayed, shuffled and smooched in gentle rhythm.

Billy held Rose's hands loosely and joined the crowd. Rose began singing the words of the song, looking directly into Billy's eyes with a happy smile on her lips, and Billy was happy that she was happy. They swayed gently to the music without moving their feet, the aching tenderness of growing love locked between them.

When the music finished, they were so wrapped up in each other that they continued to shuffle round until the next song began. Even when Jonno, dancing with Mary, brushed by them, almost touching, they carried on. They were not strictly dancing, but neither noticed nor cared.

They did not notice as the floor cleared, but a smattering of ironic applause brought them both to reality, and Billy's arms dropped to his side. They started to walk off the dance floor.

"That was good," said Billy as they neared the edge.

"You're a good dancer," replied Rose, stretching the truth slightly.

Billy started to speak again. "I like being with you," he began, but a blast of brass from the bandstand drowned it out.

"What was that you said?"

But by now Billy's shyness had returned and he mumbled a hurried, "Nothing. Not important."

The evening continued. Both Billy and Rose danced with others, but neither's heart was in it, and just before midnight, they joined up again for a slow waltz, again dancing in the same non-dancing shuffle. At one point, their faces were close, but nothing happened, and too soon the music finished. They stood for a moment.

"See you at the telephone boxes on Monday?" asked Billy.

Rose had been praying he would ask and nodded. "I'll be there" she replied softly, and they parted.

Billy had always liked girls. He had always liked looking at them from afar. He adored them. Delighted in them. Devoured them with his eyes.

But like most other lads of his age, he and his group didn't have a lot of success with them because they were too shy and inexperienced, stumbled their words when they spoke to them and didn't know how to behave.

And now he was with one for the second time. A girl. And the most beautiful girl he had ever seen.

Rose was equally shy and inexperienced, but when they met on the following Monday and Billy didn't really know what they should do, she suggested they start off at a nearby quaint tea house cafe on the hill at Hampstead to talk about it.

Billy agreed, so they took an underground train the one stop to Hampstead and when they got there, they found a small isolated booth and Billy went to the counter to order: a strawberry milkshake for her and a fizzy orange drink for himself. He carried them carefully back to their table.

They sat there silently for a few moments, sipping their drinks—Rose through a multi-coloured straw. Eventually, she spoke.

"Billy," she started hesitantly, "I was thinking... I don't know anything about you. What do you do, for instance?"

"As little as I can," he joked in his normal way.

"Oh, you...!" Rose laughed. "Seriously, what do you want to do?" she went on. "Have you any special ambitions?"

"Well, when I'm really old, I want to be able to tell everyone that I've got no regrets."

There was a pause. "That's something, I suppose," said Rose. "But seriously, what do you do now? What's your job?"

"Oh, I'm just a salesman. I work for a dress manufacturer and go round the shops and try to sell them dozens of dresses and things."

"You're an expert in women's clothing?"

"Not a real expert, but I know enough chat to bluff my way."

"OK then," smiled Rose. "How would you describe my dress?"

Billy looked carefully. "Well... it's a blouson. Casual, printed linen with a tight waist and a slightly flared hem. Dark red with polka dots, surplice neckline, probably bought from a big chain..."

Rose laughed. "OK, OK, you certainly seem to know your stuff. I bought it from Pritchard's in Belsize Park." She smoothed down the top of her dress showing above the table.

"It's very flattering. Makes you look..." Billy stopped, suddenly self-conscious as he was talking about Rose's figure. He coughed lightly. "But what about you? What do you do?"

"Just a straightforward business college. Shorthand, typing, that kind of thing," replied Rose. "It's boring."

"Why? What would you like to do?"

Rose looked a little sad. "I'd love to be a nurse, but my parents wouldn't let me study for that. I don't think I've got the dedication anyway."

"Well, I'm sure you have really."

They again sipped at their drinks and there was a silence for a few moments. Then they started to talk again at the same time, and both laughed. Suddenly, there was no shyness between them, and they began to talk properly about all manner of things: music, films, friends, hobbies and that sort of thing. They had remarkably similar likes and dislikes.

They both finished their drinks, but they carried on chatting until a waitress hovered obviously close by their table and they agreed they would like cappuccinos. The waitress went off but came back fairly quickly bringing the drinks to their table.

The conversation continued easy and relaxed, and with Billy throwing in the occasional quip they both laughed a lot. Billy loved the way Rose's whole face lit up when she laughed.

They got on so well that their coffees grew cold and although he hardly had any money, Billy brashly ordered two large replacements, although it left him with just a few small coins in his pocket. The conversation continued, turning to inconsequential matters, just like two long-standing friends.

Finally, Billy glanced at his watch, and suddenly they got a bit embarrassed at the time they had spent in the cafe and decided to leave. It was too late to go anywhere else, so without thought, they started to walk, soon finding themselves by Whitestone Pond, where Spaniards Way joins North End Road.

They crossed the road, and there before them was Hampstead Heath, dropping awaybelow them with the moon giving everything an eerie white near-day light over the wide-open expanse. They wandered onto the heath, sitting on the dry grass just down from the pond looking out on the near-distant panoply of a London ablaze with light.

"This is nice," said Rose, and Billy thought the same.

Conversation had slowed, but both were relaxed in each other's company. Time passed.

Around half past nine, Billy took Rose home, leaving her at the end of her cul-de-sac with a rather embarrassed goodbye with both wishing they'd had enough courage to kiss the other farewell.

Billy stood at the end of the road watching Rose walk to her house, the second on the left, until she was inside. He stood there for at least five minutes just looking at Rose's front door before making his way back to the coffee bar where his close friends had now gathered.

Back at Giuseppe's, he sat quietly listening to the others' leeringly crude talk for about three-quarters of an hour before telling them he had a headache and left to go home and to bed early (by his normal standards). That night, he unusually woke several times thinking of Rose.

For her part, Rose spent almost an hour daydreaming about Billy before she slipped into a deep, peaceful and uninterrupted sleep—with a happy smile on her lips.

The next few weeks were a whirl of excitement for both of them. They went to the dance hall every Saturday, and Rose met Billy's friends at the coffee bar (she especially liked Jonno), and they met up at least three other times a week.

Rose felt differently to any feelings she had ever experienced—a bursting kaleidoscope of emotion that filled her mind and body almost to bursting. It was nothing like the Hollywood films she had seen, nor like the romantic rhymes of the popular crooners she liked. This time it was real. She knew it, was certain.

Neither Billy nor Rose realised it, but they were both falling very much in love—it was their understanding and instant empathy. They were always together and soon got into the routine of telling each other little things and secrets. They were becoming two halves of a whole—the birth of their everlasting love.

Over the ensuing weeks, Billy took Rose to the usual cinemas, to theatres which she had never been to before, and to a very smart restaurant—not one of the very expensive places but one a couple of steps down from them serving good food. She didn't realise he got the restaurant name from a food guidebook and it was his first time too, and he authoritatively made the orders for both of them from the recommendations in the food book that had given him the name of the restaurant.

As they waited for the meal, as most people do both automatically looked at the dishes the waiters and waitresses were carrying past them to other tables, not knowing but wondering what the food was and hoping their own dish would be acceptable.

When it came, they ate the beef Wellington meal quietly, her cutting the various parts of the meat, pate and puff pastry into neat mouthfuls and mixing them on her fork with the vegetables. He ate the various parts separately, saving the meat until last. They were perfectly at peace with each other and chatted easily throughout.

"I've never had that before," said Rose when they had finished. "It was lovely. I really liked it. I must find the recipe."

Billy had never had the dish before either, but he didn't say anything.

It was an enjoyable evening and both enjoyed it, until Billy later went on to Giuseppe's and found the downside when he didn't even have enough money for a coffee (and five days to go until pay day). Despite that, that particular evening helped cement their friendship even further.

The meal had gone down so well—Rose was impressed at being taken to finer dining than she had ever known and mentioned it several times. Another time Billy took her to a smart-looking Chinese restaurant and as they ordered a fixed menu (they didn't know what else to eat, so went by the best sounding names), he asked her, "Do you think we should try using chopsticks?"

She nodded, and the waiter brought them a set each, but he knowingly also gave them both a fork and spoon. When the food arrived, Rose laughed at Billy's pitiful initial attempts to use chopsticks.

She just about managed but he couldn't cope at all, and eventually put the sticks down.

"They seem to have given me two left-handed ones," he said.

"Silly boy," laughed Rose, carefully picking up grains of fried rice with cautious ease.

She carried on trying to use the chopsticks, but Billy thankfully used his fork to eat his rice, noodles and sweet-and-sour chicken, and eventually attacked his spicy spare ribs, holding them in both sticky hands and attacking them with vigour like a lion with its prey. Although it wasn't like anything Rose had seen during meals at home, she found it funny.

But things were not all sweetness and light. Rose's mother Mavis was quite anti-Billy, and although she had never met him she had listened to her daughter's enthusiastic babble about him and thought he was not a suitable partner.

"He'll never be anything," she frequently told her daughter. "He'll never be able to support you."

Mavis tried everything to put Rose off seeing Billy, even putting the phone down on him when he called one day. She had high hopes for her daughter and thought Willie a better marriage prospect. He was managerial material, while she felt Billy was destined to stay a junior employee.

Rose's mother was something of a snob, always changing details of her address to make it sound as if she lived in a more suitable area, and her dislike of Billy's job was really a small sign of her haughty pretention.

Rose was still seeing Willie occasionally, although she much preferred being with Billy and, because of her mother's deafness, she was still never certain who she was going to meet when she went on dates. And because Willie was still on the scene, Mavis continually praised him as the preferred, potentially high-earning suitable son-in-law while denigrating Billy's "lowly job".

Rose's father Paul was shy now, but he had fixed principles and ideas—that's why, as a brash young man, he had volunteered and fought in the Great War of 1914 and seen pain and sights that no man should ever be made to see—and simply claimed his duty was to get Rose married, to cook and clean for a decent man and bear his children.

So, as Mavis talked against Billy and did everything she could to discourage their meetings, her husband just wanted what would make his daughter happy and didn't say anything.

Things came to a bit of a peak when after some two months of dating Billy, Rose came home to find her mother very excited.

"Willie called," said Mavis. "He said he's got a new job. It's a big promotion for him and he'll be earning a lot more money. His prospects of becoming a manager are good. Far better than a mere salesman."

Rose was unimpressed, but Mavis went on.

"He said he wants to meet you at the usual place this evening to tell you about it," she continued brightly. "I've got a feeling he wants to say something else, something important. You ought to go. He'd be a good catch; you want to grab him while you can."

Rose flushed. "I'm not for sale," she replied angrily and stormed off to her room. She had been thinking of Billy, and desperately wanted to see him. She had been thinking that way for several days.

Later, while her mother continued to flutter and repeatedly remind her to get ready to meet Willie, Rose changed to a pretty dress and left the house as if to meet him.

But she didn't go to meet Willie. Instead, she went to Giuseppe's coffee bar where she knew Billy met his friends and was desperately delighted when she found him sitting there alone.

They had a quiet evening before the rest of the gang came in, then because of their raucous shouting, they left and Billy walked Rose home.

Her parents were in bed when she finally got back indoors—at a respectable time—and she went to bed with nice thoughts, yet again falling asleep with a smile on her lips.

In the morning, after her mother had asked, rather unsubtly, what Willie had said that was supposed to be so important, there was a bit of a grumpy row before Rose stormed off to work, hating Willie.

During the day, Billy was in her thoughts, the one she wanted. And she hoped he felt the same.

Her mother's interference really irritated Rose, and so, as her feelings for Billy grew stronger, just nine weeks after meeting Billy in the club, she broke up with Willie.

And as Willie finally became just a funny paragraph in the history of her young life, Rose found herself even more deeply attracted to Billy.

As far as Billy was concerned, he still had a jaunty confidence, almost boasting, when with his friends, but Rose soon realised that he toned down when he was with her. Then he was quietly confident, but somehow humble.

Billy had certainly changed. He was still quick with the flip one-line comebacks, but while keeping his cheeky chappie outward veneer, he no longer swore or acted out his juvenile homophobic fantasies but tended to see the best in everyone. Rose still seemed the sweet, outwardly naive nice girl she had always been, although she had her moments.

One of them happened about the fourth or fifth time she met the Caballeros. Billy had taken her to Giuseppe's to introduce his friends and at first, they were a bit uncertain about having a girl with them, then during one late evening session, they were sitting quietly sipping their cold coffees when Ging automatically lifted one buttock fairly obviously and let out a long rumbling fart. There was a stunned moment, then Rose began to laugh.

She controlled herself, and before anyone could say anything, she swallowed, then replied with a low burp. Ladylike, but still a burp. It was something she had learnt at school—not that her teachers knew anything about it—and something she could do at will.

Billy was shocked. It was so unlike Rose, but it had an immediate effect on the others. They laughed.

There was another mini pause, then things settled down as normal with no one, not even Billy, saying anything. From that moment, Rose was accepted by the Caballeros and took a full share in their banter.

Giuseppe also loved her like "his boys" and showed several paternal moments especially looking after her. Billy noticed that the boys' laddish chat calmed down when she was around, and apart from a few lewd and crude remarks from a couple of them, they were accepted by Rose. She, too, discovered the difference in Billy.

The events that night showed that she was learning the ways of the boys with a rather naughty, black humour that was growing increasingly like theirs. She slipped into the Caballeros set-up easily.

When they eventually said their goodnights, Billy walked Rose home, and a few yards away from her house, they stopped in the shadow of a solid oak tree whose outline showed even darker than the black of night. Rose had her back to a low brick parapet, and Billy could just about make out her face. He kissed her, and they stood with their arms around each other for several moments.

"I love you," he eventually told her. It was the first time he had ever used the words.

Rose heard the words, and they pleased her. A sudden surge of emotion passed through. But for some reason, there was caution in her mind.

"Don't say that," she whispered. "Not unless you mean it."

Billy nodded. "I do mean it," he replied. "I haven't been able to think of anything or anyone else but you. I do really think I love you." He stopped, not knowing what else to say.

Rose's mind, too, was confused. She reached up with her right hand and touched Billy's mouth gently.

"I've... I've got... feelings for you too," she said eventually. She wanted to say more, but some natural caution held her back.

"Rose…"

"Not now, Billy."

She leant forwards and kissed his lips lightly. Then she quickly turned and hurried down the road to her house in a dream. Billy watched her, not certain if he had said too much.

When she got to the front gate, Rose stopped and glanced back. Billy was still standing there, and she suddenly rushed back to him. She stopped a few yards short, puffing breathlessly.

"And I love you too," she said, simply and obviously.

They continued to stand there, neither wanting to make the first move of parting, and although neither said a word, the three words they had already said filled the air.

Rose finally broke clear. "I've got to go or I'll be in trouble," she said.

Billy nodded, although she couldn't see him, and he mumbled, "I do love you." He just wanted to keep saying the words.

They gave each other a final peck on the lips, and then Rose left, walking backwards and facing him for the first few steps before turning and then almost running to her front gate and indoors without looking back again.

Billy watched her go. He bit the inside of his top lip. He knew they had not just spoken words. They had opened up to each other's lives.

He stood where he was for a full ten minutes before going off again, his mind a bit dazed.

Chapter 4

Now their views had been openly expressed, it became obvious amongst their friends that they were becoming a pair. Going out. Boyfriend and girlfriend.

At first, as their relationship moved on, Rose told Mary every little thing about her times with Billy, enthusiastically highlighting every new paragraph of the growing romance. But the stories slowed and finally stopped, although Mary continually pressed for details. Billy, on the other hand, never spoke about the

friendship to anyone but Rose herself.

Each liked the other's previous friendships on top of making more new ones between them and they were known to all simply as a couple. Everyone accepted them as such.

They were seeing each other virtually every evening, but because of Rose's mother's continual objections, they had to make sure she was always back in good time. It meant Billy always had time to go on to see the Caballeros boys after they had said their farewells.

The boys accepted his less frequent time with them and still took the mickey. One night, Billy got to Giuseppe's at around 9:40 and they were all there apart from Ging. The talk was about past schoolwork and Terry was telling them how he had been made to read Homer's *Iliad*. He was being over serious for the others and Billy decided to break that up.

"I know a poem," he said. "The working class can kiss my arse…"

Terry looked a bit peeved, but the others laughed. Things had been getting a bit too serious for them.

"That says it all," replied Frank. "Who the hell needs poetry? Does anyone even know any poems?"

Billy nodded and sniggered crudely.

"Hey diddle diddle," he recited straight-faced. "The cat did a piddle, in the middle of the dining room floor. The little dog laughed to see such fun, so the cat did a little drop more!"

"Hey, you're a poet," laughed Jonno.

"And don't I know it," replied Billy, still smirking.

Ging walked in and joined the group. "Hi there, Billy boy, haven't seen you for a long time," he said in greeting.

"Not since yesterday."

"A sight for sore eyes," said Ging.

"Yep, one look and anyone would get sore eyes."

"How's the bird?"

"Willy or won't 'e?" simpered Frank.

Billy tried to ignore the comments about Rose.

"You know she's a... good girl," said Jonno.

Billy blushed.

Frank noticed. "Look, the boy's blushing. Must have a guilty secret."

"Why?" giggled Ging. "He won't have done anything. He thinks getting his leg over is something to do with climbing over the seats at Griffin Park."

"Come on, even he knows," added Frank, "Just get a cider inside her and boom boom."

Billy stood up and walked out of the cafe to get away from them.

Despite evenings like that, Billy and Rose continued to see each other and continued to grow closer. From the start, they fitted together seamlessly, like bread and butter, fish and chips, sausage and mash or Rodgers and Hammerstein. They were an unbreakable team.

They were inseparable, always together, telling each other little things, laughing at little personal jokes. They were two halves of a whole.They were very much in love with each other, and although they went about with the boys, by now they were a couple, with those little knowing looks and sometimes odd mysterious sentences between them that long-married couples have.

Rose's innate shyness quickly evaporated—although only with Billy at first—and somehow the mask of Billy's normally flip one-liners slipped away when he was with Rose, and although he was still invariably light-hearted, he was much more geared to her reserve.

Rose was happy to be accepted by Billy's friends, and they were more than happy to include her, but both she and Billy were glad to be alone together.

After years of growing up with the youthful rough crudeness of his friends, Billy adapted quickly to the more adult serenity and gentleness that surrounded Rose. A part of that came because, soon after introducing Rose to the group, he was able to borrow his father's cars and act as general chauffeur to the group. As his father had a predilection for big mostly American or top end British cars, he became the focal centre for the group. It was exciting for Rose and his friends to drive round crammed tightly together and singing or joking.

One day, Ging told him, "You'll have to get your own car sometime, y'know. Without the old man, it'll have to be a Rolls Canardly: rolls down hills, can 'ardly get up the other side." He smirked.

Billy had two favourites: a huge American Packard in which he once packed ten friends, and a British Rover with four wooden floorboards in front of each front seat, but with the two central boards on the passenger side missing so Rose had to sit with her legs carefully planted wide apart when he took her out. It was dangerous, of course, but the thought excited Billy's surges of lust. Not that he did anything about it, but the thought came to him quite frequently when they were not together.

Rose and Billy still went through the rituals of late evenings at Giuseppe's and Saturdays at the dance hall, but they were slowly drifting away from the Caballeros and trying for as much alone time together as they could. Neither was really happy with others around them.

One Saturday night, they had all gone to the dance club as usual, getting to the club fairly early in the evening, but after just an hour or so of desultory dancing (or rather smooching) on the fringes of the dance floor Billy gave an almost imperceptible nod and he and Rose disappeared, creeping out to sit in each other's arms across the back seat of Billy's borrowed car.

They sat sprawled across the bench seat with shirt and blouse undone, arms holding each other firmly but gently. They kissed and fumbled quietly, enjoying each other's presence as much as the physical side of it, and giving each other meaningful but unexplainable looks in the faint glow of the car park's single light. Rose was passive during the back seat gropings, although she enjoyed them, getting her pleasure more from the feel of Billy and his close-up masculine smell.

After a while, they rested, content just to lie arm in arm, kissing only occasionally.

"It's so quiet out here," observed Rose, ignoring the occasional roar of a souped-up Ford or Vauxhall entering or leaving the car park.

"Much better than the noise inside," replied Billy.

"The music's nice..."

"If I open the windows, you can still hear it."

"Oh, don't bother. I like just being here with you."

"Me too." There was a moment of silence, then Billy spoke again. "I don't know why, but it's somehow easy to talk to you. The trouble is that I feel I'm getting all soppy talking when I do."

"It's not soppy, it's natural, lovely. And I enjoy listening to you. I like it."

Away from the cigarette smell and blare of the jazz group in the hall, they went silent again, both sitting and sharing thoughts of the romantic songs with lilting melodies and sweeping banks of violins they had heard in various films.

After half an hour or so, it started to rain, so after the mess of their inevitable gropings, they both tidied up and went back inside the club, arriving there soaking wet from the sudden downpour.The rest of the Caballeros gave them knowing looks, but Billy and Rose ignored them.

Rose celebrated her eighteenth birthday a week later on the following Saturday, four months to the day after their first meeting. Despite her mother's wish to give her a celebration meal at home, Rose was determined to meet Billy, and when she met him at the telephone boxes, he bashfully handed her a single red rose. She loved the romance of the gesture, but as he gave the flower to her Billy felt it all rather like a bit of a filmic cliche.

They had decided not to go to the dance hall that night, and so they took the underground train to Piccadilly and walked arm in arm to a small fish restaurant they had heard of with Rose clutching the paper-wrapped rose with her spare hand.

In the restaurant, they ordered plates of oven-baked salmon and new potatoes, something new for them both rather than the inevitable battered cod and chips served in fish and chip shops. While they were waiting for the meal, Billy reached into his pocket and handed over a slim, gift-wrapped parcel.

Rose unwrapped the offering, her eyes glittering as she saw a yellow box, with a slim, delicate silver-looking bracelet with a pendant letter R hanging from it inside it.

"That's the real present, n-n-not the flower," said Billy in a soft self-effacing way.

Rose smiled as she carefully took the bracelet from the box and draped it over her right wrist. She held her arm out to Billy.

"Can you do it up for me?" she asked.

Billy reached across the table and did so, but kept hold of Rose's hand, lifting it to his lips and kissing it. The waiter returned with their meals as he did so, and both Billy and Rose blushed to be caught like that. Rose hurriedly cleared away the wrapping paper from the table and put it on her lap.

They settled down to eat their fish, commenting on the funny shaped fish knives, and as an extra little celebration to mark the day, both had sauce tartare for the first time rather than the inevitable ketch-up.They preferred it.

They enjoyed the meal, and when it was over, they left the restaurant and wandered leisurely round the West End, excited by the lights, the noise and the bustle of the big city. The night sky was pitch black high above them and they were surrounded by the bright lights and busy noise and clatter of a big city, but they found a seat and sat with arms round each other in a quiet isolated world of their own.

Billy softly crooned the words of a popular song of the time. It was a haunting melody with achingly meaningful words about lost love, and the poignant lyrics hung between them.

"It's a new one by that new American singer Tony Bennett," said Billy.

Rose loved it and hummed along.

"It's so sad, but it won't be us," Billy added. "I'll never leave you. We'll never be apart."

"Never," agreed Rose.

Neither could imagine life without the other. It was something beyond their imagination. They were in love, an eternal love bound them together for all time, and although every love affair is special, both Billy and Rose knew in their minds that none was as special as theirs.

After an hour of laughing at silly things, they caught the underground home, and Billy walked Rose to her house, by now taking her right to the front door. They stood there for a while kissing frequently but not saying much.

"I love the present. Well, both of them," said Rose, holding up her flower to smell its strong fragrance. "It's been a lovely birthday, the best."

She turned to go indoors, and Billy stood there for a few minutes before going off to meet the boys.

They had been in a pub all evening and were all pretty high, and in a moment when they were being overly chatty and personal, a euphoric Billy carelessly told them about the rose. He didn't know why, it was personal, but he somehow wanted to share the moment with them.

The boys, of course, teased him so much that quite quickly Billy decided to go home to forget about the ribbing and be alone with his memories of the evening. He didn't think they would remember his "confession" but they did, of course.

Billy and Rose went out together a couple of times during the next few days, and Rose always wore the bracelet, although she kept it in her pocket and didn't put it on her wrist until she'd left the house and was far from her mother's view. It wasn't until Thursday that they went back to Giuseppe's to meet the boys. Things were just as usual there, the banter basic and bordering on the obscene.

It was Frank's birthday and Ging was teasing him as Rose and Billy walked in.

"You're only as old as the woman you feel," Ging said.

"In that case, I haven't even been born yet."

"Don't worry, there's a good woman waiting for you somewhere."

"She'll have a bloody long wait."

"Then she won't recognise you. She'll be expecting someone good-looking..."

"Belt up..." Frank saw Billy and Rose, who were now standing beside the table. "Hey, Billy, Rose..."

"What's up?" asked Billy.

"Frank's birthday," said Ging,

Billy pulled a funny face. "A person of no importance full of his own importance?" he said with smirk. "Happy birthday, mate. I'd forgotten. Want a cappuccino?"

Giuseppe had been listening paternally. "Stay where you are. They're all on me as a birthday treat now you're nearly grown up," he shouted to Frank.

Rose and Billy sat down, and Giuseppe brought the cups across and they all began sipping the steaming coffee cautiously, with Terry sensibly blowing across the top of his to cool it down but getting a smudge of frothy cream on the end of his nose. Everyone laughed at him and the evening resumed as normal.

Around half past ten, Billy had to go to the lavatory.

"Don't worry, we'll look after Red for you," called Jonno as Billy left the table.

As Billy disappeared from view, Rose watched him then turned back to Jonno.

"Red?" she queried. "What's that?"

Jonno explained. He told her that the name had followed after Billy had mentioned her birthday flower. "We'd all been out boozing and were pretty far gone," he said. "Then Billy came in, and he was the one full of moonshine with his head in the clouds. He was as mouthy as

Shakespeare and describing you as a 'red, red rose'," he said, switching to a bad accent and mimicking Billy before returning to his own voice. "You've been Red Rose ever since. We all see what he meant."

Rose couldn't help smiling. Red. She liked it, and she knew she had been accepted into Billy's closest friendship circle.

Billy came back to the table and the subject changed, but he noticed that Rose was looking at him with a mysterious smile. The phrase "red, red rose" was going round in her mind and she felt a pleasant inner glow.

Later, when he saw her home, Billy stopped her at the end of her road. "I do love you," he mumbled.

Rose laughed suddenly. "Is it me, or Red?" she asked perkily.

Billy picked up her mood change, but stayed serious. "Nothing much between you," he said, mumbling again. "I love you, both of you."

For a few weeks after that night, Rose was known to the gang as Red, or sometimes just R. They called her by that nickname for a month or so, then they got tired of it like so many other instant fads. Rose didn't particularly notice that it was being used less often, but Billy was relieved as the name always reminded him of his embarrassment when the guys had first heard about him giving her a red rose.

Things quickly settled down and, with the laziness of young men, the sobriquet faded away completely as Rose became a loved part of the group, especially when her friend Mary started dating Billy's best friend Jonno from time to time.

Billy was always ready with a quick quip or wise crack at work, and was known as quite a cheeky chap, although at home he was more subtly funny with Rose, friends and neighbours. It was his easy-going nature that allied to his studied hard work and cheerful manner that, after a year or two, earned him a promotion to become his firm's general sales supervisor, which meant that occasionally he had to travel the country to monitor and advise other sales representatives. He hated being apart from Rose when that happened and to hide her own sad dismay, she looked around for some work that would keep her busy. She took on a job as a sales assistant in a quirky shop specialising in mother-in-law wedding dresses.

Billy stuck at the travelling managerial job for about two months, but then his apartness from Rose and an incident while in the north made him give it up.

He had gone into the stockroom of one customer's shop, and as he reached for a shelf, the door closed behind him. He turned, and a pretty new accountant was standing close behind him. She was dark-haired, with a rather sullen mouth and brown eyes. She wore a low-cut beige blouse open at the neck revealing a lot of bare flesh, and Billy could only stare.

Without a word, she stepped closer and then reached across to put her hands on his shoulders and bent in to kiss him.

Billy instinctively returned the kiss, and still without a word, his right hand found itself on the girl's breasts. He was breathing deeply, and the girl pressed her body into him.

Their mouths parted, but Billy's hand remained on the girl.

"I've seen you," she told him. "You looked at me on the stairs… I thought…"

Billy could not recall the moment.

"I… I… what's your name?" he asked.

"Linda."

They kissed again, and she nuzzled her head into his shoulder. A lock of her hair fell across her face, and he brushed it away, but some-how one of the girl's hairs got in his mouth and he tried to get rid of it with his tongue. He couldn't move it and had to use theforefinger and thumb of his left hand to take it out while at the same time fumbling with his right hand to undo her blouse.

He finally got the hair, dropping it and wiping his fingers on the front of his trousers, and concentrated on the girl's blouse.

She started to kiss him again, much more passionately, and suddenly his hands were under her skirt and she was tugging at the buttons of his trousers.

The sex was quick, and as soon as it was over Billy felt dirty and ashamed.

"Look, Belinda…"

"It's Linda."

"Yes. Well, I'm sorry. That shouldn't have happened."

"But it did."

"Let's just say it didn't. I love my girl. I don't…"

"OK," said Linda, suddenly back to reality. "Let's just pretend nothing happened. You and I both know it did, but let's just play happy families. I could have…"

She stopped talking and turned away. Then she was gone, and Billy looked at the open door. Afterwards, he felt dirty, and his mind was confused. What had he done? He had got no real pleasure out of the encounter, no emotion. It had just been gratifying a basic animal hunger.

In his mind was a flash of thought. What was it his old Caballeros pal Ging had said? "The best thing any girl has is availability." He left the stockroom and left the shop.

Billy returned to his hotel feeling dirty and ashamed. He showered, then sat on his bed feeling that he should phone Rose and admit his guilt, but he couldn't bring himself to do so. For some reason, he could picture her being sympathetic and calling him a "silly man". After half an hour, he had another shower.

The next morning, he went back to the shop early and tried, unsuccessfully, to work in the office, but Linda did not turn up and he neither saw nor heard of her again.

He left early in the afternoon and went home, and when he arrived, he quickly went upstairs and had yet another hot shower before going to bed without eating. The next morning, he rang Rose early meaning to confess everything, but he couldn't find the right words. He made an excuse that he had to get to work early, arranged to meet her that evening and rang off.

He left the house and walked for half an hour before making his way to his office.

When he did meet Rose later, he kissed and hugged her but was unusually quiet and Rose knew instinctively that something was wrong. But she diplomatically, luckily, didn't ask what the matter was. She thought it must be something in his work and didn't say anything.

As the memory of the incident in the stockroom faded, Billy subconsciously began to pay even more attention to making Rose happy. He knew he loved her more than anything, and he was determined that he would never be distracted again.

The incident played on his mind though, and as soon as he could, he took another sales rep job with another dress manufacturer. Although the wages were slightly lower, it gave him more time to be alone with Rose.

He had been in the new job just two weeks when he and Rose met the boys at Giuseppe's one Saturday night—Ging and Terry almost begging to do something different for a change—and they eventually decided to go to the dance club as usual. Billy had his father's Rover 20 and drove them there, and when they got inside, Billy, Rose, Jonno and Mary stood alongside the boys, who had lined up on one side of the hall with all the other single lads watching the girls opposite.

They got to the club around 8:30, and after a fairly unmemorable hour or so of dancing, Billy and Rose stood on the fringes of the dance floor half-heartedly listening to the music and watching Ging, Terry and Frank try unsuccessfully to pick up a succession of girls. It was boring for them both, so Billy gave a nod and he and Rose crept out to once more sit in each other's arms across the back seat of Billy's borrowed car.

After the inevitable quiet kissing, fumbling and fondling, they simply sat enjoying each other's presence.

"I can't get over the idea that I used to be just like the others," said Billy eventually. "It was all so pointless. Thank goodness I met you."

Rose brushed her lips against his and with fumbling hands and croaky strained voices whispering to each other, they slowly sat with their love.

The sudden loud clattering beat of heavy rain on the car roof interrupted them, and as they sat up and started to dress again, their friends came tumbling into the car soaking wet from the downpour. The mood was broken, and Billy and Rose both silently clambered over into the front seats, giving each other exasperated looks before Billy drove them back to Giuseppe's to see out the evening.

Just as Rose had been accepted by the boys, so was Mary and she also joined in the banter.

Ging was in his usual aggressive macho mood, trying to get a rise out of Mary, and she countered in the same way.

"I bet you know some ripe and ready girls you could bring along one night," he said.

"Yeah," replied Mary. "I'll ask Elizabeth Taylor next time I'm round at her house."

"Yeah, I'd rather feel her than feel hungry."

"Are you like that with all the girls?" asked Mary.

"Only those that are available."

Mary looked at him aghast, her eyebrows raised.

"Well, women are the best alternative sex," conceded Ging eventually.

"Do you mean second best?" replied Mary.

Billy interrupted. "As the great man once said, 'Tis better to give than receive.'"

The boys laughed, but both Rose and Mary gave him a fierce look and he went quiet. It finished the conversation, and they all sat quietly until it was time to go home.

The evening had been, quite literally, a washout. But Billy's thoughts spoken to Rose in the car stayed with him, and as their romance continued to build, he started to grow a little disenchanted and distant from the other Caballeros. They were still strong friends, of course, but he was less reliant on their comradeship, getting irritable far more often over their aimless, crude, idle, salacious talk about any girls they had seen. They would sit round a table at Giuseppe's talking like young dirty old men. It was the same night after night, particularly if a young woman or girl came into the cafe.

Billy preferred the gentle attentions from and to Rose. After two, almost three, years everyone knew them as "being together" and going steady.

Jonno was also dating Mary regularly now, and he, too, was growing apart from the others of the group. They had begun getting on his nerves as much as Billy, and both of them would get sensitive about their indelicate references to both of their girlfriends, especially after Ging and Terry quickly dubbed Jonno as "Twissa": their crude references to "twice a night"!

Visits to Giuseppe's became less frequent for the four of them, and when Jonno became engaged to Mary, she and Rose also saw less and less of each other. The only real time they spent together was to spend a couple of evenings talking about Mary's impending wedding and how she and Jonno would set up home.

Billy didn't like it, but he understood. He was starting to grow up.

Undeterred by the wedding talk though, Rose still managed to see a lot of Billy. They went out on their own frequently, and thoughts of their own possible marriage began to roam through their minds. For Billy, they were new emotions—a deep swirling feeling lifting him up and round in an uncontrollable swirl of an all-embracing mass of want and need and hope and immense pleasure. He was in love.

As the thoughts began to take hold, and despite the natural feelings of youth, they both held on to an old-fashioned circumspection out of their deep respect for each other, although it often required restraint that was agonisingly and palpably painful. So, it was not until they had known each other for just over three years that they inevitably became physical lovers.

It happened one Saturday night as they sat in the back of an old Chevrolet (again borrowed from his father for the night) in the car park outside the dance hall. Naturally. Without words. Without planning.

That night, they were lying across the back seat of the car and had explored each other further than ever before, and eventually, instinctively, they made love for the first time. It was spontaneous, just a logical act between two people in love. It was not planned or premeditated. It just happened. And it was not just sex but an expression of love, each willingly giving and taking their bodies naturally with new unpractised passion.

Physically, it was quick, fumbled, inexperienced and unsatisfying. It was tentative and awkward and it hurt Rose, but she ignored the initial pain and it was over quickly. Although it had been mostly unsatisfactory, they were both glad it had happened.

Mentally, it was the inevitable cementing of their togetherness, binding them together as one for all time.

Afterwards, they clung to each other almost desperately for a few moments before Billy was struck by a feeling of guilt. "I didn't take any precautions," he mumbled softly.

Rose looked at him steadily. "Don't worry about it," she replied, equally softy. "We both did it willingly. I wanted to as much as you. We're both to blame, but I'm glad it happened."

Billy was pleased, but decided not to tell Jonno about it, and he hoped Rose wouldn't tell Mary either. They were "best" friends, but it was nothing to do with them.

They were silent again, silent and now relaxed. But the happy mood was broken fairly quickly as their friends burst into the car around them after a clownish and somewhat juvenile dash across the car park in which all were laughing at escaping the wrath of a loutish bully Ging had insulted. Billy and Rose just managed to get themselves dressed and respectable-looking in time for the others not to realise what had happened.

As life went on over time, they did not speak about what had happened, there was no need, and it didn't happen again. But it was a truth, an event, a happening, and they both knew it made them complete and that it was meant to be.

Their lives went on together—seeing each other as often as possible despite the suspicions of Rose's mother, Mavis. Billy was well aware of that mistrust, and when he was eventually introduced, he tried to turn on his natural charm to try to impress her.

He knew he had a tough job winning Mavis over through many small events. One night, for instance, he drove Rose home after a night at the cinema, taking the car right up to her front gate, and as he parked outside and leant across to kiss her goodnight, he thought he saw a slight flicker of the front room curtains, but as there were no lights on in the room, he could not be certain.

He didn't tell Rose, so when she got out of the car, she stood at the gate, watched him do a three-point turn, then stayed until his rear lights had turned the corner at the end of the road. In the car, Billy knew that Mavis was keeping a check on the pair of them and he was determined to do all he could to improve things.

He obviously succeeded, because when they had been together for more than three years, even Mavis had grown to rather like him—or rather accepted him—although there was still an underlying antipathy that he was a bit of a dilettante and not the rich super executive she had hoped for. His cheeky charm, chirpy personality and perennially happy disposition had won her over somewhat, and she could see how happy Rose was with him. She accepted him as a potential son-in-law and was resigned to her daughter marrying him.

So, it was no real surprise when, after all their time together, both Rose and Billy started some rather detailed wedding talk. They had always believed they would get married, and by Rose's twenty-first birthday, they decided to go ahead with the idea.

There was no proposal. Billy never got down on one knee to ask Rose to marry him. It was just accepted by everyone that they were engaged. And so, a tea party was arranged for that to happen—following the tradition of the times of Billy having to ask her father's permission.

Although Billy had been to the Bakers' house for cups of tea or coffee many times, because of Mavis' underlying feelings, it was the first time he'd been invited for a "proper" meal.

The tea was awkward: bulging egg mayonnaise and tinned salmon filled sandwiches cut into quarters. Mavis handed Billy a napkin—something he never had at home—and Billy rested it on his lap.

Mavis offered the two plates of sandwiches, andBilly chose two quarters of egg, but a gushing Mavis urged him to try the salmon. Billy didn't like tinned salmon but didn't like to say no, so he took the smallest one he could see. He decided to eat it first to get it out of the way. He took a small bite, and immediately turned red as he bit into a small piece of salmon bone. As he tried to surreptitiously pick it out with his fingers, Mavis saw and asked, "Are you all right?" in an obviously motherly way.

Billy struggled to say "yes" as he put two fingers in his mouth to remove the bone while still having the rest of the sandwich stuck in his teeth and on his tongue. Rose watched, rather like a mouse caught in an adder's jaws, unable to help in any way.

She sat through the rest of the meal, hardly eating anything herself and in a state of near panic. She felt for Billy's embarrassment during the actual meal, and she couldn't help worrying what her father was going to say to the boy-man she loved.

Rose had told Billy about her father's shyness and that he had been "something" in the army during the First World War. What she had not told him was that, as a soldier, Paul had been decorated for bravery, but the only reason she had not told him was that she did not really know herself. It was a subject never mentioned in their house.

After what seemed an eternity to both Billy and Rose, the meal came to an end.

Paul stood. "Very pleasant, Mavis," he said, "But now I think it's time that you and I, Billy, had a little chat."

As Billy stood, his unused napkin fell from his lap to the floor. Paul started to go out of the door to lead the way to the "sacred" front parlour, which was very rarely used.

Billy followed him into the other room scared and his mind in a bit of a whirl. There was a slightly musty air in the room from its lack of use, and Billy noticed that one of the side curtains—the one he had once seen fluttering from Mavis' spying—was still drawn shut.

Paul motioned Billy to a small armchair, then sat in a slightly larger one opposite him. Their knees nearly touched, and Paul seemed very friendly and, to Billy, rather out of character. As they sat looking at each other, Paul smiled at him.

"Relax, son, it's all right," he said smoothly. "The girls expect me to give you a bit of a grilling, a hard time, but there's no need. Rose has told me all I need to know about you and unsubtly given me my orders. I always obey a lady, so yes, it's OK for you to marry her."

Billy relaxed obviously. His shoulders, which had been hunched, dropped and he settled back in the chair. There was still a trace of salmon in his teeth and he wanted to use a finger to clear it.

"Now," continued Paul, "You'll want to know something about what you're taking on..."

For a moment, Billy feared he was going to get a talk on the sexual side of marriage, but Paul gently eased him through some talk about sharing responsibilities, always knowing when to back off from a wife's anger—"I've had my share of doing that," he smiled—and about organising finances.

"And always let her go shopping for clothes, that's most important," he said, grinning.

Billy listened, but in the way of younger men, he didn't take in too much of it. He was sure that he and Rose knew better between them.

Paul talked easily for a full quarter of an hour, longer than he usually managed, then he paused and glanced at his watch. "I think we'll let them sweat for another five minutes or so before we go back," he said with a huge, friendly smile. "Now, tell me, Billy... what football team do you support? Rose told me a lot about you. A bit rose-tinted if you'll excuse the pun. But she didn't tell me anything important."

Billy was completely at ease in Paul's usually shy but now composed and relaxed presence—his admiration for the older man grew literally by the second, and he thought he could see where Rose had inherited many of her good qualities.

Then, after about eight more minutes, Paul stood up. "Let's go and face the enemy," he said, smiling yet again.

He led the way out to the living room, where Rose and Mavis waited with a mixture of anxious emotions.

"I think he'll do," said Paul.

Rose ran forwards and kissed both men—Billy long and lovingly first, then Paul a more tender hefty peck on the cheek.

Mavis looked at the other three beneficently. She was also smiling. "Let's have a cup of tea," she said.

Billy noticed the salmon sandwich tray still on the table with three-quarter lumps turned up at the edges on it and he hoped he would not be offered another one of them.

And so, Billy and Rose got married.

Chapter 5

Mavis changed completely as the immediate excitement settled down, and although she still didn't really think Billy a suitable match for Rose, she took on the prospective dual roles of mother-of-the-bride and mother-in-law with an enthusiastic gusto.

One of the first things she did was to fix up a get-together with Billy's parents, Fred and Lynda. The meeting took place at a Sunday lunch at her house about two weeks later and was a little bit of a disaster.

Although their fathers were compliant and happy for both Rose and Billy, neither mother got on. They both wanted the best for their child, and neither thought the partnership was good enough for their long-term benefit.Maybe there was a slight bit of snobbishness about it, maybe just a natural protectiveness, but both felt they were a little superior to the other. They both wanted the best for their child. Perhaps give them the dream world they thought they had never had themselves.

Billy and Rose sat uncomfortably through the lunch, watching and listening silently—along with their fathers—to the not-so-subtle barbs flying sweetly between the two mothers. When the meal was over and formal farewells had been made with gushing but insincere promises to keep in touch, Billy and Rose went off on their own and sat despondently in Giuseppe's until it got dark.

But time, as always, allowed things to settle and their lives and plans for the wedding moved on. Billy managed to buy a fairly cheap diamond engagement ring, but had to borrow money from his parents for the small gold wedding band itself. He promised to pay it back.

They were finally married in early spring the following year—timed to get the maximum income tax and other benefits.

The day of the wedding dawned with a grey, miserable morning, and both Rose and Billy looked at it hoping it was not some kind of omen. They wanted to be with each other, but some traditional thinking insisted that they did not until the ceremony itself.

Both felt an apprehension and worry as they tried to muddle through the day, but that lifted around noon as the mist faded away like steam from a kettle, and by the time they and their families and a few guests made their ways to the local registry office, the sun was a huge pale yellow orb in a cloudless blue sky.

It was a spartan-looking office, just one small window looking out onto a car park, drab pale yellow walls and a minimum of furniture: a desk with twenty plain wooden folding chairs lined up in front of it, a filing cabinet and an out of place table with a paper covering against one wall on which stood a vase with some half a dozen white flowers already starting to droop and fade. There were a few official-looking papers on the desk.

As the formalities began, the warm late spring sunshine shining obliquely through the window somehow forecast hints of better things to come, and Billy and Rose, although still obviously a little nervous, were both full of youthful exuberance.

The actual ceremony was the last event of a busy day with the registrar anxious to get home to put her feet up.

Billy stood by the desk, self-consciously wearing a new off-the-peg dark grey suit with a gleaming white shirt and silver tie and waiting anxiously. Rose came in after four minutes looking majestically beautiful and Billy actually felt a slight jump in his chest at the vision.

Rose wore a pink flowered broderie anglaise dress, calf-length and with three-quarter-length sleeves. She had a small matching floral knotted headband worn with a bow on the left side to show off her long hair, which had been brushed back off her forehead, and to a naturally nervous Billy she looked better than any Hollywood star. In his wedding day confusion, he was even more bedazzled than usual.

Billy stood beside Rose holding her hand while the official vows were read and answered, with Mary as her lone bridesmaid behind them in a simple beige wool cocktail dress and a neat, suited Jonno somewhere near as best man.

Both sets of parents sat at the back of the room with a mix of happy embarrassment and pride, but it was obvious that they kept strictly apart during the ceremony. All four of them were overdressed—Billy's father, Fred, a junior barman in a pub and therefore unacceptable to Rose's mother, was uncomfortable wearing a rare tie and stiff collar, while his mother, Lynda, wore a simple homemade dress.

The registrar was a severe, official-looking woman in her early sixties, and Billy was so keen he interrupted her when she asked the formal, "Do you, Phillip William Saunders, take Eliza Rose Baker..." with an eager "I do" before she had finished, earning a reproving but benevolent look.

The ceremony lasted a brief twenty minutes or so and passed in a bit of a blur for the young Billy and Rose, although both grinned back and responded when the registrar finished the formal service with a smile as she told them, "You are now man and wife."

When it was over, the newly married couple and their parents drove off in two hired cars, while the two dozen or so guests followed them to a party in a pub near Billy's home where Billy's father Fred worked.

The sun was starting to set in a still bright blue evening sky as more guests turned up with presents of plates, cutlery and home ornaments—largely distant cousins of the two families but with Jonno, Mary and Giuseppe as the only "Caballeros" present.

They all stood around with obligatory mock champagne after arriving to greet and offer good wishes to Rose and Billy, then all sat down at the two long tables that formed an open square with the family-only top table. A traditional three-tier iced wedding cake filled the end of the open side. Three temporary waitresses served a wedding breakfast of roast beef and potatoes with overcooked vegetables, and there was more low-cost red or white wine. A few of the men brought their own beer.

At the end of the meal, Rose and Billy were ushered forwards to make the first cut in the wedding cake, then Billy's father Fred welcomed the guests before best man Johno tried to embarrass Billy and Rose with some risqué (and near true) tales of the couple's romance.

Then, finally, the moment Billy had been dreading: his wedding speech.

He had worried for weeks about having to stand up in front of everyone, and when the time came he started by mumbling a few words of thanks to Rose's parents—making sure to praise Mavis' dress—and then stopped.

"I've got a whole written speech in my pocket," he said, indicating the inside pocket of his jacket, "And it's brilliant. Rose wrote it. But, well, I'm just too nervous to take it out. I'd probably drop it if I did. And in any case, now I'm starting to realise I'm an old married man, Dad says I've got to start fighting for my independence and equality." He glanced down at Rose. "It's a fight he says I'll never win, but I've got to try."

Rose looked at him adoringly, but although she smiled, he got a rather disproving look from Lynda when he said that, and Mavis glanced disapprovingly at Paul.

Billy waited for the slight laugh to die away, then continued.

"Anyway, on behalf of... my wife... and me, I'd just like to wish every one of you exactly what you wish for yourselves. And I hope it makes you as happy as we both are today."

He sat down, relieved, and Rose reached across to squeeze his arm.

"That was lovely," she told him. "I told you that you could do it. That I didn't need to write anything for you."

The party went more or less without any mishap, one minor blip being when Billy's coffee bar friend Frank was showing off trying to open a bottle of champagne in front of a group of girls.

"It should come out like a virgin's sigh," he said, trying to ease out the stopper. It suddenly shot out with a loud, explosive bang. "Whoops, she farted," said Frank.

Everyone tried to ignore it.

The party broke up at around a quarter to nine without any more trouble, and the newlyweds went off to a nearby cheap hotel, cheered on by the remaining guests as they left in a chauffeur-driven hire car.

In the hotel, they quickly booked in and went up to their room. They were finally alone. They took their time undressing and, on Rose's innocent lead, got into night attire (both in pyjamas, but Rose's silk). Both slightly sheepish to start with but slowly accepting the new fact that they were man and wife.

By the time they got into the narrow double bed for the first time, both were very, very happy but emotionally exhausted, and they fell asleep immediately in each other's arms without even a kiss.

The next morning, the rattle of a trolley outside their door woke them both, lying on their right sides with Rose tucked in tight behind Billy's back and with her arm resting on his hip. He turned, her arm sliding round his body giving him a pleasant thrill, and they touched lips.

"Hello, Mrs Saunders," he said, smiling.

Rose kissed him again lightly. "Hello, Mr Saunders."

They looked deep into each other's eyes.

"I think I could like this," he said.

"Me too."

"Will it always be like this?"

"Yes, always. Just you and me."

"I'm glad we got yesterday over... um, not getting married, but all the fuss," said Billy.

"I know what you mean. Now it's just us, we can start our lives."

"I love you..."

They kissed again, more strongly this time, then got up, leisurely dressed and packed, and went to the downstairs restaurant for a light breakfast snack before the pre-paid hire car picked them up to take them to the station for the start of their honeymoon.

The train took them to St. Austell, the nearest station to Mevagissey, a small fishing village on the south coast of Cornwall where they had booked a room in what sounded like a suitable guesthouse fairly close to the harbour.

They arrived just before lunch and started their honeymoon amongst a crowd of elderly other guests, fussed over by the attentive landlady herself, Mrs Griggs.

Billy and Rose were conscious of their youth amongst the other guests and also the fact that it was just the first day of their lives together. They were complete innocents, and although quite at ease with each other, both felt out of their depth as a married couple with the staff and others staying in the guesthouse.

It was a long week, slow, but for Rose and Billy not a moment too long. They were deliriously happy as they instantly settled into their new status together and floated blissfully into their holiday.

They had a lovely week, just the two of them together behaving exactly like what they were: newlyweds. They went walking hand in hand on the beach, investigated the local sights with Billy fantasising about (and almost believing) the many local myths and legends about mermaids, devils and kings that proliferated in that part of the world. They just sat in the scenery simply enjoying being a part of it all. They had picnics, stuffed themselves full of rich cream scones, and sometimes just sat under a tree, with arms around each other and watching the waves roll in. On some evenings they sat quietly drinking half pints of cider in the village pub, accepted by all the locals who could see just how much in love they were.

They spent the first afternoon wandering round the narrow, winding cobbled streets of the village, and went to look at the busy harbour with painted fishing smacks bobbing on the waters of the inner quay and a few fishermen sitting chatting on their boats as they worked repairing their nets. They were both fascinated by the lighthouse away to their right on the breakwater. It was the first time either had seen one.

On the advice of Mrs Griggs, they explored the surrounding area. They left the village and walked slightly north-east along the coast, aiming for the headland of Black Head, the sun blazing above them glistening off the English Channel on their right. It was sublime—Cornwall at its best.

"It's so glorious," said Rose.

They sat on a grassy bank above the sandy beach of Pentewan, and while Billy just lay back and enjoyed the novel experience of the moment, Rose sat picking a posy of the wildflowers growing around them.

It was too hot to just sit, and they reluctantly got up after almost an hour, both perspiring profusely, and carried on towards Black Head. Mrs Griggs had given them a small parcel for a picnic, and they stopped under a tree above the headland to eat it: two enormous pasties, a couple of crab sandwiches and another duo of scones. It was delicious.

After they had finished eating, they had a short kiss and cuddle, then stood and made the return journey back to the guesthouse. They had a short walk to the harbour after a filling supper and went to bed reasonably early.

There was not a lot to do in Mevagissey on Sunday, so after a quiet morning strolling round the town for a couple of boring hours, the couple spent most of the next afternoon at the Mevagissey Museum on the East Wharf in the inner harbour, lapping up facts about the village's Bronze Age history and finding fascinating facts about the smuggling that had once been the main source of money for the villagers.

They spent too long there really, and as clouds started to darken the sky, they went to a brightly lit fish and chip shop for supper. They looked at the alien names of the fish on offer—mackerel, bream, pollack, wrasse and garfish seemed quite exotic to them both—but settled on cod for their own meal.

Later, still a bit bored, they decided on a rare visit to a pub, choosing the Harbour Tavern because of its views over the quay and the high ground towards Portmellon, and spent a desultory hour or so doing nothing but drinking a glass of mead, a local drink made with honey. Rose suggested the drink with a slight laugh when she saw it advertised as "Cornwall's legendary love potion" and it made them both slightly tipsy. After a small glass each, they went back to the guesthouse hanging on to each other for support and giggling at everything.

Rose and Billy woke up the next morning. The bedroom was bright with sunshine despite the thin curtains being drawn—Mevagissey being noted for its bright artist's light. They lay on the bed under an old-fashioned sheet and blanket, their arms loosely round each other's waist, faces centimetres apart but their foreheads touching. Rose had her eyes shut, daydreaming romantically about now being a wife; Billy, with his eyes fixed on Rose's face, too close to be fully in focus, was thinking how beautiful she was. They lay there contented until Rose opened her eyes.

Billy kissed her lightly. "Hello, Mrs S," he said, repeating himself. He liked saying (and hearing) the words.

"I still don't feel like Mrs Saunders," she replied. Then, after a beat, added, "But I am. I am." She smiled, and it was her turn to kiss Billy gently.

"Yes, you are. A real missus."

"Married, eh?" whispered Rose. "We've got each other now. For life."

"You're right. The rest of the world can go…"

"Just us."

"That's right. Just us. We've got everything. We don't need anyone else."

Their bodies had pulled apart, but they were still close and facing each other. Billy pulled Rose close again and they kissed before making slow love. Afterwards, they held each, both choking with love but neither saying a word. There was no need. Both knew.

Despite the single episode in the car outside the club and Billy's stockroom incident, they had married as two perfect innocents despite trying to listen to half-hearted and embarrassed advice on sex from parents and equally innocent friends, but neither understanding nor really believing any of it. Despite their previous fumblings on the back seat of a car or in the last row of the cinema, neither had a real clue about the ha-ha hilarity of the act itself.But over the honeymoon, they were starting to discover things for themselves and learnt from and with each other.

They finally got out of bed, dressed, smoothed the sheet and blanket as best they could and went downstairs. It was too late for breakfast, but Mrs Griggs insisted on cooking some bacon and eggs especially for them, then they went out into another brilliantly sunlit morning.

Rose had suggested a lazy day on the beach, and as they had learnt that the best place was Polzeath, just outside the village, they walked there and climbed down the steep two-hundred-step stairway to its sand and shingle. They had again brought a picnic of pasties and relaxed, completely at ease just being with each other.

By Tuesday, they had both begun to get a bit restive. Although they were enjoying the holiday, it was their final joining in marriage that they really relished. Although quite content just spending time together as husband and wife, they didn't realise they were just filling time.

They decided to go window shopping, resisting the temptation to buy souvenirs in order to save money before taking a slow walk to nearby Chapel Point, loving the sight of the clear sea through which they could see the underwater rock formations and an occasional flash of a fish—or it might have been a grey seal.

They sat on the grass at Bodrugan's Leap, where a local dignitary was said to have jumped into a boat from the clifftop to escape murder by Henry Tudor's men, and fed the gulls, cormorants and oystercatchers, fighting off the attacks by the impatient birds trying to snatch the food from their hands before it was thrown to them.

It was yet another bright morning on the following day, and they strolled around the harbour again, wondering what to do. They were going through the motions of a holiday and enjoying them, but their real pleasure was just in being together all the time. So, while it was really quite a mundane holiday and they did all the things they were supposed to do, they were simply enjoying a heaven of their own that didn't require outside help.

Billy spotted a few men and their sons dangling lines over the side of the harbour wall and they went to have a closer look. They discovered they were fishing for crabs using rods or just bits of string with bacon tied to the end.

"That looks like fun," said Billy. "Want to try it?"

Rose shook her head fiercely. "No, I don't think so," she replied. "I wouldn't be able to handle it if I caught one. Slimy things. And those claws... so big..."

Billy laughed, and after a while, they moved on to see if they could find a coach tour inspecting the surrounding countryside. They discovered an agency advertising several on boards pyramided outside on the street, and booked one that seemed suitable and was affordable. It began half an hour later, so they went for a tea—and a Cornish cream cake—while they waited, and then joined the bus, getting seats about halfway along the off-side.

It turned out to be the best side because they had the best views, and Rose, in particular, enjoyed the ride as it rested her aching legs. The wild unspoilt scenery was all both had hoped for and, for townies Rose and Billy, a splendour they could hardly believe.

The next morning, Friday, was the last day of their honeymoon, and together they decided on what they regarded as a bit of an adventure. They didn't have too much money to spend, but they agreed to splash out on an exciting sounding sea trip. Once again, it was a novelty for both—neither had ever been on a boat before.

They walked to nearby Heligan and were lucky enough to book the last places on a ride that was not really a sea trip, but what turned out to be a packed ferry to Fowey, crossing the sheltered St. Austell Bay.

They sat on the starboard side of the boat, the Bessie James, for the three-quarter of an hour outward trip, looking for dolphins. Billy thought he saw one, but he was the only person on board who did, but even without that, it was a relaxing and very pleasant day in the sun.

On the pre-reserved return journey, the boat slowed, and the crew pointed out a shoal of dolphins romping about a hundred yards away, and that thrill was improved when another passenger, a middle-aged woman who suspected Billy and Rose were on honeymoon, offered them both a cold drink from a bag she was carrying.

Billy and Rose left Mevagissey on the Saturday, returning to the apartment they had rented roughly midway between their two sets of parents to begin their marriage properly.

They went back to work on the Monday, hating being apart after their first full-on twenty-four hours a day week-long honeymoon. For both though, there was added joy at getting back to "their home" after work in the evening.

Chapter 6

The apartment was really the upstairs floor of the house owned by a friendly woman in her mid-to-late fifties, Sally Brooks, and it was about five or six miles from both of their parents.It was clean and in a reasonably nice area—and cheap. Billy and Rose regarded it as home when they moved in and settled down quickly.

Rose especially fitted in immediately to her new life after the wedding, enjoying the new freedom from strict (and, she had often thought, unnecessary) parental control.Both she and Billy enjoyed the different freedom that being married gave them.

After the wedding, they saw both sets of parents regularly, having Sunday lunch with them in turn, but while Billy's family fell instantly in love with Rose, her mother was still slightly antagonistic towards Billy, more or less daring him to put a foot wrong in his treatment of her daughter.

Gradually, Mavis saw how good he was with Rose and how happy he made her, so on top of Billy's natural charm, good manners and obvious devotion for her daughter, she began to really like (almost love) him.

Rose and Billy quickly settled into a routine marriage. They bought furniture and carpets and rugs on the never-never, and decorated the chimney breast of their living room with a hideous grey wallpaper that was faux brickwork. They were inordinately proud of it.Eventually, they got a kitten, donated to them by a neighbour.

They were very much in love, besotted by their love, and they each knew (or thought they knew) that no one else in the whole history of mankind could have ever been so happy.

Things went well, and although there was the usual minor bickering, they were so devoted to each other that their petty differences didn't linger. Their marriage followed what they thought was a fairly conventional path, and they allowed the new releases of speech and behaviour to blend into their own dual way of life—their still juvenile thoughts of a liberated emancipation played a big part in things.

They didn't have children, not by desire, it just didn't happen and neither was too bothered at first. They were an ideal married couple happy in their own togetherness.

They had the normal married couple intimacies, and had a very active sex life. It was natural, the survival of the species, and they were young and they enjoyed it. And they were married.

They laughed a lot—both at and with each other without rancour—and it was often so loud that all their neighbours (even those across the street) heard it and chuckled with them.Life was funny, loving, and they were excited with each other.

Rose quickly got into the habit of cooking meals for the two of them, and proved to be very good and inventive. One day, she had a day off from work and spent the whole day in her kitchen preparing a special evening meal. When Billy came home, he found there was a beef Wellington she had lovingly made during the day—a recipe she remembered from an early date when they had their first restaurant meal together.

Billy was amazed that she had remembered and enjoyed the meal.

"It was better than that restaurant," he told her as he helped her clear the table.

"I'm glad you enjoyed it," she replied. "I've never cooked anything like it before. I didn't know how it was going to turn out."

"I don't know why you were worried," said Billy. "You seem able to do just about everything."

Rose laughed and turned to kiss him. "Thank you, sir," she said, bobbing a small curtsey.

"No need to thank me," he said. "It's just that I'm discovering that you're a better cook than my mother…" They kissed again. "That's why I love you."

They made love on the floor, the kitchen pots and pans above them and the dirty supper washing up still in the sink.

Rose giggled afterwards. "I can't imagine my parents doing that!" she said. She was herself living proof that it wasn't a new invention made up by Billy and herself!

Another evening, when Rose went into the kitchen to make a cup of coffee, Billy followed her, suddenly grabbing her round the waist and whirling her round and round, giggling in a crazy frenzy of "dancing" until they both collapsed to their knees, puffing but still laughing. His arms were still round her waist and he pulled her body close and kissed her.

"I love you so much," he said.

Rose looked back at him, her eyes wide open and looking deep into his. "Me too," she replied.

The physical side was still important to them both—they never missed a chance to kiss or explore each other. Put another way, they couldn't keep their hands off each other.

There was another day when they were relaxing with the new television they had rented and Rose casually said she was thirsty, so Billy got up from the settee and went into the kitchen. He got a bottle of cola and a glass and returned to the sofa where he ceremonially held the bottle in his right hand at its base and put his left hand behind his back like a sommelier at a posh restaurant.

"Would madam care to check that the bubbles are at the right temperature?" he said with a phoney French accent.

She laughed, and they forgot both the drink and the TV as they embraced and loved each other.

One summer's evening they even made love on the lawn in the back garden, indifferent to the thought that they might be seen by their landlady or the neighbours. He would always call it his "lovelorn garden" afterwards, and although she didn't think it particularly funny, she always laughed, because it was him saying it.

They really were both besotted with each other. They slept close together, arms around each other, and one night, when a loud noise woke Billy at around 4:30, he got out of bed to investigate. Nothing seemed wrong, so he climbed back into bed, but he was by then wide awake.

The duvet made him overly hot, so he threw it off again, looking at Rose beside him in a deep, deep sleep, taking steady, measured breaths. The streetlamp outside the house threw a weird half-light into the room, and he could see her nightdress had ridden up to her waist. He reached across and gently put his hand between her legs. She didn't wake, but her breathing seemed to speed up a bit and a silent smile appeared on her lips.

Billy lay there for about three minutes before he, too, fell asleep again with his hand still on Rose.

When they later woke up, he told her, "I love you." It still sounded slushy and cinema romantic to him, but he meant it and somehow Rose knew that he did.

The marriage wasn't only physical though, and as weeks and months went by they continually discovered new things about each other.

One day, for instance, she watched him in the kitchen preparing a slice of bread.

"What are you doing?"

"Making a pickle sandwich. Do you want one? Here, I'll make it. A Michelin-starred mustard pickle sandwich. You'll love it."

"Why are you putting so much butter on?" she asked.

"You can't eat naked pickles!"

She laughed. "Idiot," she said, and walked over to take the knife from him. "Here, I'll do it," she said.

He let her, and she scraped off half the butter he'd already spread on the slice of bread.

Billy gently pushed Rose out of the way and took the knife from her. "Right, that's fine. Now I'll do the hard part." He added a thick layer of pickle. "Here, how's that?"

Rose bit into it. "Delicious," she replied, her words muffled by the mouthful of pickle.

Billy never lost that early happy feeling when Rose came into a room, and they both held hands and cuddled each other whenever they could. It was a true partnership—two elements capable of being independent, but better off when one entity.

And although they were a perfect team, it didn't take Billy long to find that, like almost every other newlywed man of the time, he'd married not only the woman of his dreams but a cook, cleaner, advisor, bookkeeper, housemaid, mentor, financier, accountant, banker, gardener, planner, secretary, legal sorter-out and lifelong best friend all rolled into one. Not only that, but she was also glad to do it and enjoyed the responsibility.

Rose took on all the responsibilities of the house and their marriage naturally and willingly, and as he had no knowledge or interest in that kind of thing, Billy gladly left her to do it all. He was useless with money matters and left things like savings and paying bills to her.It worked for them.

Rose budgeted precisely, and while not exactly sorting out piles of coins and notes on the dining room table for each regular bill, she always had money available for every payment. She even carefully allowed Billy a small weekly "pocket money" allowance. Billy liked it like that. And they were never in debt.

They often say that girls "marry their father", but Rose's choice was very different. Her father was a private person, organised, almost shy (although he often opened up with Billy), but Billy was outgoing, friendly towards anyone he met and somewhat chaotic. And instead of just being a wife who cooked and cleaned—her father's idea—she and Billy became more than just lovers and husband and wife, they became friends. True friends. Neither liked being without the other.

One day, when Rose was getting ready to go shopping, Billy kept asking if she had put certain items on her list.

"Don't be long," said Billy wistfully when he could no longer delay her.

"I won't."

"Promise?"

"Yes."

Rose picked up her bags and walked to the kitchen door.

"Remember, be quick," said Billy.

"Of course."

Billy walked across to open the door for her, and she went out. He closed the door, and almost immediately opened it again and called her back. She was by the back gate, but turned and went back.

"Don't be long," he repeated.

She kissed him and laughed. "I'll be back in a flash," she replied. "I'll miss you."

It didn't take long before everyone—especially their neighbours—knew them as a happy pair who enjoyed their life together. They were equal partners.

"We are equal, but Rose is better," Billy joked, but Rose would prod him on the arm whenever he said that.

Not that it was always perfect between them. Billy's refusal to take serious matters seriously always hit a bad note with Rose. Often, in exasperation, she would break off a serious one-sided conversation to tell Billy, "Oh... you... silly Billy." But she could never be really cross with him and later that developed into a gently reprimanding "silly boy", which he claimed was a promotion and always amused him. It was, at least, better than Jonno's "uncouth lout" comments.

But they rarely argued. If one was annoyed, the other always knew and backed off. On those rare times, they would call each other by their full names—her Eliza Rose, he Phillip William—and it would be a bit of a tension-breaker.

Like true friends, they knew when to talk and when to sit silent and listen. Rose, in particular, was good at that. They shared those little knowing looks where you could fleetingly almost see the electric magnetism flow between them.

After a year or two, Billy was promoted to sales manager with a big pay rise, and occasionally had to travel the country—he hated being apart from her.

They still saw Billy's best friend Jonno, who had by now married Rose's friend Mary from long ago, but they were the only coffee shop Caballeros they still saw regularly. For a while, they met frequently as true friends who gave both Billy and Rose their affection and support. The four of them spent their time doing this and that together.

But Jonno and Mary now had other interests and did things that were too expensive for Billy and Rose to even consider. They kept up

Saturday evening meets to go to the dance club though, sometimes linking up there with the other Caballeros after meeting at Giuseppe's. It was never the same, and they gave that up after Giuseppe sold up and new owners took over the coffee bar.

Life moved on for Billy and Rose as they settled easily into a regular life. They did normal things—loving the cinema, especially seeing all the new Hollywood films as well as supporting the home industry offerings from Pinewood, Shepperton, Denham and Ealing Studios. Billy preferred the loud, glitzy musicals, but Rose's preference was for light romance or comedy.

They went to museums and historic houses, to some fascinating and interesting exhibitions, to educational lectures (Billy didn't like them and got restless), and once to the final of a beauty contest.

"But you're prettier than any of them," Billy predictably told Rose, and he genuinely meant it.

Once they could afford it, they also began going to see live theatre shows in the West End, and on special occasions they would splash out on a meal at an overpriced "name" restaurant too. But both preferred more intimate meals cooked by Rose at home.

Both were growing up, and life was good.But Rose and Billy were still happiest when alone together.

For his birthday one year, Rose decided to give Billy a real treat. She wrapped the football scarf and book she'd bought as a present, then silently laid out the carefully measured ingredients for a feast of crispy duck, something Billy had frequently seen on Chinese restaurant or takeaway menus and thought sounded "posh".

When he finally came into the kitchen forty-five minutes later, she had just put cinnamon sticks, star anise, orange peel and spring onions in a frying pan and turned on the heat to make the seasoning. She turned. She had a small dab of white flour on the tip of her nose, and he bent forwards to kiss it.

"I always said you were well bred," he joked, and they were suddenly in a tight embrace kissing with their lips tight against each other and loving with a deep and indescribable emotion.

"Happy birthday... old... man." She smiled at him and silently handed over the present, and he ripped the gift wrapping off.

"Oh, it's lovely. But you shouldn't," he said, still sleepy. "I'm not old. Older, perhaps, but not old," he replied, swallowing deeply to hide his emotion. "In any case, I'm thinking of putting my birthday back to tomorrow... as you know, tomorrow never comes."

He was just twenty-six years old.

Rose looked disappointed, but he laughed and grabbed her by the waist and gave her a long, lingering, romantic kiss on the lips. "But I love the 'not birthday' present. And the food looks very edible..." he added, looking at the mass of ingredients laid out haphazardly on the table.

Then, singing the music of a popular love song very off-key, he whirled her round and round in an enthusiastic dance.

"I love you, Rose," he said, both of them panting for breath, and they kissed again, holding each other close.

Fat sizzled in the frying pan and spat and was ignored by both as it got too hot on the stove.

Their romance was deeply engrained in them both—a love that was all embracing, almost achingly beautiful for both.They had grown up—together—and by now the meaningful words "I love you" did not sound quite as sloppy and sentimental as they were at first... nor as mechanically dutiful. Both loved saying them to the other—and repeated them frequently (perhaps too frequently).

They grew with each other, and together they lost their individual immature shyness as both became rounded human beings—Billy to the point of near arrogance.They had settled to become a very happy, very normal couple.

Chapter 7

By now, they had moved to their own independent flat in an apartment block about half a mile from Mrs Brooks. It was not very big, with just one bedroom and a living room with an open fireplace enclosing an electric hearth, along with a miniscule kitchen with a built-in electric oven and stove, and a combined toilet and bathroom with a handheld shower on the wall over a bath. Not much but it was their own, and for the first time, they were completely on their own.

To their neighbours on both sides, they were just an average, middle-class couple who plodded along minding their own business but living quietly happy, for each of them being together an everlasting magic. They were so strongly bound together that they both felt it was a miracle of love that somehow went above any normal.

Money was not plentiful, but thanks to Rose who did, after all, take after her very prudent (to the point of mean) father, her natural frugality and thriftiness kept their finances balanced, and they paid their bills and were starting to build up a small nest egg of savings.

Things seemed to be moving along serenely and they were deliciously happy for over seven years.

Rose's mother Mavis had now accepted Billy completely, and she now boasted to her friends and acquaintances how good a husband he was. Rose, she was now convinced, had made a good choice, and she often spoke, obliquely she felt, about their making her a grandmother.

Surprisingly, Billy was the first to pick up on the not-so-subtle hints, and in their now not-so-frequent bouts of sex brought a hint of expectation to proceedings and he also suggested Rose stop her contraception. Although their initial early marriage hard sex drive had abated, Rose readily agreed and joined in willingly.

Then one Sunday they got a message that Rose's father was feeling a little poorly and they cancelled their regular lunch with her parents. With the sun shining in a bright, clear sky, Rose felt free and dressed up specially hoping to please Billy more than usual. He noticed.

They went to Hampstead Heath as they had once before they were married and wandered down from Whitestone Pond for a while before finding the spot where they had sat that first time. They looked over the London scene and sat or lay there fully relaxed for a while.

"One day, I'm going to conquer that town and give it to you as a present," said Billy.

Rose smiled but didn't answer.

After almost an hour of simply lazing in the hot sun, they stood, dusted each other down and walked back to find a small trattoria fairly nearby, where they enjoyed pasta lunches and tiramisu. They didn't go to Giuseppe's.

"It's been a lovely day," summed up Rose when they got home.

It had been almost idyllic, but then within five weeks both Rose's parents died. Paul first from a stroke followed by Mavis just eight days later apparently from a broken heart. Rose was devastated, but Billy calmly and conscientiously saw her through her personal crisis and it made for an even tighter bond between them—unlikely though that had seemed. Billy came through responsibly when it mattered—when he needed to for Rose's sake.

The two funerals took place with a quiet, private ceremony two weeks later in a joint grave.

And after all the official paraphernalia and kerfuffle that followed, Rose (and therefore Billy) inherited several thousand pounds and they were able to put down a sizeable deposit on a move to their first suburban home.

It was a very ordinary bungalow in a row of similar-looking properties, with a modest-sized lounge, dining room, bedroom and a narrow kitchen. It had a miniscule, grassed area at the front and a long narrow shaded garden at the back.

There was still quite a substantial mortgage remaining so there was not an abundance of money to spend, but Rose and Billy were able to start enjoying occasional luxuries and outings. Luckily, they preferred their own company together and didn't particularly want to go out with others.

They both loved eating out and were frequent regulars at a nearby French bistro for *"un diner pour deux"*. She loved its *poulet à l'estragon* (chicken with tarragon), while he normally ordered the duck *à l'orange*. The staff all adored Rose and laughed at Billy's never-ending optimism, and they were quickly dubbed *"Les Romantiques"*.

As they started to head towards middle age, the actual physical side of their marriage had faded a little, although they still had their moments, and after the first few years of unbridled passion their lovemaking settled down and as they both got more experienced and learnt each other's pleasures it became a more enjoyable more mental experience.

Despite the physical side of their marriage slowing down now though, both still got a vicarious thrill when they held hands while out walking, and alone at home, they still enjoyed the privacy of their own nudity.

There was complete mental togetherness, but just being together and only linked together physically in that way was usually enough. The flames had burnt themselves down to an ember, and instead of a raging inferno there was now a brightly glowing fire giving out just as much heat—a steadier and even warmer heat. The magnetism still flowed between them.

Over the years, Billy had grown more mature, but although he took a big interest in outside events, he was still able to cut them off from his everyday reality. He had enough matters to concern him, so he tended to joke and be light-hearted about things.

His warm personality endeared itself to almost everyone, and all who met him felt his instant friendliness, but Rose was very much his main responsibility.

She shared a reciprocal feeling, but Billy's apparent thoughtlessness over important situations would sometimes exasperate her.

"Why can't you take more responsibility, deal with things, you... you... silly man?" she would ask.

Billy would smile, nod or promise to change, but he would always continue in his blithe, haphazard way, letting Rose carry on doing most of the essential chores that had to be done. And Rose, in the end, was always happy to do them.

Rose's adolescent juvenile prettiness had now blossomed into a delicate, more adult beauty, and she hardly ever wore make up; the natural beauty of her features ensured that it didn't make much difference. But she had started dying her hair blonde to hide the wisps of grey that were starting to creep in. Billy, who still combed his hair with a quiff but had given up the teenage gel so that it often flopped down over his right eye, especially thought she was still a stunning-looking woman.

They enjoyed their seventh wedding anniversary alone, although throughout the day various friends phoned to gush congratulations. Rose took it all graciously, but Billy routinely joked that he "only hung on because it was cheaper than paying a cook and a cleaner". He also reminded others that "you get time off for murder", Rose looking on with almost resigned pleasure at his comments. In the evening, both were quiet, simply going to the favourite French restaurant and enjoying a light meal. They enjoyed the lone evening together.

Although they were married, they were the best of friends and still very much in love like newlyweds. They had built up a solid wall of friends over the years—true friends not just acquaintances, because they both had a rare knack of attracting honesty and affection. Once met and liked, others quickly settled into the unspoken acts of harmony and they both had them round as guests and went to their houses for meals.

One of them, Matt Lucas, was a journalist and they joined him and his wife on several occasions. One time, he invited them to a book launch. After the formal business, which Rose enjoyed but Billy found boring, they were standing by a hefty buffet table during the reception. They were supposed to meet the author and offer praise, but Matt suggested they just enjoy the food.

"He's a boring old fart," he told them.

"Oh, surely not. He writes such interesting books. He must be quite exciting to meet," replied Rose.

"Don't you believe it. Writers are usually boring if they aren't talking about themselves and their... 'art'."

Billy interrupted. He couldn't care less. "Well, I'm going to get some nosh," he told the others.

"Don't take a plate. That way no one can see how much you're eating," said Matt. "Just pick up things as you want them. You'll get far more."

Billy took note, but Rose was still intrigued by the author. "I'm sure he tells some fascinating stories..."

"Even us journos can't make up their kind of stories," said Matt.

"Surely they're reality though. Writers just use their experiences."

"Just have some food, Rose," interrupted Billy. "Matt's right. I know. You can't bluff a bluffer..."

The conversation petered out and they eventually went home—Billy quite full but Rose still a little hungry as she had been too busy trying to meet the author.

Money was easier now as Rose carefully managed their joint income with almost religious frugality, and although they were far from being rich, they could afford little (or even medium-sized) treats more often now and then, so because of the food situation the previous evening, Billy took Rose to a small restaurant he knew for a treat. She put on a new gown: a pale green plunge-fronted tie-waisted midi dress.

"You look good tonight," said Billy. "You've done your hair different."

"No, just as usual."

"Well, whatever. I really fancy you."

"Don't be silly. At my age?"

"If I was twenty years younger..."

"What was it Ging used to say in the coffee bar?" sparked Rose perkily, flattered by her husband. "You're as old as the woman you feel."

"Rose!"

And suddenly, they both were twenty years younger.

The mood stayed with them through the meal and on the way home, and it was still with Rose the next morning. She got up before Billy and was in the kitchen getting things prepared for their evening shepherd's pie when he finally appeared. Rose turned to him with a saucy look.

"Come get me, tiger..."

She took Billy by the hand and led him into the living room. She had a dark ribbon holding her hair away from her face, but now she tugged it off and the new white-blonde tresses curled around her like a picture frame. She gave Billy a lopsided smile.

"Come on then," she said, her voice gravelly and slightly distorted.

Billy moved over, and after a few minutes, they fell to the floor, holding each other and laughing for a few moments before their kisses drowned out any conversation. For a while, both felt like their younger just married selves.

When the little playful romp was over, they carried on cuddling and laughing, still on the floor, until Rose suddenly sat up. "Good grief, my potatoes will be soggy," she said, her voice now normal.

Billy held her down, looking at her chest. "Don't ever get soggy potatoes," he grinned.

"I'll just go and turn off the gas," she said primly, but with a smile returning to her face.

Billy stood and turned to help Rose, but Rose, although managing to kneel on one knee, had trouble standing up. She was puffing noticeably, and Billy had to pull her up as she was a bit unsteady on her feet. He held her for some time until she seemed to recover.

Then she went back to the kitchen and carried on with her cooking, but as she did, she reflected—the Miss Prim and Proper before she had married Billy would never have acted as she had just done. The smile returned to her lips.

Finally, goodbye, Miss Prim. Welcome, Mrs Me, she thought.

Billy had straightened the messed-up furniture and rug in the living room but then followed her into the kitchen. She still had her back to him but sensed he was there.

"I'm getting too old for that kind of thing," he said, bracing his shoulders.

"If you're achy now, what are you going to be like when you're an old man?" she chided, still concentrating on her cooking.

Billy laughed. "I may be too old for that kind of thing, but I've no plans for senility," he said. "I may have to grow old, but I don't intend to grow up."

"But it was fun," said Rose over her shoulder, still not turning.

"All I want is to make you happy," replied Billy, suddenly getting serious. "Nothing more. Anything else would be a bonus."

He again felt he was being "slushy", but he meant every word, and Rose knew it and believed him.

Life literally plodded on uneventfully. Billy and Rose still had their small disagreements like any other couple, of course, but they were always quickly forgotten and generally their life together ran smoothly. They were a relaxed, normal couple.

Rose's inability to stand up by herself that once after the falling down romp worried Billy though, and he made special efforts to help her around the house. But over the next few weeks, thanks to the closer than normal observation, he noticed that she unusually complained quite frequently about not feeling well, but she steadfastly refused to go see a doctor when he suggested it.

Despite that worry, although both had suffered minor ailments—colds and that kind of thing—it was Billy who showed a first sign of "real" illness. He began to get some quite severe pains in his lower left stomach area, and over a week or so of coming and going, it got so bad that, unlike Rose, he had to go and see the doctor. The GP was concerned and got a nurse to take blood for a test and made an appointment for Billy to go to the nearby cottage hospital for tests.

A week later, Billy had a colonoscopy, an unpleasant internal examination of his stomach and bowel area through his bottom. It was lucky he took the indignity, because the test showed some nasty internal infestations.

Rose went with him when he went back to his own surgery to get the result a week later, and both were relieved when the doctor first told them that Billy did not have the bowel cancer he had feared.

"Unfortunately, you do have this thing called diverticulitis," he said, explaining that Billy had developed some small bulges on the lining of the intestine and they had become badly infected.

He put Billy on a fluid only diet for a few days and said a district nurse would call on him to inject twice daily doses of an antibiotic.

The nurse came and began giving Billy the two daily injections in his stomach, and after three days, she showed Rose how to give the jab, and left her with Billy roaring with laughter as she practised injecting a potato. There were a lot of laughs as Rose practised throughout the week before she was deemed efficient enough to give the daily dose to Billy.

Rose was completely unflappable, her always calm demeanour allowing her control of every situation, and she instantly picked up the nursing skill to help Billy. He had complete faith in her ability, and the stomach injections soon cleared the problem. He was grateful.

"Thank you… Red," he told her when the nurse gave him the all-clear. He did not know how or why her old nickname came to his lips.

It took Billy a few months to really get over things—his own illness as well as Rose's standing difficulty adding to signs of something not quite right—but he did get better and as things settled down to normal, Rose began to notice that he became more intense about their intimate times in bed—almost as if he were willing their bodies to make a baby.

But for all that, nothing came of their attempts, and after almost eight years of happiness (and slight financial hardships), they decided to take a summer holiday. They remembered how much they had enjoyed their honeymoon—a relaxing holiday by the sea when they had revelled in being together.

The extra glow of delight at that holiday had lasted several weeks, and because they had enjoyed it so much, they decided to be adventurous and for the first time in both their lives they agreed on a seaside abroad.

After lots of talk, they decided on Italy, but as it was to be their first ever time overseas, Billy decided they should do a bit of sightseeing first. He put a lot of effort into researching and planning it, and on a late summer's day at the beginning of August, they made the journey to Luton Airport for a cut price flight to Rome at the start of a two-week break.

They spent the first two days in the Eternal City, loving every minute of it. The did all the usual touristy things, seeing the Colosseum, Pantheon, and the Forum by cheap city bus tours, and spent a whole morning in Vatican City—an experience they both enjoyed because of Michelangelo's Pieta statue and his painting on the Sistine Chapel ceiling. Their feelings were a bit soured when they were faced by a beggar pleading for a few liras for her children by the entrance to the richest city state in the world.

"It's so unjust," said Rose as they passed her.

When they left the Vatican, the beggar had gone, and they wandered round for a while before finding a small trattoria in a side street where they, obviously, ordered spaghetti. They were delighted when the proprietor came to their table for a chat (in English) and ended up singing a romantic ballad to them before getting his wife to come from the kitchen to drink glasses of the lemon liqueur limoncello, "on the house", in a kind of grandparental way.

"We Romans love lovers, and you are obviously lovers," he told them with a huge beam on his face.

When Rose and Billy left the restaurant, they were (literally) full of good spirits and exceedingly happy—lovers being loved in a fairy-tale place.

"Rome... well, it's just what you expect Paris to be," was Billy's take on things. "A lovely city, and lovely people."

Billy had worked out a plan for the holiday and hired a car, but characteristically had not taken into account the difficulties of driving on the "wrong" side of the road from the "wrong" side of the car, the somewhat different approach to driving by Italian motorists or the intricacies of finding the way in a different country. In his own confident, brash way, he didn't let Rose see his discomfort.

It was easy at first as they drove slowly and ultra carefully from the airport to take the E45 road south, and after making good time, turned off the main road from Rome to head towards the mountains and across country. It was quite a shock as they made their way towards to the small mountain village of Isola del Leri.

Neither Billy nor Rose had ever seen mountains before—they were far steeper and taller than Hampstead Heath—and as they got higher, they made many stops to point out to each other the buzzards, kestrels, golden eagles, peregrine falcons, raptors and kites that hovered over the valley as a heavy sun lowered itself reluctantly towards the horizon.

They got to Isola in the early evening, the sun still shining but now weakly, and booked into a small room in a cheap family run *locanda*, sharing a bathroom with the other guests and sitting with them that evening over huge shared bowls of spaghetti and pizza.After the meal, they sat in their room, holding hands and looking out of the window with awe at the still visible splendour of the view.

The town was only about seven hundred feet above sea level, and was actually a kind of inland island, entirely surrounded by two separate branches of the River Liri, with two waterfalls, the Cascata Grande and Cascata del Valcatoio in the old city, coming down from the Simbruini range of the Apennines and both dropping an impressive thirty metres or so.

They had only intended on staying in Isola for one night, but the town proved so instantly magical that they extended their stay and spent three idyllic days in the town, relaxing completely and ridding themselves of all the bad memories of the previous few months.

They kept the car in a garage (Rose only slightly resenting the waste of rental money) and walked endlessly, exploring the medieval bridge and the twelfth century fortified Castello Boncompagni Viscogliosi, the sixth century castle of San Casto at nearby Sora (a popular site for lovers) and looking at the amazing panoramic views of the town's roof garden, standing high at eight hundred metres and displaying many really ancient trees. It was touristy, interesting and tiring, so they just spent long spells sitting in a cafe by the Cascata Grande just gazing in absolute reverence at the falling waters and having what they were told was the traditional lovers' kiss inspired by its magnificence.

They were enchanted by the town. To them, it was a fairyland filled with people so completely different to themselves, and those people took them to their hearts because of their natural, naive exuberance. It was a long way from their usual suburban London.

On the evening of the second day, they were in their room after a tiring day sightseeing, and while Rose changed for the evening meal, Billy sat on the bed bare chested and in trousers only. Rose slipped on a floral blouse, but stopped in front of Billy without doing up the buttons.

"I'm really enjoying this holiday. Thanks for organising it," she told him.

Billy looked up at her, smiling, "Yes, it's nice, isn't it?" he replied.

"It was a great idea. Just the two of us..."

"Yes. If only..." said Billy.

"What?"

"Well, wouldn't it be lovely if we had a baby to complete the family? We can afford it now."

"Just."

Rose looked into Billy's eyes and saw the fervour and intensity glowing in them as he spoke of having a family, and she felt the same potency of need.

The three days passed quickly, but by the end, both Rose and Billy had really seen enough of waterfalls and mountain views. They decided to move on and look for an Italian seaside, and from Billy's original research, Positano on the Amalfi Coast sounded a likely place for the last days before driving back to Rome and home.

They got the car from the garage and left for the two-and-a-half-hour journey to the pretty hillside township, driving down the coastal cliff road Via Guglielmo Marconi before turning into the one-way Viale Pasitea, which took them right into the town itself.

When they arrived, they again found a garage, this time at the top of the town, where they again left the car and walked down the hill (Billy carrying their large suitcase uncomfortably). As they had saved money in Isola, they upgraded themselves to a suitable small *albergo* with windows looking over the placid Mediterranean.

After settling, they went for a walk round the steepslopes of the town, and as dusk started to creep over the Amalfi Coast, they stopped off at a jolly trattoria for their evening meal.

Positano, the pearl of the Amalfi Coast, was a cliffside village with pebble beaches (Spiaggia Grande and Fornillo) and steep, narrow streets, terraces, stairways, colourful houses, boutiques and cafes, and they both immediately found it even more wonderfully blissful than Isola. They both relaxed physically and mentally, and although they couldn't really afford it, they spent far more than they should by going to the abundance of restaurants in the town almost every day. It was not expensive food, but the total soon added up.

It was near the end of the season, and although the town was quite busy, it never had the feeling of being overcrowded, so during the day they spent their time walking the narrow serpentine streets, taking in the difference of the delightful small houses, and window shopping—although they did not actually buy any of the high-priced clothes or tatty touristy souvenirs.

Despite her natural frugality, and knowing they couldn't really afford it, Rose easily slipped into Billy's devil-may-care attitude to money and they took expensive boat tours to Capri and the Blue Grotto, and delighted in a quite sinful trip to Pompeii and Vesuvius with lunch and a tipsy-making wine tasting.

They thoroughly enjoyed the tours and organised trips, but they both very much preferred the times they were on their own staying near Positano itself.

Once, they spent the whole day walking romantically hand in hand between the town's two beaches along the two-kilometre Sentiero degli Innamorati, trudging uphill by about a hundred and forty metres.

The sun was high and warm as they strolled the twelve walkways of the *sentiero*, the Path of Lovers, and they took frequent rests on the eight viewing platforms that allowed them to appreciate the magnificent scenery both on the land around them and away out to sea.

They thoroughly enjoyed the quite special views, so different to any they had ever seen, and when they reached the Spiaggia Grande, they sat on rocks just above the water line and had a picnic of cold pasta and panino sandwiches made of ciabatta bread washed down by drinking in turn from a shared bottle of slightly warm prosecco.

On another day, they got a bus to the Positano suburb of Nocelle, from where they set off enthusiastically along the ten-kilometre length of the Sentiero degli Dei, standing at five hundred metres above sea level about halfway up Mount Sant'Angelo a Tre Pizzi. Legend had it that it was the route taken by the Greek gods to save Ulysses from the sirens living on the islands of Li Galli.

As they wound their way through the mountainous route, they passed two shepherds leading mules carrying wood and farm milk to the local villages, and they took in the incredible beauty that showed just why the name of the trail translated to "Path of the Gods". Billy and Rose took in the lovely aromatic smells of nature and the views of gorges, cliffs, precipices, dry stone walls and woods of the Amalfi Coast, and the whole atmosphere was heady and enjoyable.

They were completely at ease with each other, small personal intimacies and jokes passing secretly between them—sometimes sounding almost rude to outsiders. She would call him "a doddering old man" or "you silly boy", while he would tell her she was "a kept woman" or "just the hired help". It was affectionate banter, part of the married couple speak that exists amongst two people at ease with themselves, and if taken like that, quite charming.

The two weeks passed by slowly in a whirl of enjoyment—it was as near perfect as it could be—but too soon it was the last night of Billy and Rose's holiday. They had seen and been told about the many dances in the posher, more expensive hotels and dance halls, and they decided to celebrate the end of the trip by going to one of them. They discovered a quite fancy club in a narrow side street that seemed to be one they could afford.

The hall was in the basement of a big building, poorly lit and crowded. Pop music was continually piped at the crowd from a cassette hidden away in a corner, too loud for comfort but all right for the swaying mass. Billy and Rose danced close for a while (they had to be close as there was not much room on the floor), and when they eventually sat down at an empty table to one side, they ordered non-alcoholic cocktails to cool down. They were ridiculously overpriced, which was irritating.

As they drank them, Billy and Rose had to almost shout to make themselves heard.

"It's just like that hall where you picked me up," said Billy, laughing despite everything.

"Where *I* picked *you* up?" replied Rose, mock angry but also laughing.

"Yes, some fanciful tale about selling a raffle ticket."

"Did you ever buy one?"

Billy changed the subject. "I can't remember," he mumbled. "Oh, this noise. Shall we go?"

Rose nodded, so they finished their drinks and left.

They were both exhausted, not only by the noise but by the exertions of their hectic week, and as soon as they got back to their *albergo*, they went straight to bed. It was hot and they lay on top of the blankets. Away from the overly loud noise of the dance hall it had been a magical night at the end of a magical week.

They could still hear music and singing and laughter all around them, much softer now, and they were almost drunk with the overall atmosphere.The street singing and jollity wafted on through the window and the mood stayed with them both.

"This has been a lovely holiday," sighed Rise. "I know I said it before, but I've really, really enjoyed myself. It's the best."

They made love, physically and mentally, completely taken in by the mood of their surrounds but absorbed by each other.

And the moment it was over, both knew the miracle that they had created a baby. Both knew the very instant their first baby was conceived, an electric-shock-like thrill running through their bodies and brains as they lay there. How they knew they couldn't explain, but it was a certainty, and they were both quietly but deliriously happy—full of a deep, deep love for each other at somehow knowing the miracle of conception.

Eventually, the music outside faded, and the soft swishing of the sea lulled them to a deep, satisfying sleep in each other's arms, both of them thrilled, excited and happy at the knowledge that they were now a family.

They returned home from the holiday ecstatically happy, but two weeks later Rose was sick, and when she saw her doctor she was delighted when he confirmed she was pregnant. That evening, when Billy returned home after work, she gave him the news and was overjoyed when he was as delighted as she was. They kissed and then stood holding each other for five silent minutes delighting in their joint happiness.

Billy was really delighted, as if no one had ever fathered a child before. He finally whooped out loud with joy, grabbed Rose and tried to whirl her around.

"Careful," she shouted, smiling with a shared joy.

"Of course, you're a delicate lady now."

"Just a mother..."

Billy let her go, but obviously led her to a chair. "And our baby... hopefully he'll have your looks and my brains," he told her.

"Oh no," said Rose. "*She'll* have *my* looks and *my* brains!"

They both laughed, and Billy knelt down beside Rose's chair and hugged and kissed her.

"Our baby. You clever little woman," he said.

He felt elated and clever, empowered by creation and somehow on a different plane to others who were not about to become fathers. He celebrated an overwhelming passion not only for Rose but for what she was growing for them inside her body with an almost religious ferocity.

It was a difficult pregnancy, and for almost two months, Rose, at thirty years old, was sick almost every morning and tired easily.

Things settled, however, and she seemed perfectly normal when she went for her first mid-term test in the ninth week of her pregnancy.

Billy was working on the day she went for the first scan—much to his distress—but as he couldn't go to the hospital's maternity ward with her, he arranged for her old friend Mary to go with her.

Rose went into the scan with a bit of apprehension, but the junior doctor was experienced and, although only twenty-seven years old, gave an air of confidence. He asked Rose to lower her trousers to her hips and lie on a bed on one side of the consulting room while he prepared things. Then he stood by her side and carefully pushed up the bottom of her blouse, so her abdomen was completely exposed.

He put his right hand to his mouth and coughed softly behind it, then began pressing down on her slightly distended stomach area rather forcefully, which was slightly uncomfortable for Rose, and he began feeling in various places.

The doctor pursed his lips but didn't say anything, then reached across and picked up a stethoscope from his desk. He put the earpieces in his ears and bent down to listen to Rose's stomach, again moving the cold bell around to several spots.

When he had finished, he deliberately took the stethoscope out of his ears, replaced it precisely on his desk and turned back to Rose.

"You can get dressed now," he said, going to sit sideways at his desk.

Rose finished straightening her clothes, and he indicated another seat in front of him.

"Let me explain what I've just done," he said. "When I was prodding you, I was feeling to see if the baby's head was in the right place, to make certain baby was sitting correctly in your tum. Then I listened to hear the baby's heartbeat. It was quite regular, and everything seems in order. The baby's fine and is growing at the right rate, and although we can't really tell for certain yet, things appear to be normal. No need for you to worry."

He gave Rose a professional smile, and she grinned back feeling giggly, but they were both distracted by a slight sobbing noise. Mary, who had been watching carefully, had burst into tears.

And that was all there was to it. The whole scan had taken just under half an hour.

Rose and Mary left and went to the hospital cafe for a cup of tea and a chat about the scan, but Rose was anxiously in a hurry to get home. They said their goodbyes and parted.

Rose got home and twittered about, busy doing nothing, waiting for Billy. When he got back from work that evening, she was watching through the living room window, and when she saw him walking down the road, she went to meet him at the front door.

"Everything was fine, the baby's all right," she told him.

Billy kissed her, smiled, and they went into the living room and sat on the settee for more than an hour oohing and aahing and treasuring the thought.

Everything went as expected as the pregnancy progressed. Rose's sickness had disappeared, and she felt well when she was called in for the twentieth week second scan.

This time, Billy went along to the maternity ward with Rose, sitting on a chair slightly behind her but able to see everything.

The procedure was exactly the same as the first scan, but this time carried out by a young midwife, a rather older woman than the first-time doctor. She prodded and listened to make certain that things were all right and proceeding well.

"It feels perfectly normal so far," she told the delighted—and re-lieved—parents.

She got a tape measure to try to assess the baby's length, then after watching for a moment, she had another feel of Rose's stomach. Her eyebrows raised slightly, and she bent down to put her ear on Rose's growing bump.

After a moment, she straightened, bobbing her head up and down knowingly a couple of times, and with a huge grin on her face, she beckoned Billy over urgently, taking his hand and quickly putting it on Rose's stomach. He felt the baby kicking vigorously, and a tremendous surge of emotion flooded inside him, an abnormally strong bond not only with Rose but with the creation she was forming inside her.

Life seemed to be too good for Rose, Billy and their unborn baby, but after another two and a half weeks, Rose unexpectedly became listless, anxious and depressed. The doctor told her she had pre-eclampsia, high blood pressure, and although Billy was very considerate and did what he could, it did not really help.

Rose tried to carry on as normal, but she really wasn't feeling very well and had to spend long hours either sleeping with her feet up on the settee or in bed, and after about ten days, she was physically sick, pale and feeling really ill. Billy called for an ambulance, and after a quick check, the paramedics decided to take her to A&E.

The doctors and nurses there were rushed off their feet, but they were concerned and meticulous in their examinations, and after three hours, they decided to keep Rose in the hospital overnight. They didn't say what they had discovered nor what the problem might be.

Rose was transferred to a ward, where Billy was allowed to sit by her bed. She lay propped up by two pillows with her eyes closed at first, but she opened them, saw Billy and tried to smile. Her eyes were wet. Billy pulled the chair closer to the bed, leaning forwards and holding her hand.

"Rose..." he began, but there were no words he could say.

They were still for about a quarter of an hour before a nurse came to look after Rose, pulling back the curtains around her bedspace.

"You'll have to wait outside," she told Billy. She was friendly but firm.

Billy left and stood in a corridor outside the ward, his shoulders hunched, stunned.

Eventually, the nurse came from behind the curtains and walked up to Billy. "You can go back now," she said. "I've given her something to make her drowsy."

She followed him back to the bed and drew the curtains back. Billy saw Rose was already asleep.

He stood there, feeling as if he was somehow responsible for her being in hospital, although he was not, of course. It was a biological misfortune of some sort, but he was mentally trying to take the "blame" from Rose, although it was not her fault either. He stayed by the bed for half an hour before he went home exhausted.

The next day, Billy visited Rose in her ward. They smiled wanly at each other.

"How are you feeling?" asked Billy brightly.

Rose frowned, and her mouth drooped. Her face suddenly seemed clouded. "Well, I felt awful just after I woke up," she replied, speaking very slowly. "I had a really bad pain in my stomach, and the nurses called a doctor to look. It was a bad stabbing pain, but it suddenly went away. I feel fine now."

"That's good," said Billy. "You sure?"

Rose nodded. Tears rolled down her cheeks, and conversation became difficult. Both were rather relieved when a doctor came and asked Billy to wait outside.

"Sorry, Mr Saunders, we're taking her up for a D&E procedure now."

"D&E?"

"Yes, dilation and evacuation," said the doctor. "I'm afraid the baby is dead. We have to remove the foetus."

"Dead? Does Rose know?"

"Yes, we told her." So matter of fact. He'd faced this situation so many sad times before.

Billy was stunned, shocked. He couldn't speak, but he stepped aside as a porter and a nurse wheeled Rose's bed away. He was in a lonely agony of thought and sorrow and lack of understanding. He couldn't believe what he'd been told, didn't want to believe it, and he wished he could be with Rose so they could help each other.

"I won't stay. Just look after her," Billy told the nurse, taking a cowardly way out.

He went home sorrowfully. The baby was lost. So was Billy.

Rose left the hospital after a week during which Billy visited her twice every day. Billy collected her in a taxi. They didn't speak and even when they got home, there were no words, although both shared the other's grief. It was a tangible, haunting feeling between them and there was no need to say anything, but that unspoken grief bound them even closer. They both felt it. Both mourned alone and together.

Rose had carried the baby proudly and lovingly for a few days over five months before the baby was stillborn. The doctors never gave them a reason for its death, and neither Rose nor Billy really wanted to know. It was the same even when the embryo was cremated a couple of days later after a medical examination. Once again, neither Rose nor Billy felt they could attend the brief ceremony. Their dream was shattered.

It had been a dreadful day when it had happened, with Rose in agony and Billy desperate but unable to help, and neither would ever forget the moment the kindly but pragmatic doctor had given them the news. Both were completely devastated, but they knew life had to go on. Their lives together.

They were both heartbroken, of course, but they held themselves together simply by being together. Although both had been distressed at first, the disappointment faded into an unspoken fact over time. They hid their grief, but each was strong with the other and very slowly the obvious pain subsided and there was just a dull ache in both minds. Even that faded after a year or more, although it was still there a layer or two down in their subconscious.

They consciously continued trying for a baby for the next few years, without discussion and somewhat half-heartedly, and after a while the need faded. Rose, although joining in willingly, actually began to find the act rather comical.

They had no more babies. They accepted the fact that they were not to be parents and got on with their lives, satisfied with their own togetherness.

Their love for each other was as strong as ever despite the tragedy of being childless.Although both thought of the searing, aching heart-break, and what might have been, neither spoke about it to the other. It would have been too painful, even many years later.

They gradually settled down to their old happiness. But it fairly soon became quite noticeable that Rose had begun to forget things, had suddenly started to repeat questions, forget names, misplace things.

Chapter 8

It was two weeks before Rose and Billy's golden wedding anniversary—fifty years of almost perfect bliss during which they had come to be regarded by everyone (friends, neighbours and casual acquaintances) as a routine married couple growing old together in a dull life with no excitement or anything special.

They didn't think they were dull, but nevertheless they both agreed they didn't want any celebration of the anniversary. A quiet meal at home, with no one else around—with Rose already planning a beef Wellington to mark their first ever restaurant meal together. As Billy's best mate Jonno had died of a heart attack seven months before, and his wife Mary (Rose's best friend) had become a recluse and refused to see anyone ever since, it was easy to manage, and they just hoped they wouldn't upset any of their other companions by not having a party.

They had moved some three years before and were now living in a small semi-detached house called Glebe Cottage in Avenue Road on a moonscape housing estate far out in the suburbs on the fringes of the countryside.

Like most houses built for mass ownership between the two World Wars, it had a narrow hallway leading from the front door, with a living room immediately on the left and the main sitting room at the back, with a kitchen at the far end. On the immediate right of the hallway was a flight of stairs, turning left at the top with three more steps leading to the two upstairs bedrooms, bathroom and toilet. It was a virtual replica of Rose's pre-marriage home.

Rose and Billy slept in the front bedroom, and the back room was used more or less entirely as a wardrobe. Billy had acquired two low shop racks from his firm and he kept them in this back (spare) bedroom, and all of Rose's dresses, skirts and blouses were hung neatly washed and ironed on them. His own clothes were similarly hung in a wardrobe built into the wall of the same room.

Billy liked Rose looking good, and she enjoyed it as much, and as a result she had a bigger than usual collection of outfits because he was able to buy things from his firm at less than a third of the cost price, as well as being able to pick up the odd demonstration gown previously worn only once by a model.

Rose was always very well groomed, although she was happiest with a plain blouse tucked into neat trimmed full-length trousers or a wide, swirling skirt, often with a scarf or kerchief tied round her neck to add a touch of brightness. She liked looking smart but was not precious about it.

The house had a small square garden patch at the front and a long, rather narrow garden at the back where Rose liked to potter and look after the abundance of flowers she grew from seed, while Billy occasionally, very occasionally, mowed the two lawns with a robotic non-thinking lack of enthusiasm.

From the outside, it looked exactly like every other house on the estate, and Billy would often joke that he hoped he wouldn't get lost and go to the wrong house.

"If I did, purely by mistake mind," he would joke, "I hope the girl who answers the door is an attractive eighteen-year-old blonde." He had long ago forgotten the episode in the stockroom.

If he had met a young blonde, it would not really have made any difference anyway. He and Rose were getting older now, both in their seventies (Billy at the higher end and Rose at the lower), and the more naturally youthful urges and physical side of their togetherness had faded. Theystill held hands when out together, and frequently kissed and cuddled, although more with emotion than passion. They were still a couple.

Rose's forgetfulness was starting to get worse, and there were frequent occasions when, for instance, she would go out to the kitchen while watching television to make them both cups of tea and come back without them.

"Oh, did you want a cup of tea then?" she would answer Billy when he asked where his was.

Rose's body had by now begun to fill out, but although she began to show signs of her age, she was still comparatively slim and her face was youthful. Billy never really changed, and although in his case his face was fuller, he retained his almost permanent smile and the hint of mischief in his eye.

That was on the outside though. Inside, both knew they still had something special, super special, in their deep love of each other. They had no real need to express it; it was all encompassing for both.But they did mention it occasionally.

There was the day, for instance, when Billy started a two-handkerchief cold and felt terrible. He didn't complain, but Rose made him lie down and then sat by his side holding his hand as he slept. After half an hour or so, she bent forwards.

"I love you," she whispered.

He didn't open his eyes, but murmured back. "I heard that," he said, then sneezed violently and went back to sleep.

Both were happy working, but they were starting to get tired with the daily grind and began to think of retirement.

"But we're not old, just older," Billy would say. It was something he had said in their early marriage and he still meant it.

They did eventually retire, on the same day, and almost immediately set up their own dress shop—Rose having worked out some plans in the couple of months before.

Billy always claimed it was a "going concern". "At least," he joked, "It's always going downhill."

The shop only lasted for five months before they closed it down. Running it proved too hard for them at their advancing age. There was little money coming in, but large chunks of their savings going out. They settled for a happy pensioned life together.

Retirement did have one benefit however. Billy had had to give up his company car when he retired, but with help from the more than efficient mechanic who'd been servicing it for many years, he and Rose found and bought themselves a small, well-used second-hand Honda for running to the supermarket or on occasional trips. Rose, who had never learnt to drive, was quite content to let Billy do the chauffeuring. She was a calm passenger who always had complete faith in her driver. They didn't use the car very much and after the failure of their shop even less.

As he was now at home all day most days, Billy was able to see that Rose's signs of forgetfulness were increasing. One day, he saw an opened letter on the kitchen table, a final demand for gas, and it worried him. He took off the glasses he now needed for reading (although his long vision was also fading) and put them on the table by the side of the letter. He rubbed the back of his hand over his brow and ran his hands wearily through his hair, now snowy white and starting to recede at last at the temples. It was so unlike Rose, who had always been so meticulous about paying bills on time, so he asked her about it.

"I thought I'd paid it," she replied dismissively.

Time seemed to slow down as they settled into their retirement. They were doing the normal things, shopping, the occasional cinema, going for drives, walks in the park, and all seemed to be going well. They watched television most evenings, and sometimes met friends either for lunch or for evening meals in each other's homes.

Most of the time, Rose was normal, talking well, pottering around the garden (which was a passion) looking after the multi-coloured flowers she nurtured, dusting round the house—although she let Billy do the hard work vacuuming the carpets—and doing various other things that needed doing. But the small aberrations seemed to increase. Slowly, in fact, but at a headlong rate in Billy's concerned mind. Rose's memory was getting worse.

"I didn't know we were meeting Henry and Louise tonight."

"I told you yesterday."

"Oh yes. I think I remember now."

She started repeating sentences and asking the same question over and over.

"We haven't heard from Jonno and Mary lately. I wonder how they're getting on. We should have them round. Do you think we should phone them?"

"Jonno died."

"Oh no. How sad."

About five minutes later, she'd say, "I think you should get in touch with Jonno to see how he's getting on."

At supper parties, which she prepared as thoroughly as always, she was a charming hostess, and if she did repeat a question, the guests thought she was getting hard of hearing as she was growing older and simply hadn't heard the answer first time.

It became so noticeable though, and that worried Billy. He would lie in bed at night, and while Rose slept soundly beside him he would try to think what he could do. It was obvious something was not right with her, but she wasn't exactly ill so it was no use taking her to see a doctor. What could he or she do about it anyway?

On top of the vague absent-mindedness, she started having too many aches and pains in the neck and shoulders and she seemed to get a lot of headaches. She was forgetting far more things these days.

"Do you know where the egg whisk is?" she asked.

"I thought you'd put it back in the drawer by the oven after we washed up yesterday."

"It's not there."

Billy wandered back into the living room and as he sat in his armchair, he noticed the whisk in an otherwise empty fruit bowl on the sideboard.

He got up again and silently took it back to Rose in the kitchen.

She would often get up while they were watching television saying she'd remembered something that needed doing and wander into the bedroom, but when she came back she had not done anything. She'd forgotten what needed doing.

Billy never said anything. He had got used to her forgetfulness.

Rose had never had a really serious illness in her life before starting to get her terrible headaches without any obvious cause and Billy's concern was even more worrying. Although she was reluctant at first, he eventually decided she did need medical help and insisted she see their GP and took her to the surgery as soon as he could.

The doctor carried out a meticulous examination and gave her a prescription to stop the headaches before deciding to send her for a more detailed analysis at a specialist unit at the cottage hospital. He was a thorough, conscientious man, and while not thinking it was the case, he said he wanted Rose to have a brain scan to eliminate the possibility that she had suffered a stroke or that there might be some kind of physical brain damage.

It was raining and a dark, dismal day when they went to the hospital for the scan, but in the corridors inside there was a funny, fake air of mock jollity. The medical staff hurried along with serious concentrated faces, mostly heads bent in thought, but the back-up staff were generally all smiles to try to give reassurance to the sick and maimed.

The radiography department was at the far end of the hospital, and Billy ushered Rose to it slowly and deliberately, holding her arm fairly firmly. They got there four minutes before the appointment time.

The department itself was in a small add-on block off a side corridor and was simply an open corridor with half a dozen seats, a water cooler and four doors leading to the private consultation rooms.

They sat side by side in the corridor waiting room, along with another man waiting to be seen by the medics. Billy watched him as they waited. He was always moving, gulping at a coffee in a plastic cup gripped tight in his right hand, taking quick nibbling bites from a sandwich still half-wrapped in a plastic cover in his other hand, constantly eating and drinking in never-ending motion.

They waited for ten minutes, then Rose was the first to be called in, and after a brief chat with a nurse, who took a sample of blood from her left arm for a test, Rose was sent along the corridor to the radiography department. Billy, leading her along, chattered nothings to try to calm her natural concern. When they got to the department, a receptionist told them to sit while waiting to be called, then another nurse brought Rose a rather large plastic mug with cloudy liquid in it. She said it was a contrast dye that would help show up any abnormalities revealed by the scan.

Rose drank the liquid slowly. It had an unpleasant, bitter taste but she managed to finish it before the nurse returned and told her it would take about twenty minutes to work. Time dragged, but Rose was eventually taken into the CT scanner, with Billy again made to wait outside.

Rose felt rather nervous when she saw the apparatus: a computerised tomography scanner. It was a fairly tall but long piece of equipment with a hollow space running through it, but the radiographer, a reassuring young man with a scar down his left cheek, gave her a seat by its side and explained the procedure.

He checked that she didn't have anything metal on her, a watch, jewellery or hair pins, and then while making sure things were all right with the machine, he chatted away soothingly.

"All this came about because of The Beatles," he told Rose. "The guy who invented it worked for their record company, and it was some of the profits from their records that paid for the research. Blame Ringo for being here," he joked, turning back to her.

"No need to worry," he went on in a supportive voice. "It's rather like having an X-ray. You must have had one of them, so you'll know you won't feel anything. The difference is that you'll be on that bed and then you'll just slide gently part of the way in. I'll be behind the screen over there, and I'll be taking the pictures. We'll be able to talk to each other, and I'll probably tell you to do a couple of simple things before I bring you out again. It won't take too long. OK?"

Rose nodded, and the operator pointed to the scanner.

"OK then, let's do it. Lie down."

Rose sat on the edge of the bed and started to lift her legs up.

"No, love, the other way. Head first."

Rose got in position on her back, shuffling until she was comfortable, and the radiographer smiled at her then walked behind a screen.

"Right, here it goes," came his voice, loud and rather metallic sounding.

The scanner moved gently until Rose's head and shoulders were inside the hollow.

"Breathe normally," came the voice. "Very still now... that's it."

A small ring rotated round Rose's head, and she watched it with her eyes following it while she kept her head rigidly still.

"Again, don't move..."

That happened several times, then after about ten or eleven minutes, the bed started to slide back out of the hollow. The radiographer reappeared at Rose's side.

"I can tell you at least you've got a brain," he said with a broad grin. "I got some pretty pictures."

He helped Rose stand up, and as she adjusted her clothes, he told her the scans would go to a doctor for analysis, and she'd be told the result after a few days.

"That's all there is to it, love," he finished. "No need to worry, was there? You can go home now."

Rose left the scanner room to find an anxious Billy standing, waiting outside, and when he'd checked that she was all right, he drove her home. The other patient had vanished.

It took more than a few days, and it was actually sixteen days before Rose was called back to see her GP to be given the result. The doctor started by telling them the scan was all clear, but he now suspected what the problem really was and sent her on to the hospital's memory clinic to check.

Billy again took her to the clinic, and after a twenty-minute wait sitting in the corridor again, Rose was called into a consulting room where a dull-looking, dispirited doctor was waiting for her. Billy was yet again told to wait outside. The room was purely functional, painted a noncommittal off-white and with a desk, a bed covered with a blue paper sheet, a cabinet of some sort and a hand basin.

Rose sat facing the doctor, and he shuffled a few papers before explaining the test.

He began asking a series of formal questions, the date and some other routine questions, then fairly early on he gave Rose an address to remember: 24 North Street, Brighton, East Sussex. He asked Rose to count backwards from fifteen, and when she had done that (with difficulty between six and eight) he asked her what the address was that he had given her. She told him it was Glebe Cottage in Avenue Road, her own home address.

In all, the doctor had a standard list of twenty-six questions and Rose answered thirteen of them correctly, but as that put her in the lower range showing dementia, he threw in a couple of extras to help him make up his mind. He asked Rose the name of the prime minister, and she said it was Margaret Thatcher although Tony Blair had taken the role almost two years earlier, and when asked when Christmas was, she replied, "The day after Boxing Day."

The test took just twenty minutes, and when it was done, Rose went back to sit with Billy in the corridor.

The nurse came out to them after a short wait and told them the doctor wanted to analyse the results with his colleagues and would call them back to get the result when he had done so. Rose and Billy were not satisfied, but there was nothing they could do, so once again they went home.

They were called back to the specialist memory clinic by a phone call from a vague receptionist a week later. Another week after that, Billy sat side by side with Rose on the hard-backed seats in the clinic's corridor waiting room silently but with their breathing perfectly synchronised.After a short wait, they were both called in by the doctor.

The doctor was curt. He glanced at the notes in front of him, then gave a quick upwards glance at Rose.

"You have dementia," he told her in a rather ill-advised directness, rather cruel in its simple straightforwardness.

Rose did not show any emotion. She simply nodded.

The doctor closed the folder and stood. He was indifferent. Rose was his twelfth dementia test of the day.

"We'll be in touch with your GP," he said, and the consultation was over after just a couple of minutes.

Billy led Rose out of the clinic without saying a word, and they drove home. It was terrible news, but neither really understood what it meant and therefore they didn't speak about it. Rose was ill, doctors cured illnesses. Life went on.

They didn't realise completely how different things would be for them, how much life was about to change so drastically, and that it would now be up to Billy to manage that life for them.

It took almost two weeks before they heard from their GP. He called them both in for a face-to-face consultation, and at that meeting, he started by getting an assistant to bring them all a cup of tea. He was very considerate as he told them about the letter he had received from the memory clinic.

It had said that Rose actually had the Alzheimer's form of dementia.

As they quietly drank their tea, the doctor explained the likely path of the disease and how it would probably affect them, then answered Billy's inevitable questions. Rose didn't say a word throughout the visit—she hadn't mentioned the problem since she had first seen the GP.

She still refused to talk about—or even acknowledge—the Alzheimer's as things settled down in the weeks after the trauma of the testing and diagnosis. She was frustrated. She had heard the doctor's verdict, and while she refused to believe it, she became very aware that she was becoming increasingly forgetful, misplacing her glasses, not knowing where a certain pot or pan was, and Billy had to search daily for her keys, purse or whatever.

He found a pile of small notes she had written herself; the actual writing got scrawnier as he read through them. All were reminders of "important" things she had to do and the items were the same for days on end.

It scared her, but she struggled to keep her life normal and she never let the always optimistic Billy know how she felt. She could see that for some reason he was being extra considerate—even more than usual—and was fearful that if she did tell him it would worry him even more.

Rose's memory became noticeably worse and there was a general deterioration in her physical condition although there was an immediate whirl of panic as Billy tried to come to terms with the illness (although he was told by several people and official bodies that dementia was not a disease but a social problem). All the time Rose remained blissfully calm—she couldn't, or wouldn't, relate the dementia to herself.

They settled into a routine, with Billy slowly taking control of their two lives.

The one thing he couldn't do was cook (he had never needed to learn as Rose had always done it for him), so he began taking her to local pubs and small restaurants for meals, but he found that gave him another small problem. Luckily, the owner of the local pub, who also happened to be the chef, was friendly and helpful, and would often make special dishes of Rose's favourites even though they were not on the menu. But there was an especially high step in the doorway to the pub.

It all helped as they drifted through the next two years with Rose slowly becoming more and more incapable of looking after herself. Her memory continued to get worse, she continued to mislay things and she frequently wandered round as if in a dream. Although it sometimes drove Billy to the point of despair, she remained ignorant of her slowly worsening condition. Her basic nature stayed the same, however, and her health stayed good. She was generally happy.

Billy, of course, was affected by it all. He hated seeing "his" Rose deteriorating mentality, but he accepted it and was unknowingly determined to do all he could to help her. He still loved her so much. Their roles switched somehow seamlessly, and instead of Rose doing everything for Billy, he now spent his time looking after every minute detail of her life.

Chapter 9

Rose had a generally unwelcome, helpless feeling as the reality of the Alzheimer's hit her. She still refused to admit it out loud—especially to Billy, in some vague way thinking it might stop him worrying—but deep down she knew she needed help. It scared her beyond belief.

Billy did worry though, and he quite decidedly and unquestioningly became that help. There was never a moment's doubt—he didn't actively think about it—and he automatically stepped forwards.

To begin with, he contacted various organisations and people—social services, councils, charities and the like—to try to get some hints, and various people called on Rose and him to offer support, most no doubt filled with the fervour of those devoted to the idea of helping. In Billy's eyes, most of them rather than doing good were do-gooders. No one seemed to him to have any real ability to help.

There was, for instance, the prim and proper woman from a charity who told him that Rose smelt—she was quickly shown out of the door—and there was another whose only idea was to move a wall calendar to a more prominent position so Rose would know the date (she didn't look at it even once).

As Rose's condition started to grow worse, nothing practical was offered, and Billy was convinced that even without training or actual knowledge, he could do the job better than anyone.

He learnt "on the job". It was not easy, mind, and at first the small things in caring for Rose proved especially hard. The major things like cooking and housework—things he had never done before—were easier and usually obvious to learn, but dressing her, for instance, was a bit of a problem to start with.It took Billy a couple of weeks to get used to the idea of doing up her blouse, jacket or coat buttons the "wrong" way round. And although he tried twice, he could never manage to cut her toenails!

He got up around six in the morning, often when it was still dark, leaving Rose still asleep while he got things ready for breakfast. A bonus with that, however, was that when he drew the kitchen curtains, he would usually see the milkman running to the front door. They would wave and became quite friendly in a remote way.

When those early chores were done, Billy would return to bed, lying wide awake until Rose woke naturally when he would always make certain she at least had a strong, reassuring hug. He made sure there was another when she went to bed and before she fell into oblivion.

Finances were a problem, a big problem, for Billy, who had absolutely no idea of money matters as he had always left that kind of thing to Rose. He looked up her files and discovered savings and insurances he knew nothing about and he wondered, without figuring it out, how she had found the money to set them up.

He suddenly found he had to deal with regular bills, standing orders and things like that. It was a hazy mystery, but he knew he had to cope somehow.

Things were getting worse almost by the day, and Rose was called in to the memory clinic for a medical update. It was the same procedure as before, and once again Rose got thirteen questions right (Billy, sitting in this time, played along mentally and got twenty-five of the twenty-six, failing only with the first name of a famous TV actor). When they had finished, the doctor got them to wait outside while he analysed the results.

While they were waiting, Rose became restless to see the doctor again.

"Won't be long," said Billy cheerfully.

"Peanuts," replied Rose. But it was not what she said but the vehemence with which she said it that worried Billy.

When they went back into the consulting room, Billy told the consultant the story, but he simply nodded.

"That's quite normal. It'll get worse," he said nonchalantly.

Billy didn't know what to say.

The new test did not make any difference, although Rose was given a daily pill to take—a prescribed drug called galantamine, which would hopefully slow down the advance of the dementia, but despite that Rose continued to worsen.

Over the months, walking became difficult for her, and she often stumbled and wobbled unless there was something close to hang to, and Billy always had to be careful that she didn't fall. He always held on to her, and it seemed that the physical contact was essential for Rose. If he was not holding her, she invariably clutched at his arm, once again seeking reassurance.

She became doubly incontinent, and he discovered, almost by chance while shopping with her one day, incontinence pants, and in that respect, it was like looking after a baby.It took him weeks to discover that he had to change them for Rose every three or four hours.

He was actually living their two lives as one, but he did it because it needed to be done. It was tiring, not only physically but emotionally, and Billy slept largely from exhaustion and usually without full satisfaction because a part of him was always aware of Rose and her needs.

The small things that needed doing became trifling, such as when he noticed that Rose was walking apprehensively round mats on the floor, and when he queried it with the doctor, he found that people with Alzheimer's often saw them as gaping black holes. It was a simple problem and he just moved them.

While often irritating, over the ensuing days, months and years (sometimes in minutes or hours) Billy not only picked up the basics but learnt how to look after Rose. By now, he had a routine that seemed to work.

Billy fed Rose at the dining room table, usually porridge or two pieces of toast and a rich raspberry jam for breakfast and something easy to chew for the main evening meal. She usually accepted the offerings, but there was one morning when the sun shone through the windows throwing weird slivers of light across the table, crisscrossed with shadowy dark lines. The weird patterns freaked Rose and she froze. She wouldn't eat and had tears rolling down her cheeks. Billy had to give up and throw away the half-eaten slice of toast. By lunchtime, Rose had recovered and let him feed her lunch, eating avidly.

Their lives were like that—ups and downs.

Billy finally mastered the secret of dressing her fairly quickly, but some days Rose was uncooperative and made things difficult. One morning, he put Rose in a colourful organza blouse and trousers, but by mid-morning the sun was shining bright, and the temperature started to rise from spring pleasant to summer hot. Billy noticed a trace of sweat on Rose's top lip, so he felt her forehead and as she seemed to have a bit of a temperature, he went upstairs and got a short-sleeved plain white lightweight cotton dress. Although he managed to get her blouse and trousers off, she objected to the dress and wouldn't lift her arms.

Billy struggled, almost resorting to force, and eventually got her dressed up again. Then an hour later, he saw she was shivering. He went upstairs again and searched in her clothing drawers until he found a lightweight polyester sweater which he managed to get on with Rose being very cooperative this time.

But that night she reverted. Billy was tired and Rose was not cooperating, and he struggled to get her up the stairs and into the bedroom. As he started to undress her, she tried to walk away, and he angrily pushed her down onto the bed. He was immediately ashamed of himself and tried to hold her so he could apologise, but she wouldn't let him. He got her into her nightclothes with difficulty and then into the bed. He walked round to the other side and, with a deep sigh of relief, got himself ready. By the time he'd got into bed himself, Rose was asleep. Billy lay there for over half an hour blaming himself for his angry actions before he, too, fell into a deep sleep.

Rose's signs of dementia were increasing noticeably and rather rapidly—she was repeating herself, forgetting things. Once, after night had fallen and it was about two in the morning, Billy woke to find she was not in the bed next to him. She had got up and gone to the toilet but had then got lost. Billy found her in the darkened spare bedroom, empty but for two twin beds, scared, not knowing where she was or why she was there.

Once, she went wandering in the pouring rain and a resident two roads away from their house in Avenue Road saw her and, realising she was soaking wet and that something was wrong, he took her into his house and asked where she lived. Rose told him "Glebe", and while his wife looked after her, he went to nearby Glebe Avenue to try to find her home. Luckily, one of the other residents there recognised Rose from his description and took her back to a distraught Billy, although she seemed to have recovered by then and wondered why she was so wet, asking Billy in an innocent way.

On another day, Rose was being particularly troublesome asBilly was trying to do the housework. She had refused the lunch he had made for her and was generally being awkward and kept wandering away from him. Billy was not in the mood to put up with Rose and eventually shouted at her.

Luckily, he realised he was again growing angry, and as he had found he needed some essential spray polish, he told her they had to go to the supermarket for it. Rose accepted the idea meekly, and as he manoeuvred her into the car and strapped her in, she relaxed so completely that Billy abandoned the shopping and hit on the idea of taking her for a drive instead.

Rose enjoyed it so much that the next day he tried it again, and after that, Billy decided that daily drives would become part of his caring routine.Luckily, Billy enjoyed driving, and when they were out together Rose was so calm and he always knew where she was and that she was safe.

It soon became a regular feature of their daily lives, Billy quite often driving as much as a hundred miles in an afternoon. Sitting in the car, Rose always settled right down and was so quietly serene that he just kept driving. After just a little while, he began recognising the various scenes in the different routes he decided to take—things like scaffolding, a cut hedge and the like.

On one trip, many miles from home, he was attracted to an enormous wild bush set back on an empty open patch along a small country lane. It was, unusually as it turned out, roughly seventeen feet wide and about twelve feet high, covered almost completely in vivid purple clusters of flowers, and Billy felt compelled to stop for several minutes to gawp at it. Rose didn't seem particularly interested.

A week later, Billy decided to return for another look, and he visited the stunning flowering bush several times in the next couple of weeks becoming almost obsessed with it.

On one of his visits, he saw a man standing outside his house just a little way down from the bush and stopped to ask if he knew what it was.

"A hydrangea," he was told.

A week later, he returned, but he'd forgotten the name and stopped to ask again. Unfortunately, it was the same man.

"Exactly the same as last week," he replied tartly to Billy's question, "A hydrangea!"

Billy drove off, but he didn't return to "his" bush again.

Billy quite enjoyed the driving, and he knew Rose was safe and relaxed, but all the time, on every drive, Rose sat silent.

The daily drives continued, and they were generally a huge success.

And then there was the singing.

Finding things to keep Rose interested and amused had become difficult, so with the festive season approaching, Billy had decided to take her to a Christmas carol concert at a nearby church to help pass the day. It bored him, but Rose joined in the traditional old favourites, singing every carol with obvious gusto and glee. She loved it, and her face glowed when the concert was over and he drove her home.

Rose had always sung a lot around the house, although Billy had not noticed it particularly, so with the obvious delight she had shown over the carols he asked some questions. Looking into it, he was surprised to learn that music was, apparently, the last part of the brain to die. None of the experts had told him.

He quickly moved on and soon discovered a group called Music for the Mind—all by himself again. He took Rose to the next session the following Tuesday, and once more Rose sang with abandon. There was a fair group of dementia sufferers, many old, and their carers, mainly young, at the session, and the songs were all old favourites—First and Second World War favourites and other traditional sing-alongs like "My Old Man Said Follow the Van"—and Rose loved them all. When group leader Margot Cox began singing Vera Lynn's "We'll Meet Again", the whole audience's eyes, including Rose, misted over. It was as if Vera herself was singing and although he didn't really like the music (he much preferred the old Hollywood musical style), Billy's eyes were as damp as everyone else's.

Rose had a really great time. As her brain had been going, there had always been music in her mind, although she couldn't let anyone know. She loved it—the music, the atmosphere, the singing.

Before that first session had finished, Billy was determined to bring Rose again, and when they had sung the final song of the day, he approached Margot to talk about it. Margot was very friendly—and helpful—and tried to include Rose in the chat as best she could.

The result was that, after that first time, Tuesday afternoons became "a must" for a regular visit to the singing sessions.

Billy noticed how involved Rose became with the singing, and although he did not join in—he couldn't hold, or even reach, a clear note—he joined in the sessions enthusiastically. He noted, particularly, that although she had difficulty remembering most things, Rose knew all the words of every song they sang.

She and others all sang the long-established songs with enthusiasm, and Margot coaxed and persuaded them to musical heights they had never before thought possible. It was clever, planned and successful with most of the ageing singers whose brains were falling apart.

Rose enjoyed the singing, and Billy the companionship, so much that after two or three months he began taking her regularly to a second, separate, singing meeting run by Margot and her partners in another district on Thursday afternoons, where he met a different set of carers.

The second time they visited this new group, Rose started singing away lustily, but Billy could not concentrate. He let his mind wander, and as the group singing moved on, he noticed a girl on the far side of the semi-circle. She was about twenty years old, pretty, with blonde curls framing her oval-shaped face—and she was wearing a very tight sweater.

He fancied the girl. There was something appealingly attractive about her and his mind began fantasising. He started daydreaming while the singing went on around him. The girl was singing along with her patient and the others, oblivious of his lewd thoughts, and while Rose was still enjoying the sing-song, Billy let his imagination run riot.

He didn't realise that the singing had stopped and that Margot had turned to a solo version of Gershwin's "Summertime", but the line about "the livin' is easy" somehow hit through. Billy instantly snapped out of his fantasy. *How ironic,* he thought. Life was definitely not easy. Reality was always there.

With the driving and the music, Billy was learning how to help Rose almost daily and, as he told himself, without help.

There was, no doubt, information available, but where? How could Billy and the hundreds of thousands of others in the same circumstances find it? There was no system in place to help discovery, all had to find their own information—on the small personal things as well as the major necessities.

He didn't mind having to do everything, or even having to teach himself how to do it, but he did get a bit niggly when it came to some of the smaller things, like the drinking mugs. By the time he began thinking about it, he was having to feed Rose, and he found it was easier to use a mug rather than a tea cup, and he reckoned she might feel better with a brightly coloured mug, so one day while shopping he bought two: a red one and a yellow one.

He gave Rose the brighter yellow mug, and she passively allowed him to feed her from it, but weeks later Billy learnt by accident that dementia patients react better (appropriately in this case because of her nickname with the Caballeros before they were married) to the colour red.He switched Rose to the red mug, and from then on, she would usually put both her hands on it while he fed her as if to show it was hers.

That had been another exasperating matter, and Billy had been angry about the apparent lack of information and help over small things like that at first, but by now he had finally settled down knowing that despite everything, he had found his own solution for Rose's welfare. After more than eighteen months during which they had settled into the round of the two weekly singing sessions on top of the daily drive, Rose was still enjoying every moment of both. She knew everyone connected with the singing sessions, by sight at least—although she couldn't have told you their names—and she loved the regularity as much as the actual singing.

There were still the down moments though, such as when Rene Patrick, a tall, wiry bottle-blonde who was Margot Cox's main assistant and the girl who collected the entrance fees, was not there for one of the Thursday meetings, and Rose sulked. Rene had a very severe manner and a somewhat sharp tongue, but she was really helpful and Rose missed her—she was a regular component of the whole day.

Rose refused to sing and was disruptive, and it took her the whole of the following week to get over the bad mood. Billy had to work hard to control her. But he accepted it stoically and finally helped Rose settle down. It was just another little drama, a blip on her normal happiness.

Usually, Billy looked after Rose with affection, although sometimes he felt as if he did it all with somewhat of a feeling of duty. After all, she had tended to him when he was ill, and they had married in sickness and in health, but there was more to it than that. He did it because it needed to be done and because he loved her and wanted to do it. Billy could not actually say his life was a bundle of fun, but he was looking after "his Rose" so he was fine about it.

But it was physically hard as well as being emotionally wrenching, and Billy was looking haggard. He was tired, and on edge a lot of the time,

It was not surprising, because Rose's deterioration had been inevitable, although quite slow and unobtrusive. Seeing her regularly, Billy had not really noticed it, but he now realised how far she was slipping away from reality—and from him. There were many times when the light seemed to go off behind her eyes, leaving an expressionless, vacant blank in her eyes when she looked at him.

She was having delusions—often talking about "the baby there on the floor". It took Billy some time to put two and two together and realise there was some hidden memory of their stillborn baby.

Other disrupting thoughts also seemed to grow in her mind, and she often seemed to be living in the past.

There was the night when he had undressed her and got her into the new silk pyjamas he had bought her. He had tucked her into bed before going into the bathroom to clean his teeth wearing only pyjama trousers. He could hear her chattering away in the bedroom, and when he went back into the bedroom, she was standing by the side of the bed completely nude—her pyjamas were lying crumpled on the floor.

"I can't find my nightdress," she said, a tantalising provocative gleam in her eye.

Billy did not react—he could see her pyjamas, not a nightdress, on the floor beside her—but he looked at her and could not help his old passions taking flame.

He quickly took off his trousers, and they stood there for several moments both completely nude, suddenly quiet for no apparent reason but just looking at each other with the old feelings surging through them both like a river in flood.

Billy knew it was stupid, wrong, but without a word, he moved towards Rose and hugged her, their bare bodies touching. They kissed, then got into bed together still in the nude. They held each other close, and it was as if they were twenty years old again. It was not lust but love. They fell asleep in each other's arms for the first time in many years.

It was a rare magic moment for Billy. They had always had a lot of laughs in their long life together—their whole marriage was built around light-hearted good humour. But as he now looked after her, it was different. There was still laughter, a lot of laughter, but it was somehow not so relaxed—and that was palpable.

It was like an adaptation of the old Longfellow poem maxim: when she was good, she was very, very good, but when she was bad, it was horrid.

On one of those bad days, Rose had been "messing around" all day, and by the time he took her up the stairs to go to bed, Billy was getting exasperated. He always guided her up and down the stairs, always one step below her to either encourage her up or to stop her falling down. There were fourteen steps, and from experience, he knew that if he could get past the tenth, things would be all right. So, when she stopped moving halfway up and refused to go on, he was angry and shouted at her for five minutes until he managed to get her to the top and into the bedroom.

There, she refused to help him get her undressed and into her pyjamas, and he again lost it completely and pushed her quite strongly back onto the bed.

"Why don't you just do what you're told?" he shouted, and immediately felt remorse. It was the second time he had really lost his temper with her, but it was not her fault and he knew it, but he would always remember the moment.

They were rare moments, luckily—Billy generally kept his cool and most of the time was committed and staunch because of his love for Rose. People called it dedication, devotion, duty, but he simply thought of it as something that a husband did for the woman he loved. He didn't think too deeply about it, it was just something that needed to be done so he did it—to help make her life easier and hopefully happier.

When people said how much they admired him, he became embarrassed and simply told them, "Well, she cared for me all the times I was sick. It's just my turn now."

Most people were rather considerate towards him and Rose though—either that or just ignored the illness. But not everyone. On another bad day, Billy took Rose to the hairdresser she had always used, but Rose made a bit of a fuss when the girl got soap in her eye while washing her hair. The next time they went there, the girl refused to take Rose in her chair.

It was all taking its toll on Billy's health, but luckily for him a chance remark at one of the singing sessions seemed to offer the solution, and finally the last piece in his personal carer jigsaw fell into place: respite clubs.

It was through someone at a Tuesday meeting that he first learnt of the respite clubs that some care homes ran. He investigated and found the Calder House Thursday Respite Club, a care home that ran weekly meetings for non-residents arranging all sorts of activities to keep them occupied while their carers got time off to do whatever they wanted without the responsibility for a couple of hours.

It sounded ideal, and Billy quickly enrolled Rose. The club was run from a first-floor room in the same named care home by a happy group of female carers and a solitary male helper, Jules. They were all instantly friendly and made both Rose and Billy feel welcome from the start.

At the respite club, they spent their time doing activities like handicrafts, and (again) singing. Like the driving and the music sessions, Rose loved it.

Everything seemed good, but it continually annoyed Billy every time he went to collect Rose, because he would always make a point of arriving ten minutes or so before the end of the session to join in the final moments with the patients (always getting a cup of tea and an iced bun) and would invariably walk past a group of four or five other carers chatting downstairs from the respite room before dutifully collecting their charges at the last possible moment.

Why did they abandon their loved ones? How could they not care? He mentioned it to one of the girls who assisted at the club.

"They just can't cope, bless 'em. You have to be strong-willed to cope with seeing your loved one in distress. Don't blame them because they can't, poor dears," she told him.

All went well for several months despite the advancing horror as the disease took hold and Rose started losing her memory for words, although she now made many references to "the baby" and seemed convinced there was actually a baby in front of her. Billy never knew what to do or say.

Then tragedy struck suddenly. Real tragedy.

Rose was no longer able to spend the hours in the garden that she used to, and knowing how much she loved it, Billy drove her to a noted nursery about seven miles from home. Rose was in her element, but then, after more than twenty-five minutes of pottering about, she said she was not feeling too well. Quite by chance, they were in the aptly named Rose Garden, surrounded, rather bizarrely, by a large collection of red rose bushes, one or two with buds or flowers.

Other customers tried to help and helped lift her onto a chair where she seemed to recover. Billy got her back to the car and took her home.

Then the next night, he was once again taking Rose up the stairs to bed when she collapsed on the tenth stair going up. Rose literally just folded down, face down. Billy was scared, but he wanted to get her off the stairs and clambered over her, not thinking for a second that it was dangerous not only for him but that it could have sent them both slithering to the bottom.

It needed huge strength to haul her up. And it was not until later that he realised how stupid he had been, although he did not know what else he could have done.

Having got Rose to the top of the stairs, Billy got her undressed and into bed as quickly as he could. She never realised exactly what had happened.

Then it happened again the following night, exactly the same thing, then for a third time on the day after that.

Billy still stubbornly refused to seek help, but a week later, he was actually on the way to taking Rose to her respite club when she passed out in the car. Billy drove on to the home to get assistance, and when he arrived a nurse immediately dialled 999 and called an ambulance.

Doctors in the emergency department saw her straight away although there were many people already waiting, and in view of various incidents that occurred while she was in the department, they arranged for her immediate transfer to a ward for further observation.She was, they told a distraught Billy, severely dehydrated, almost to the point of dying.Before she was admitted, he had cared for Rose on his own for many years, and it had not occurred to him that, especially in her deteriorating condition, she needed a lot more than usual intakes of liquid.

Chapter 10

Billy soon discovered that the "incidents" in A&E related to "a seizure" and although he never discovered what that actually was he was told it could have been life-threatening.

"Do you mean she could have died?" he asked. He was sitting on a hard-backed chair by the side of Rose's bed in the ward.

"I'm afraid so, yes," replied the female doctor looking after Rose, taking her pulse.

Although she had an oxygen mask over her nose and mouth, and a wire leading from a cannula in her left wrist to a bottle on a stand, Rose's arm was limp in the doctor's hand and she looked peaceful. She was sleeping, and there was a slight smile on her lips.

Billy couldn't get his mind round it. Rose... dead?

"She seems to have got over it now," the doctor continued. She had a slight Baltic accent and "it" came out as "eet". "She must sleep, it will help her. Then when she wakes up, we must carry out some more tests."

There was nothing Billy could do, and after sitting watching Rose for a while he went home.

He was back early the next day to find Rose awake, and he was comforted to see her propped up against three pillows. She didn't seem to realise what had happened or where she was, and although the oxygen mask had been removed, there was still an IV pole by her bedside with a wire holding a plastic bag filled with a colourless fluid dropping from it to the cannula still fixed to her right forearm.

Billy returned for several days after that, seeing Rose apparently improving physically. She still seemed rather frail, small and confused, but in his eyes probably no more than she had been before collapsing. He began to feel much better.

But that feeling didn't last.

Parking at the hospital was always a nightmare, and its delays invariably put Billy into a state of panic because he was late. As he hurried down the half mile or so of corridors and took the lift to the second-floor ward, he hoped Rose was all right.The relief when he saw her was tangible, butit was not the same when the doctors came round.

Rose had been in the hospital for two weeks before he saw the female doctor again. Dr Kristina—Billy had heard the nurses call her that, but he never did discover her surname—quickly brought him up to date on Rose's condition.

"I'm not sure at the minute, but I think she may have damaged some connection with the brain," she told him. "I think it is likely that she has lost the power to walk. There are more tests we must do. Her electrolytes are all over the place. There is a chance she may be permanently bedridden."

It was all matter of fact, but the news rocked Billy.

"Electrolytes?"

"They are the things that keep your nervous system working. They keep you hydrated, and that makes your nerves and muscles work properly. Rose's electrolytes are all over the place. We are trying to rehydrate her and hope that makes them work properly again, but we don't know yet."

"Could I have done anything to keep her electrolytes right?"

"Not really. It's a question of diet. You couldn't have known."

Billy looked at Dr Kristina mutely, but his expression held a question.

"I know it will be hard for you to understand, but your wife is very ill," added the doctor sympathetically.

Billy did not want to admit it—facing facts was still difficult.

Over the next few days, Rose had the IV drip removed and was put through several tests to establish her electrolyte levels, and at the end of them, Dr Kristina saw Billy again and confirmed that Rose would never be able to walk again.

"I'm so sorry," she said with genuine sadness.

Billy continued to visit Rose every day, and she certainly seemed to be getting better. Her memory was still bad, and she didn't have any recollection of her collapse or early days in the hospital. But she was generally cheerful, and Billy was happy with the way things were going.

It was during her third week in the hospital that Billy was introduced to Scott Forbes, a fairly young man working in the hospital's family help group. At first, Billy still didn't think he needed any family assistance, but after a few meetings with the charming Scott and the nurses attending Rose, they persuaded him to think about things seriously.

In bed that night, in the dark and alone, he did think about it, about the several years he had looked after Rose alone, all the hours and minutes during which she had been steadily deteriorating. He had done his best, but now that best was not enough. He realised that they both did need help after all.

He didn't really want to remember the tough days, but he knew they had been rough, so the next morning he agreed to the suggestion that Scott should start looking for a suitable home where Rose would get that help.

He admitted that if Rose was actually bedbound he really didn't have the experience to carry on looking after her on his own, and although her physical condition had improved tremendously during her weeks in hospital he began thinking Rose needed permanent medical help.

"She will certainly need professional care," said Scott.

Billy finally asked for help, and Scott told him that both he and the doctors suggested they find a specialist home that would not only look after Rose physically but also with her ongoing dementia.

Billy hated the thought—"I don't want to abandon Rose," he repeatedly insisted—and tried to put it out of his mind, but then he woke up in the middle of the night a few days later and realised Scott was right. The next morning, he agreed to the move, and Scott set about forming a hospital team to help guide him through the process.

Within a day, Billy was introduced to a middle-aged woman called Dorothy Blair who told him during his lunchtime visit that she was preparing a list of possible homes that would be suitable for Rose. She told Billy that once she had the list, she would take him to see all three, and then it would be up to him to decide which was the most suitable.

By the end of the day, Dorothy rang Billy at home to say she had selected three possible homes and would pick him up on Friday morning to take him round to see them. She said that to start with she had chosen homes that took NHS patients.

"Fees for care homes are really astronomical at the moment," she told him.

"How much are you talking?" asked Billy.

"In the thousands a week," said Dorothy.

"Thousands? A week? I can't afford that..."

"Well, I don't know how you are financially, but I promise you that if you can get state help, it will be beneficial," added Dorothy. "Using us, the NHS, is what we're here for."

Billy noted what she said and told her he was grateful and appreciated her thoughtfulness.

True to her word, Dorothy, a friendly soul, called on Billy two days later exactly at the 10:30 time she had promised.She had a small four-door saloon which she drove with care, and she took him to the first of her selections. It was about three miles from his home and turned out to be two houses joined by a narrow corridor. It seemed pleasant enough, and Billy was made to feel welcome by the home manager as she showed him round, but there was something about the place that didn't sit right with him. It seemed at first glance too cramped.

After that first home, Dorothy drove Billy to the second choice. She chatted away during the drive and said the home they were going to was, in fact, a privately run home that took NHS patients.

They arrived at Peace Hall Care Home after a fifteen-minute drive, approaching it along a winding, tree-lined private road that took them to a car park in front of an imposing, purpose-built three-storey building. As they walked from the car Billy noted the immaculate gardens in the centre of the three-quarter circled building and its surrounds.

The reception hall was also imposing, with leather easy chairs and a settee set on one side, and the reception desk tucked away on the other. Dorothy had a word with the receptionist, who said the home manager had seen them come and was on the way down.

Seconds later, the manager Becky Watts was with them. She greeted Dorothy like an old friend and shook hands with Billy.

"Let's go and look at the room I've got in mind for your wife first, shall we?" she asked, leading Dorothy and Billy to a door a little way down the corridor.

She punched in a number on a security pad to open the door to a stairwell, pressed a button to call a lift on her left, and took them to the first floor, where she again punched in security numbers to open a door into a corridor leading to the rooms. "It's to stop the residents wandering off," she explained.

The fifth room on the right, 153, Becky said, was the only one available.

It was a simple room, plain and freshly painted in a neutral pale yellow, with an in-built bathroom/toilet that had a walk-in bath, a wardrobe and a quite wide single beech wood hospital bed with padded retractable side rails taking up one side of the room, and with a small TV set alongside a music player on a shelf on the opposite side. There was a heavy recliner chair sitting looking out of the ceiling-high window over the central garden. It was not big, but there was a feeling of roominess that was ideal for a bedridden patient.

"We don't call them patients. This is their home and they are residents," said Becky when Billy mentioned it.

When they left the room, they walked slowly along the corridor, which was liberally covered with bright paintings and posters, and Billy noticed that many of the other rooms on both sides (all exactly the same) were occupied with men or women asleep in their beds.

They came to a large lounge which was packed with patients in various stages of dementia—all shapes and sizes, men and women, some with thinning, wispy hair, others with their hair smartly cut and coiffed. Some of the patients seemed perfectly normal, some were asleep in easy chairs and others just sat and stared into space, while five were closely watching a huge television screen hanging on one wall not really able to comprehend what they were seeing: an advert offering cheap cremations.

There was a goodly number of nurses and carers in various coloured tunics to denote their rank and job—about two-thirds young girls— and they flitted round talking, stroking, helping. Most were laughing, while a rather well-built events lady wearing a very bright blouse was reading a story to another small group on one side, and there was soft easy music playing in the background.

Billy, Dorothy and Becky stood by the door, watching as the story came to an end and nurses and carers began moving the patients out of the lounge for lunch. Becky led them further down the corridor to a large dining room set with many white-clothed tables, and again Billy watched silently for a few moments as the patients were settled in their places, some chatting but mostly just sitting waiting for their meal.

After several moments, while Billy admired the slick efficiency of the carers, Becky suggested they also have some lunch. After a word with one of the carers, she led them back along the corridor to room 153, where they sat round a moveable overbed table by the big recliner chair. Billy was given a straight-backed chair, while Dorothy sat on the bed and Becky on a low three-legged stool.

Three plates of food arrived—mass produced food, hardly Michelin-star standard but well-cooked and tasty and served by a pretty Nepalese girl.

"They are so patient," said Becky.

Although the girl generally kept her eyes lowered, Billy did catch her eye on one occasion. He noted the friendly, eager-to-help look as she asked him, "Ice cream or pudding?" She pronounced it "eyesh cream".

As they ate, Becky told Billy a bit more about Peace Hall. "Relatives can visit any time—in the daytime only, of course—and they're encouraged to join in the events," she said between mouthfuls. "We have specialist nurses on duty every day—two at a time—and a local doctor and consultant nurse visit at least once every week."

When lunch was over, Becky called another Nepalese carer to take Billy back to reception while she and Dorothy went to her office to discuss things.

As he waited, Billy thought that the whole place felt right. Perfectly right. He couldn't say why, it was just an instant, instinctive feeling and he knew it was the right place for Rose.

Ten minutes later, Dorothy returned and told Billy that suitable terms had been agreed and said she had agreed financial terms with Becky, and if he wanted the home, they could take Rose immediately.

Billy had decided that Peace Hall was his definite choice and told Dorothy to go ahead and fix it, but she said he should look at her third choice before making a final decision.

By now, it was dark and too late for the third home, so Dorothy drove Billy home with a promise to pick him up again the next morning. Billy said his goodbyes, but didn't go indoors, instead driving to the hospital for a quick visit to Rose. She was asleep so he didn't stay long.

Dorothy was again exact with timing when she collected him the next morning, Saturday. The third home on her list was close to the first she had shown Billy. Another converted house. Billy thought it "quite nice", but he still favoured Peace Hall, and he told Dorothy when they got back to the car.

"I thought you'd say that," she said with a smile. "It really is a good place. I was lucky they had a room available. I'll phone them when I've dropped you off, and it should be fixed first thing on Monday. Scott will tell you the arrangements when everything's sorted."

Dorothy left him and Billy never saw her again, but despite forgetting her name, he was to be continually grateful for her kindness and consideration and especially for her selection of Peace Hall.Finding the home had been an understated, easy job for Billy, and he was grateful to Scott and Dorothy and the NHS for making it so simple for him. Arranging the funding was not so simple though.

All seemed to be going well, but the ugly, heavy hand of rigid bureaucracy overrode everything. Billy had a phone call, an e-mail and a letter telling him to contact a direct line at his local county council and it took no fewer than five attempts covering more than an hour and a half before he finally got through.

"What do you want?" asked a rather brusque voice.

"I'm calling because you asked me to," replied Billy, quoting a reference number.

"Hang on." The line went dead for several minutes, then the voice came back. "Can I speak to Mrs Saunders?"

Billy explained that Rose was in hospital and that he held power of attorney over all her affairs, and that was greeted with a sigh.

"But we need to know about her financial situation," said the voice. There was no sympathy, no compassion.

"I can give you all that," said Billy. "Look, the easiest thing is for me to call in and—"

"You can't do that. It's not allowed."

The phone went dead.

Billy thought of ringing back to complain, but he had to go to the hospital, so he left it at that, but when he arrived, he saw Scott and told him all about it.

"Leave it to me," said Scott in a way that showed he had faced the situation before.

Later, as Billy sat holding Rose's hand, Scott returned with another young man, a social worker attached to the hospital. He said the council had given him permission to carry out the checks and showed Billy a form he needed to fill in, and as Rose was drifting off to sleep, Billy went home early to get out his account file and fill it in.

The form was an official county council means test, and as Billy had split his and Rose's money and pension incomes to separate accounts (luckily), it was comparatively easy to fill in. The next morning, he returned it, and the same young man glanced at it and took it away.

"Seems to be OK," he told Billy, "I'll talk to the council and sort it. They're always happy if someone does their job for them." He smiled and walked away.

The form was satisfactory, and Scott told Billy the next morning that the council social services would be paying the majority of the fee for Peace Hall, with the NHS adding a bit for the medical care.

"They'll ask you for a donation, but it won't be anywhere near the frightening amounts you've heard."

And so, it was fixed.

But there was one last blow to come.

The day before the transfer, Dr Kristina saw Billy and told him that he shouldn't build his hopes too high. "I think you can only expect another three months. Her condition is still very serious," she said.

The news hit Billy hard and he couldn't think about it, didn't know what to say, and the move went ahead.

Chapter 11

The sun was shining when Rose was transferred to Peace Hall Care Home by a windowed transport ambulance three days later, and Billy arrived in the home's car park as she was being taken in on a wheeled stretcher. He was given a cup of tea and two biscuits as he waited in reception for her to settle in.

Manager Becky Watts soon came down and took him to the first floor and Rose's room, number 153, then she left him with her. The thoughtful staff had decorated the room, and there were red and yellow roses, three balloons and a welcome card waiting for her arrival.

"We always remember this is their home. We just work here," Becky told him.

Rose was in bed, still wearing a rather ragged and slightly frayed hospital nightdress and with her eyes shut and drowsy. The ambulance journey had been tiring for her, but when Billy held out his hand to hers, she gripped it tight. She muttered something too softly for Billy to hear, and they stayed hand in hand for twenty minutes or so before she fell asleep.

Billy walked down the corridor until he found the nurses' office and asked if he should bring Rose any clothing. He was given a list—trousers, tops, sweaters, nightclothes—and without going back to room 153, he left Peace Hall and went home, where he looked in Rose's chest of drawers to see what was available. Like most husbands, and despite his years in the fashion business, he didn't know what clothes his wife possessed.

In the event, Billy found several sweaters and blouses, two pairs of trousers, two old pairs of pyjamas and a fairly new nightdress. Then, feeling rather flat, he went to bed. The house felt lonely, and he climbed the stairs slowly, and was consciously grateful when he passed the tenth step.

He didn't know what Peace Hall preferred its residents to wear, so the next morning he went shopping to buy Rose two new specially designed nightdresses that buttoned at the back like a hospital gown, and straight away took them and the pyjamas along with the other clothes to the home in time to give Rose her mashed-up lunch. It turned out the nightdresses were welcome as the preferred form of night attire as they were easiest to put on and take off and far easier to cope with Rose's incontinences.

With Rose taken away from him, his life was, in all honesty, a bit of a hazy blur in his mind, but he quickly discovered emotions he never knew he had. He had a constant feeling for Rose—something he had probably taken for granted in the past.

With nothing else to do on the first weekend after she'd gone to the home, he went to the seaside to visit friends living on the seafront in a small bungalow just above the beach. He wanted to explain things to them, but he found it very difficult to talk about it and they did not press him.

He stayed with them overnight, sleeping on a sofa, and took them to a pub for Sunday lunch, but he left early in the afternoon and returned home feeling desperately alone. Although he knew there were thousands, possibly millions, in the same position, he felt as if he were the only one. He was devastatingly, achingly, constantly lonely.

The next morning, he went back to see Rose. While at the home, he checked with the staff, and as a result of what they told him, he went home and sorted out several easier to put on outfits and took them along the next day. The clothes he didn't take he took off their racks and crammed them in alongside his own jackets and trousers in the wardrobe, then he took the two racks to the local dump. Going through the clothes and things that Rose and he had gathered together, his love for her grew ever more tangible and added to the feeling of helplessness and his need for her voice and her being.

He spent three days clearing the rest of the house, collecting all her jewellery and putting the various necklaces, bracelets, brooches and earrings in an ornate box she had kept on top of her personal bedside table—she didn't have much, always preferring small, subtle, unostentatious but pretty items,

In the lower drawer of that table, he found a small baby toy, battered and obviously much hugged and sat on the bed on Rose's side holding it on his lap for more than twenty minutes and staring into space, his mind a blank.

Billy called on Rose every weekday over the next two weeks, trying to figure out in his mind how he felt about her moving away from their home to the care home. He didn't want to bother the busy staff at weekends when most visitors called on the patients as he knew they would be busy. It gave him time to do various essential things around the house.

He quickly discovered that when Rose went into the home he had to assume all the various jobs she had being doing. Dusting and vacuuming were easy, he worked out how to operate the washing machine and dryer, and he found he actually enjoyed the neatness of ironing. Cooking was largely controlled by ready-made meals heated in a microwave whose controls he quickly mastered. It literally took years before he had the courage to boil or fry things and even then, when he used a frying pan, the smell of burnt oil pervaded the house for days.

For most other things, he would call in "a little man", an expert. Luckily, he could afford it.

He discovered that Rose's control of their finances had been excellent, and even in the early days when she started to lose her memory, she had split their joint bank account into two separate accounts to cover taxes, and arranged powers of attorney should anything happen to either of them. She had been so, so organised, and explained it all to Billy, but he did not really listen as he had no interest—then.

He opened letters addressed to her, and after a month, he found a direct debit form from the local council, and although it did not give any payment sum, he filled it in and returned it.

He had made himself form a routine to organise his solo life, and still visited her every day—without his visits to Rose and the home he felt a little at a loss.

It was the same most days and evenings. Almost every night, as he went to bed, he would take out his hearing aids and sit on the side of the bed listening to the silence. It seemed to hit him then that he was all alone in the world and he felt sorrow for his own loneliness. But even then, he didn't blame it on her leaving him.

He woke up at 2, 3, 4 almost every morning and lay on the bed in the pitch black of the night with a blank void inside his skull and a hollow feeling in his chest.He took to leaving the door to the bedroom open as it made him feel less as if he were in a prison cell.

As he settled into the pattern of life on his own, he was sad in the mornings because he didn't have anyone to say "good morning" to; he was sad at night because he had no one to kiss and say "sweet dreams" to.

He was all alone, yet everywhere he went in the house, there were reminders of Rose: pictures on the shelves, a scorch mark on the carpet where she had rested a hot iron, her handbag still on top of a bookcase.

He could never escape her, yet he was always alone. Yes, he had been alone at times before, but he had never, ever, been lonelier.

Acquaintances would ask how he was more often than usual, and his most regular answer was that he was either muddling or plodding along. The trouble was that was exactly what he was doing.

He kept himself reasonably busy, seeing friends, neighbours or acquaintances for lunch or on visits as often as he could, but he realised they had their own lives to lead and weren't always available.

But there was always the moment when he'd said his goodbyes, locked the house door behind him and closed the curtains and was alone with the spirit and feel of Rose all around him, but alone.

For a while after Rose went into the home, Billy slept with the landing light on and his bedroom door open. He felt noticeably alone, and he didn't want to be alone in the dark.

The loneliness sat on him with a palpable feeling. He was sensitive to its dark air of desolation and gloom as it wrapped itself round both his mind and his body. Even when talking in a group, he felt that sense of forlorn seclusion.

He would lie in the half dark of his bed thinking that the phrase about the sound of silence was true—you could actually *hear* the silence. There was the nothingness of loneliness.

Luckily, he had the daily call to Peace Hall, and for the short times he was there, he was actually with Rose—physically, at least, if not in spirit.

But still, after every visit, he would get home, and as he walked through the door, he would lock it automatically and then both he and the house felt even lonelier than ever, missing someone else, missing her.

After years of agony at home, now this.

As for the visits, some were good, some were bad, some were very good, some very bad. One day, he had fed Rose and was delighted she had eaten every mouthful. As he sat there, Rose fell asleep, and after a while Billy started to wonder why he wasstill sitting holding her hand. *Because I love you,* he thought, *and because I want to be with you.*

"I love you," he whispered, saying the words without emotion but as an honest statement of fact.

Her face took on an emotional look although she was asleep. He hoped it showed a love returned.

Day after day he was alone, always thinking of Rose. And when he went to bed, his last thought on turning out the light was of her, that he had lived another day without her. He always held her hand when he saw her and was delighted when Rose was the one to take his hand first. When he held her hand, she gripped his fiercely. He noted how small and delicate her hands were.

One day, as she reached up towards him, he leant forwards towards her—her fist was clenched tight—but at the last moment, her palm touched his cheek and rested there lightly. She smiled, and it gave Billy an extra surge of emotion, although she was simply conscious that she could feel somebody she could trust. The smile stayed on her lips, and she seemed to look straight into his eyes, but he had a feeling that she didn't really recognise him.

Other times, far too often, he would find himself sobbing away for no immediate positive reason, with tears filling his eyes and rolling uncontrollably down his cheeks. In practical reality, his optician told him he was suffering from dry eye—a misnomer if ever there was one, because it was a condition that

made his eyes water—although he knew that was not the only reason for his tears.

Eventually though, Billy managed to go about his lonely days without consciously thinking of Rose, although she was always there, sitting on his mind.

On one of the better days, Rose was talking as usual—a jumble of disconnected words that didn't seem to make sense. Billy knew she was in a deep conversation with someone, but he had no idea with who or what it was about.

"I think that maybe perhaps..." she said, then suddenly laughed. "Oh, Billy," she went on. "Rose said..." and she was off again on her garrulous vocal rambling.

During every visit, Billy gave an outward air of cheerful near normality, but he was struggling to cope, with reminders of Rose constantly bringing tears to his eyes. Everything he did, said, felt, gave him a reminder of the girl he had loved for most of his life.

Living alone, he became used to locking the street doors, drawing the curtains and being lonely, although very occasionally he would turn to the empty settee opposite him or look across the double bed and expect to see Rose there.

"I'd give anything to just have one more conversation with her," he regularly told himself."Just one more."

He would bring her name into everything he said: speaking to checkout girls in shops, people at bus stops, strangers in pubs.

He ate too fast without bothering too much about his manners as he wanted to watch television, and always before he finished the meal, he would belch very noisily out loud—there was no one in the house to hear him. He grinned as he remembered how upset he had been after she had been introduced to the Caballeros and he discovered that Rose—young, innocent, naive, sweet, gentle Rose—could burp at will... something he could not do!

He slept alone in their old double bed, often waking in the stark dark nights **for no reason** to suddenly realise there was no one alongside him or realising that the dark hump he could see on the other side of the bed was simply a pillow and not his Rose.

In the mornings, he often woke and lay there, immobile. He was wrapped in a warm cocoon of duvet and indifference. He wanted to get up, but he did not want to move, to stand and rejoin the sorrow of loneliness.

Generally though, he did sleep reasonably, although in patches and short bursts, but usually when he was wide awake early in the morning he would stay in bed with the lights off, normally trying not to think and get back to sleep. Most mornings, he was reluctant to get out from under the duvet. He had no incentive to get up. He was very lonely.

Billy had always been interested in the news, reading middle-of-the-road newspapers at first and later almost religiously watching TV bulletins. But now his interest was fading, and he just couldn't be bothered. It was all part of his general lack of enthusiasm for anything that didn't centre around Rose. That had become something of an obsession.

He often didn't change his bed sheets for a month or so, until even he realised they smelt, and at least once or twice a week he didn't shave or wash properly. He had no one to have a smooth chin for, no reason to go to a barber to have a haircut in order to look respectable. He usually wore the same shirt for a week or more.

Luckily, living on his own, he did not need to spend a lot, and with his and Rose's pensions, it was easy to keep ahead of the game. So now, alone, while he was not rich, he could comfortably afford most things. He quickly realised how to monitor larger expenses, making sure the money in each of their accounts would cover standing orders and things like that, but in general, he tried not to think of money. That was something Rose had always done for him.

Apart from her physical presence, he missed the feeling of her "being" everywhere in the house around him. He missed her hanging onto the handle as he pushed her shopping trolley round the supermarket, and her small hand clutching for his when they went for walks in the local park.

Days ran into each other, and he lost track. Any day was like the day before and the day after: Monday, Tuesday, Saturday, Sunday or bank holiday. He got up, visited her in the home or muddled his way through, then went to his lonely bed.

Ghosts of their past clung to the walls of the house, to the furniture, curtains, cushions. There were reminders of Rose in every room, every nook and cranny. Her handbag was still on top of a bookcase, there were tubes of skin lotion, pots of cream in the bathroom, her old toothbrush.Every time he made the double bed in the morning he noticed that "the other side" was still smooth, untouched. All reminders of Rose, a permanent link, but in reality they only added to Billy's loneliness.

The slovenly mood passed slowly, and Billy fairly quickly slipped into a daily routine where he got up and shaved, washed and dressed, went downstairs to open the curtains, put on the television (usually a talking news programme) then had his morning pills, morning tears and morning cup of tea. He tried not to think of Rose, but it was impossible until something important happened in the day, like bringing in the milk or looking into the usually empty post box.

Once in a while, he'd go for a drive in the countryside, following the same routes he'd once used for Rose's daily drives, and although he tried to convince himself that "once you've seen one tree, you've seen 'em all" he had a weird, eerie, inner feeling of a "presence" that bound all of life together. It made him feel small and somewhat insignificant, but he always muttered a few words to whoever—or whatever—for having him as part of it.

Unstable though Rose was mentally, she was the only stable thing in Billy's life. He often went for whole days without meeting or speaking to anyone else—he was truly alone on those days, but her presence was always with him, always tugging at his emotions.

Although he sometimes tried not to think of her, pictures of her would gather in his mind and it inevitably brought physical tears to his eyes. She was still always a part of him. He loved her as much now as he had when they first discovered each other.

After persuasion from Rose's nurses, he made himself go for short, lonely walks in the streets around the house although he had difficulty walking—nothing too long, just a short, slow stroll to give him a change of scenery, but they always hurt. He'd had had his knees examined and X-rayed before Rose went into the home, and nothing was found, but they were the main reason he found walking difficult, so he had to force himself to take the quarter-mile slow stroll every day.

He stuck at it for a while, but it soon got boring, and instead he found a nearby park where (in spring and summer) he could sit in the sun. Sometimes there would be mothers and children, and he enjoyed watching the sheer enthusiasm and love of life of the youngsters running round and rolling on the grass with their compulsion to kick, throw, fall over, chase and generally have fun. He loved the "company" and the noise.It was the same watching most dogs enjoying their freedom when their owners took them for walks in the park.

Mostly though, he enjoyed the days when the park was empty. Then he could sit in the sun enjoying the noisy company of all manner of birds as they soared and dived around him and the trees.

He knew he was letting his standards slip, leaving dirty dishes in the sink during the day, only washing things up before settling down to late night television, letting unironed bits of washing litter around for days, hardly ever opening windows to let fresh air in, and no longer shutting doors, but surprisingly leaving toilet seats down as he had when Rose was at home!

He had rarely sworn in front of Rose, although she knew all the words, but now that he was alone in the house without her, he often shouted obscenities at himself when things went wrong or he dropped things or banged himself against a jutting wall or table, using four-letter words or combinations of swear words in anger or anguish.

He was lonely and he knew he was, and all the small shared intimacies he noticed between all the couples he met just increased the loneliness.

But there were always the visits to see Rose. It elated him on one wintery day in December when she seemed to be asleep, but suddenly opened both eyes wide and flashed a big smile at him.

"I love you," she said, then shut her eyes again.

Billy squeezed her hand. "I love you more," was all he could reply. There was a sudden lump in his throat.

It somehow summed up Rose's first year in Peace Hall: low lows but very high highs.

Chapter 12

The second year of Rose's stay in the room at Peace Hall started in much the same way—Billy visiting every day of the week to help feed her in her recliner chair and trying to fill time on his own for the other hours of the week.

He still felt as if he had abandoned Rose, but that feeling passed as he continued to see how she was cared for, how much she really did need medical help as well as love.

The nurses and carers tried to speak to him about the years he had been the sole carer for Rose, about the problems and events he and she had faced, but he honestly couldn't remember most of that time. Over that first year, they had all grown to like Billy, and with the added thoughts of the love they felt for Rose, they adopted him as "one of the family". One of them, Bethany (all the staff wore name badges with their first names only) was particularly concerned about Billy, noting the tears in his eyes when he was with Rose. On average, it took around ten or fifteen seconds before his eyes started to fill.

Bethany was wonderful. She was a very big woman of Jamaican descent, and her clipped tones and manner bore a very Caribbean air. Billy always joke-complained that she bullied him—she didn't—but she played along with it and seemed to enjoy the banter.

"You a man, you need to be bullied," she would insist.

Billy always called her Big Beth (not in her hearing, mind) and that described her perfectly. Big Beth was a big lady and Billy adored her, even when she suggested that he cut back on his daily visits.

"You be no good to her if you ill yourself, innit."

Billy, she repeated, just had to do something to lessen the emotional pain.

"You have to t'ink about yourself," she insisted.

"I do," he always replied, somewhat truculently. "But I can't leave her. I want to come and see her. I need to, it's a compulsion." He became serious. "I just couldn't leave Rose. She's a part of me and I'm a part of her and I have to see her, be with her, hope that I might possibly help her in some way even though she doesn't know it. It's upsetting, yes, but there's no question that I couldn't come."

It was a long, impassioned, rather overdramatic plea, and it was a message he repeated over and over to the nurses and carers who listened, although it was Beth, in particular, who continually insisted that it was better for him to cut back on the daily visits.

Billy listened, and although he would argue, when he was alone, he couldn't sometimes help asking himself, "*Do* I really need this?" He always answered in the affirmative.

The continuous, but gentle, inducements finally worked through to Billy's brain, and Big Beth, with help from other members of the staff, finally persuaded him to cut back his visits to alternate days, three times a week. He did so, taking his time to slowly accept things.

As he had visited regularly when she first went into the home, almost every single day, he found the change hard. Slowly though, as Rose got worse and stopped recognising him, he slipped into the three times a week routine, accepting life as it had to be. He would drive to the home almost religiously every Monday, Wednesday and Friday, no matter what the weather, and sat with Rose who spent most of her time sitting in her chair in her room either chattering away to herself or sleeping. She was always dressed in thick sweaters, loose T-shirts and trousers, but although the temperature in the room was well controlled, she occasionally felt cold and Billy would put an extra blanket round her shoulders or, once, his own outdoor anorak.

On every visit, Billy was overcome with an emotion over Rose such as he had never felt before. It even went beyond his previous feelings for her, much as he had thought that impossible. He would sit by her recliner chair, holding her hand, sometimes stroking her cheek or forehead, smoothing her hair and muttering words she couldn't hear.

"I love you," he told her. "And you're still just as beautiful as ever."

Rose would stare into space, smiling at… well, Billy couldn't say what, but he hoped it was at him.

The tears continued every time he saw her stuck immobile in her chair, and they quickly filled his eyes. They simply highlighted his loneliness.

Once in a while, Rose would mutter something intelligible—"It's nice" or "That's good"—and Billy would try to look as if he was part of her conversation and would agree with her—"Yes, it's nice" or "Very good".

Generally though, Rose was helpless, incapable of any meaningful actions on her own, and because she couldn't do anything for herself, Billy also felt helpless because there was nothing he could do to help her. Except unimportant things like the day he arrived to find her in her chair and she had pulled her sweater and vest up showing her bare stomach.

"Come on, you're too old for that," he laughed. "When you were eighteen, I'd have paid to see your tum…" He felt he was actually doing something helpful as she passively let him straighten her clothing.

There was no way he could help or do anything though when an outbreak of some sort of stomach bug suddenly caused Peace Hall to close and Billy missed his three visits a week. He was distraught.

He worried, every single day, every single night, about the closure. Would Rose catch the bug, how would it affect her, would she have the strength to resist and fight it off?

The nurses asked what they should do if she did pick up the germ. It could be fatal in her condition, but it was possible to treat it in a hospital with its greater facilities. Should they send her to hospital or try to treat it themselves, they asked him. The lifesaving, life-ending decision had to be his to make. It more than worried him.

"Why does it have to be me?" he queried. "I'm no doctor. It's a medical issue."

Luckily, the decision was never needed as Rose didn't pick up the bug. But Billy woke every night, usually between 3:30 and 4, and lay awake for the best part of an hour agonising over it. What if she did catch the killer disease? If they were able to cure it, would it recur? Was that likely or merely possible?

He knew that whatever he determined had to be in Rose's best interests, whatever would keep her happy and pain free. He could not decide, could not pass a possible death sentence on "his Rose", did not know if his thinking was of her wellbeing or for his own sake.

The complete shutdown of the home lasted for two weeks, and it was a relief when things started to get back to a little bit of normality. A room was organised with a glass window down one complete side so that visitors could at least see the patients without being open to them to either catch or pass on anything nasty. There was a two-way microphone so they could converse.

It was not ideal, but at least it was something and for Billy at least it meant that, although he could be in the same room as Rose, he was with her but not really with her. For her part, she slept in her chair through most of his visits.

So, every other day, he drove to Peace Hall to see Rose, and every other day, he would go home emotionally drained, going to bed early and climbing the stairs to bed (still automatically counting the steps as he used to do with Rose and always glad to get past the tenth) and climbing into bed thinking of the next visit.

It was a desperately lonely time, even more so than normal, and Billy dreaded the thought of an emergency phone call, knowing that the persistent ringing could well be Peace Hall calling with bad news.

Then Billy got a message that the home was opening up again as usual with the proviso that visitors (and staff) wore full safety aprons, gloves and masks. The next day, Billy was back.

The partitioned visiting had lasted for just over a week and a half before the home reopened fully and Billy was able to sit holding hands with Rose in her room once more. She blissfully slept throughout in her chair with a slight smile on her lips, only waking briefly to let him feed her lunch.

Ten minutes after he had arrived for his reunion, Big Beth came into the room to see him.

"How're you?" she asked as she straightened Rose to a more comfortable position in her chair, "You managing?"

Billy nodded. "I'm just about getting over that decision about sending her to hospital," he replied. "It was probably the hardest thing I've ever had to do." He paused for a moment. "It's not fair to ask people like me about what should be a medical thing. It's like asking us to sign a death warrant."

"You have t'do what best for her."

He paused again. "Everyone says that, but how do I know what's best? I don't."

That was true. It was something he and Rose had never discussed, never had reason to discuss. Why would they? They would have been young, and talking of your own death was too far off on the horizon, not even a vague thought. But she was here now, he was able to touch her. She was Rose, and he still couldn't bear thinking of her not being there.

After four weeks of heightened hell, the disease had passed, although for a further month visitors (like the staff) had to wear face masks to prevent any cross passing of any remains of the disease. Billy was glad when he eventually didn't have to wear it and Peace Hall life returned to its routine. Situation normal.

There was an abhorrent moment a few days later when Billy had to sign a "Do Not Resuscitate" form. It was a horrible thing he had to do. It made sense, but he felt as if he had signed her life away, and after signing the form he sat in her room alone with his morbid imagination, and knew the blankness of absolute helplessness.

The break had helped Billy though, and although he did not realise it, his mind somehow wrapped itself round the fact that Rose was likely to be taken from him suddenly, at any time. He was not at all religious—at least, he didn't need any organised religion—but he had a vague belief in an all-powerful being who controlled every single thing on Earth. So, despite his beliefs, he got into the habit of saying a short prayer every night. As he turned out the light and waited in the dark for sleep, night after night (unless his emotional exhaustion made him fall asleep too quickly), he tried to recall religious phrases from childhood visits to the school chapel, but couldn't, so he simply implored "dear God" to "continue to look after Rose and keep her as happy and content and as healthy as she can be for as long as she can be."

After a pause, he would add, "I love you, dear God... in my own way." He never asked for anything for himself.

Billy had always been an optimist and lived for the moment, so the traumas of the unexpected closure were quickly forgotten, gone, and he couldn't recall them no matter how hard he tried. He only knew that Rose had survived and was here now. That was all he cared about. It was emotion. It was love.

Billy had, in fact, forgotten most of the bad times since Rose had become ill, but there were a few incidents he did recall that he wished would go away: his loss of temper, the time her incontinences had inadvertently made her relieve herself two ways while he was cleaning her, but memories of the slow, general decline were gone. His mind had wiped the unpleasantness away. With it, unfortunately, also went most of the good memories of their marriage.

All the staff at Peace Hall were lovely and tried to steer him away from the dark memories and moments. They were brilliant. *All of them real saints*, thought Billy.

There was Beth, of course, with Dipankar and the very English Diana along with two more nurses from India, Ashish and Kuwarjeet, with the carers who were mostly Nepalese girls—Ditya, Kiara, Aabha, Chadani—and two Nepalese boys, Tenno, very shy and quiet, and the other, Kamal, very chatty (his English was almost good). There was also the very demure, sweet Japanese girl Hanako and a six-foot-four Serbian, Bogdan, built like a rugby prop forward but with the gentlest hands anyone had ever known. He would often sympathetically—but deliberately—give Billy a huge man hug, which he knew embarrassed Billy but amused him.

With manager Becky included, they had become his new family.

Outwardly, Billy was the same as he had always been: light-hearted, friendly, always ready with a smart answer or comment. No matter how he felt, he always forced himself to be chirpy with the nurses and carers, but they knew the visits affected him, really upset him, in abig way.

One day, he was sitting with a sleeping Rose, his hand resting on her arm, when Beth came into the room.

"How you gettin' on?" she asked. "All well?"

"Just growing older by the minute," he replied.

"Why you say you old? A young handsome lad like you. If I were no married, I could fancy you." She paused with a smile on her lips. "Mind you, only if you had more money than my old man…"

Beth would always swap mock flirtatious jibes. It was her way of cheering people up, so Billy replied in the same vein.

"It wouldn't do you any good," he said. "The worst thing about getting old is that nowadays, when I'm hot in bed, it's because the duvet is too thick."

Beth laughed. "In that case, lover, I jess don't want to grow old," she said in the same mood. "But you a naughty boy for t'inkin' that."

The phone in her pocket rang, and after taking it out and glancing at the screen she added, "Got to go now. That pretty Dr Jenkins is waiting for me advice. And he young!"

She left the room, and Billy turned back to the still sleeping Rose, all jokiness gone. He took her hand in his, but she suddenly pulled it away from his grip and reached forwards.

"My baby…" she said. "Awack bang."

The inevitable tears started up again in Billy's eyes. Life returned to its new normal.

The year dragged on, one day very much like the day before, with Billy continuing his three-times-a-week lunchtime visits, both pleased and upset to hear Rose now talking more. Until now, her "conversations" had been made up of words used randomly, usually in the wrong order. But now she began making animal-like noises interspersed with the words.He loved seeing her still smiling and laughing a lot, although no one ever knew what was making her laugh.It beat the days when she had slept throughout the visit.

Much of the time, Billy didn't know what to think. Did he visit Rose out of pity? For his own sake? Because he felt it might help her? He just felt pleased when he was with her, even though it ripped at his heart to see her in the condition she was.

She would sit there, occasionally still propped up in bed but usually in a heavily padded mobile recliner chair and would stare sightlessly out of the window. They used a hoist to get her from her bed to the chair, and Billy only saw that once and felt it so undignified for her that he refused to watch it again, preferring to wait in the corridor outside.

Rose's view from the chair had her looking out into the car park at first, but then they moved her to a room looking out on a grassed central area with a fountain spouting endlessly. She enjoyed the bright colours of the few flowers dotted around, until her sight started to fade. But for her, it was always the same view, day in and day out.

After her eyes had failed, she stopped hearing things as well, and in her mind's distorted memory, she retreated into a happy world of just her mother and occasionally her father and (mysteriously at first) two couples: her twenty-six-year-old husband Billy and herself just as they had once been fifty years before, and the Billy and Rose of now.

The two couples were four separate people in Rose's mind, and she would sit with the real Billy by her side "conversing" with the Billy she had known when they were first married.

"Hang on a moment, Billy's just telling me something," she would say out loud, retreating into her mental haven with the young man of her dementia-fuelled memory.

She chattered away to him, laughed with him, was happy in their own limited world.No one could ever know what was going on in what was left of her disease-ridden brain, but in her mind, she had visits to theatres and cinemas, mainly to see music shows, and she "lived" the excitement of running a house and looking after her newly married husband.She didn't need any more.

When she spoke to him, Billy was often confused as to which Billy she was talking to. He hoped there was a vague trace of the current him left somewhere in her brain.

It confused Billy the first few times he heard of the "new" couple, and he only realised what was going on when one day she spoke of "Billy's black hair, so lovely". As a young man he'd always had jet black hair smoothed down with a straight parting on the left side and a quiff on the right, but now his hair was white and thinning, and the quiff was a little meagre, although still there.

Billy got a little jealous of the "other Billy" at one stage, wishing Rose would come back to him in real time, but she only retreated further and further into her past. She was happy holding hands with the modern Billy and living in happiness with the younger man of her dreams.

She kept trying to put her fingers in her mouth, and during his visits, Billy had to be alert to stop her. It was only a reflex action, a return to babyhood, but he still tried to stop her. It was hard work sometimes because her grip and her arm strength was surprisingly strong.

Then names faded and finally words disappeared almost completely. She held Billy's hand during visits but still broke off to talk in weird animal sounds, apparently to her husband. The noises would flow out, not in any understandable order, and more often than not in a very loud unRose-like way. She had always been rather soft spoken, but now she almost shouted the internal conversations she shared with the world.

She was not the only one though. In her new room, she had competition. The woman in the next room was vying for noisiest patient, and at the moment, she was winning.

"Help me," she shrieked. "I don't know where I am." Her voice was strident, shrill and rasping. "Help me," she repeated. "I want my husband."

It upset Billy when he heard it, but it was not the worst time. Night times were probably the worst, and at home with nothing else to distract him, his mind thought of Rose and the dreadful disease that was eating away at her brain and he couldn't stop the tears that automatically came to his eyes. He would force himself to think of other things, and then his own mind became so active that he couldn't sleep. He became overtired, and that somehow meant he couldn't fall asleep and he thought of Rose. It was a peculiar secondary symptom of her dementia.

Billy was, and always had been, fiercely loyal, and as he lay in bed, he could not help images breaking into his mind of Rose in her recliner chattering aimlessly. He felt his lips twitching and tears rolling down his cheeks yet again. He tried to switch off the images, but he couldn't. Even in half sleep, he couldn't abandon her.

He tried to recall memories of their early life together and couldn't. He tried to summon up thoughts of holidays, of outings, of visits, and couldn't. The past evaded him, and his only thoughts of Rose were of the way she was now: blank eyes, a being lost in a body, a mind which just didn't register.

He wanted the happy times, but all that existed was the terrible enormity of Rose's illness.He still loved her with a deep intensity, and often when he was alone it felt like an ache in his chest. He could not express it in words, but it usually brought tears to his eyes.He cried a lot, too much, with his lone thoughts.

He frequently woke with a strange feeling, alone, although in a strange, mysterious way Rose was always "with" him in his mind, in his being, in his mental emotions. His eyes continually filled with tears that rolled for no apparent reason, and he left them to dry in the corners of his eyes and on his cheeks. It happened too often for him to bother wiping them away.

In the mornings, he would always lie in bed trying not to think of Rose, and after ten minutes or so he would force himself to get up and make himself concentrate on shaving, bathing and getting dressed, although on some days he didn't bother about such basic cleanliness. The loneliness was still there, but the morning mental haze thankfully pushed it into the background.

Despite that, one morning, he found he had prepared two cups of tea for breakfast, one in each of the red and yellow mugs he had bought at the start of Rose's dementia. He had not been aware of making them, and he reluctantly poured the red mug down the sink without feeling.

On every visit to Peace Hall, he took dozens of photos and short videos on his mobile phone, and very soon he had a collection of over a hundred stored in its memory, often looking at them while at home. Sometimes when he woke in the middle of the night they gave him an ethereal feeling that somehow brought him and Rose together. After a while, he had some of the photos printed and framed, and put them on the mantlepiece and on the shelves and ledges of his living room.

Despite the photos and all the other recollections of her in every room around the house, he tried not to think of her. The memory was always too hurtful, but she was always there in her chair and making noises, not as she had been in the good years.

He always left the curtains open until it was quite dark outside, drawing them closed as late as possible. When they were closed, he was alone, cut off from the rest of the world. He wore his loneliness—it caressed and weighed on him like a blanket on a hot night. It was not only Rose's condition that upset him though. It was the thought of her and all the other residents of her home, of the thousands, millions, suffering like them around the world. It was the futile nothingness that upset him. Bodies just living out their physical lives.

Billy was starting to feel his age. He felt wobbly, needing to be near a wall or something for steadying support when he moved around the house, and he now used a walking stick for confidence when he went out. He noticed that he was automatically keeping his feet wider apart when he walked.

Slowly though, over the year, he had somehow started building a bit of a new social life for himself, and now he was starting to meet neighbours and friends more often, and the "old Billy" often came through in those meetings. But it seemed there was no escape from the present—everyone seemed to have a mother or aunt or grandfather who suffered from dementia. But none of them knew anything about the disease, any more than Billy had before it had affected Rose.He could not escape it.

There was the time, for instance, when he was joking with a neighbour and his wife who had come round for tea. The wife was trying to convince the husband that he had to take more exercise, and Billy was jokingly backing up his laziness.

"If God had meant me to walk, he'd have given me eight legs," said the husband.

"Only you could have said something like that and meant it," countered the wife.

Billy was in no mood to take that without a quick quip. "Why do wives always talk like wives?" he asked.

"Silly boy," said the wife, echoing Rose's saying.

Things like that always made him think of Rose, and although he tried not to let it bother him (the memory was always too hurtful) she was always there, in her chair and making noises, not as she had been in the good years.

And so, that second year drew to a slow and rather unhappy close.

Chapter 13

It was the start of his third year alone, and Billy was determined to get his life sorted. He knew he had to do something, and he set about a determined effort to widen his social life.

When Rose had first gone into Peace Hall, some of his neighbours had brought him small pots and plates of fresh cooked dishes and invited him for meals or afternoon tea, and a few friends had rallied round and tried to help him.

They would invite him out for meals, but every time, he was conscious of the fact that the table was for three or five people and he was always the odd one out.

It was the loneliness that got to him. Even when he was with friends or neighbours, he felt very alone. In big groups, he was invariably the sole lonely one. It never left him.

He got on well with his neighbours and seemed to have an affinity with the widow living opposite and the widower down the road. He understood their similar unspoken loneliness, their solitude. The difference between them was that they had all lost their soul partners, but he could still see his Rose.With the others, friendly though they were, he always noticed the invariably moment when husband or wife would make a little personal comment that only they understood and made him an outsider.

Sometimes, when he was out with friends or neighbours, he heard the couples niggling at each other, probably over some minor parochial matter. *Don't do it*, he thought. *Just bite the bile back and get on. Don't risk losing what you've got. It's lonely on your own.*

But he still went with them for lunches or very early evening meals or even on rare occasions short outings. He needed their company.

The enthusiastic initial blast had lasted for about five months before tailing off to just a few good-hearted souls who cared. And while Billy still accepted every small kindness gratefully, he was not too upset as some drifted away. They had lives (and problems) of their own to deal with.

His own life trundled on.

Billy had never been so lonely, even when he met people. Some days he didn't leave the house but sat watching TV or pottering about doing nothing jobs, and on those days, too many, he didn't see or speak to a single soul. They were depressing days, and in the evenings of those days, he always vowed to go walking or go to the club across the street. Life was beyond sad.

One evening, he did venture across the road because he had not seen a single person all day, and he just wanted to speak to someone, anyone. He quite enjoyed the friendly banter that went round between the regulars—men and women of various ages from houses near him. The "conversation" was mostly trite and banal and Billy tried to ignore it or tried to subtly take the rise out of the speaker. They often didn't realise.

"I've got forty toilet rolls," one staid grey-haired woman suddenly announced.

"Oh my God, I'd see a doctor," said Billy straight-faced.

"Oh no, I mean... well, Maggie said she used the cardboard rolls in the centre when we plant seeds. It protects them from birds. That's what I've got."

Billy could see there was no point in staying at that table and moved across to sit on a high stool at the bar with a group of older men, and because they had nothing else to talk about, he suddenly found himself telling them about Rose's decline.

"Don't think about it, old chap," said one of the regular Saga louts.

Billy snapped again. "Don't think about it?" he shouted back. "I've been waiting for a phone call telling me she's dead for years, and you tell me not to think about it! Do you know how hard it is, waiting. Not knowing."

The others just looked at him, silent, and he stood and stormed out.

Billy continued to go to the club fairly frequently after that and was soon accepted as one of the regulars, although he always left earlyish with the excuse that he had to have his supper. In reality, he preferred the loneliness of his home to the loneliness of a crowd, and often wished he had a son or daughter to share his TV or to talk to. Preferably a daughter, as she would be more like Rose.

During his various visits to the club, several of the men urged him to join in on Saturday mornings—"no women, real men's talk"—and one Saturday Billy did so, and found himself surrounded by a group of around six sour old men with beer sagging bellies and little apart from monosyllabic grunts at each other. What little "men's talk" there was was about women!

They revelled in relating the usual ailments of old men, and only one of them seemed to have a sense of humour. Billy stuck it out for about forty minutes before making an excuse to leave their company and go back home to his loneliness.

Back home, he made himself a cup of tea and muttered to himself that it was "a crowd of boring old farts boring a crowd of boring old farts".

That visit was one of the reasons he now made a conscious effort to see old friends he hadn't seen for years and a few more of his neighbours, and he began a fairly organised search around the various pubs and small restaurants in the area for lunches or lunchtime drinks with them.

Many of Rose's acquaintances and old work friends also got in touch, and for a while, Billy had a busier social life than he'd had for several years, juggling it with his regular visits to see Rose.

Seeing Rose was still his main priority, and being with her was the most important part of his life as he worked everything around his three-times-a-week trips to see her. He couldn't think of a time without her, could not abandon her.

So, although he continued to visit Rose on a regular basis and quite enjoyed being with the neighbours most of the time and reminiscing with friends from past days, he made himself fix on other things like going to the cinema or theatres, although he did not enjoy those as much because it was not the same without having Rose to immediately discuss their merits or faults.He was particularly conscious of seeing others in couples discussing the show or film either at the interval or on the way out at the end of the programme.

The visits to see Rose were still the most important part of his life, and he was always pleased when he found her happy, like the morning he drove to Peace Hall relishing the late spring freshness of the day. He found they had taken Rose, in her recliner chair, out onto the recreation room balcony so she could sit in the sunshine. She had her eyes shut and seemed to be asleep, but she was smiling as he sat down and took hold of her hand.

Rose's fists clenched tightly; the index finger of her left hand locked awkwardly over its middle finger. Billy tried to prise them apart, but Rose's grip was too strong.Using his other hand, he stroked her forehead and cheeks. She still had remarkably smooth skin, despite the age lines on her upper lip and round her mouth, and her hair, too, was remarkably silky, and all the nurses and carers had always said they were jealous of it.

"I love you," she announced, her eyes still shut.

Billy welled up with emotion. It was a rare moment of "conversation", although Billy chatted easily with all the staff and was always ready with a quick quip or wise crack—just as he had been at work or when going out with Rose, although at home or with close friends he had been more subtly funny and was regarded by them as quite a cheeky chap. He was the same with other visitors.

One day, for instance, he was talking to the Indian nurse Dipankar, who was feeding Rose some medicine.

"It's always raining here," she said, looking out of the window.

Billy smiled. "In England, we have four seasons." He counted them out on his fingers, "Winter, winter, winter and winter. And it always rains in winter."

But still, despite the home and his neighbours, Billy had never felt so alone. When he met people, he was alone. When he spoke to neighbours, he was alone. When he went for lunches or drinks with friends, he was alone. Even when he got up in the mornings and drew the bedroom curtains, he paused in front of the windows in the hope that he might see someone outside, anyone. He was alone.

He knew others, neighbours, friends, acquaintances, whose partners had died, and he felt a certain affinity to them. They enjoyed his company too. Apart from anything else, he was a good listener as they revealed themselves. They also listened as he told them that the first few days, a week, after Rose had moved into the home, it had seemed natural, just an extension of her month-long hospital stay, but that it had slowly hit him. She was gone. After their lifetime of years together, he was alone, and a feeling of loneliness fell on top of him, a shroud that felt like a blanket enveloping him. A thick, heavy, woollen cover.

They all understood each other, but there was always something that put him apart—their spouses had gone, forever, but Rose was still physically there for him even though maybe not really living.

He didn't say anything to them, obviously, but he knew in his own mind that with death there was finality. A line had been drawn.But with dementia, there was no line. There was a physical presence, but no person. There was a voice, but no contact. There were eyes, but no sight. Ears, but no hearing.

Other people didn't realise that when someone developed Alzheimer's they were not the only one to suffer—the close relative or carer did too.It was the same with any disease, really, but they could discuss it, share it. With dementia, it was a one-way feeling, despair, a living death, and for the person watching and loving, there was the hourly knowledge that the real thing could hit at any moment. Dementia was really the same as death, but there was no final cut off—just the anguish and grief.

On his visits to the home, he would see it all again, and wonder, *What kind of life is this, this living death?* And thought, *But at least they are still here.* At those times, he was almost clinically depressed.

Billy was living in limbo. He liked theoutings and lunches, and he worked hard to arrange them and make them happen. But he was always glad at their ending when he was able to retreat to the routine of being alone in a house which should have held happy memories but was just a cocoon around his loneliness.

He knew and recognised what was happening to him, and he tried to find things to keep himself occupied, although far too often he simply wanted to sit and feel sorry for himself.

He thought, briefly, of going on a luxury cruise, dismissing the idea quickly because he knew he would be a singleton amongst many couples.

"They're only floating care homes anyway." He remembered he had always told Rose this as he justified their joint dismissal of the idea.

When he was alone in the house, he dug out old photos of Rose from the albums where she had meticulously stored them, and either put them in frames (especially those in which he also featured) and put them on show in every room in the house, including the lavatory. He even put one in the wardrobe so he could see it whenever he took clothes out or (rarely) hung them up again.

He wrote letters full of irrelevant nothings to everyone he could think of and was occasionally pleased to get a reply or, better still, a phoned answer with a human voice.

He was a social creature by nature, and he enjoyed being with friends and neighbours. He really needed the bustle and bantering, the conversations and contact with other people, but that only made it worse when he left them.

He loved the company of his lunches and meetings, but a desolate feeling of loneliness would often sit on Billy as he tried to watch an afternoon game or a comedy show on TV.It was only when he was with Rose that he felt complete, like the cold and frosty morning when he had had to scrape the ice off his car windows before setting out to see her. He arrived dispirited and chilled from driving to the home in heavy rain, with bad drivers racing past him dangerously, shooting spray over his windscreen and blinding him for seconds at a time. He got soaked dashing from the car to reception, and by the time he got to Rose's room, his hands and nose were freezing cold.

He sat down beside her and tucked his hands in turn under her armpit and next to her thick woollen jumper, and as his hands warmed, he knew that he still really needed her help.

His hands were starting to feel alive when Nepalese carer Chadani came in to feed her lunch. It was a slow process—Rose was pouching her food (holding it in her mouth) and needed to be encouraged.

"Eat your food," Chadani repeatedly told her. "Shwollow."

Somehow Rose seemed to understand and did swallow the food.

Billy helped by stroking her chin or cheek to remind her to chew and it worked most of the time. He went home feeling that—despite the continuing rain on the drive home—they had both played a part in looking after each other.

Billy slept alone in their old double bed meagrely, badly, often waking up in the dark lonely hours when the moon was resting behind the clouds and the windows were simply slightly lighter patches in the dark blackness to realise that there was no one alongside him, and suddenly knowing that the dark hump he could see on the other side of the bed was simply a pillow and not his Rose.

In the mornings, he always woke with a dry mouth and a head full of sad memories. He would close his eyes again and lie with them shut as he tried to recall a happy day: a scene with Rose in a forest with sunlight glinting through the trees, slanting down on the remains of their picnic.Still on his back, he would open his eyes and look to his left. An empty space. She was not there. Reality kicked home and he slowly got out of bed. Another day was starting. Like yesterday. Like tomorrow.

In the mornings, he was always reluctant to get up from under the duvet. He had no incentive to get up.

He bathed and shaved with an empty mind, trying not to think of that picnic. Hard boiled eggs. Tomatoes. Cakes.He would dry himself, dress and go slowly downstairs to open the curtains and make himself a lone cup of tea.

Once, Billy invited a group of former colleagues for an evening meal and arranged a Thai takeaway for them. It was a failure. One didn't like "foreign" food, they now had nothing in common, and with no previous experience (Rose had always organised things like that), Billy's first attempt at hosting left a lot to be desired.

The event ground on slowly, drably and with difficulty, and after things were over one of the guests realised he had missed his last train home and Billy was unenthusiastically forced to invite him to stay the night, offering him a rather narrow sofa to sleep on. For the first time since Rose had gone to the home, he shut his bedroom door when they went to bed, cutting out the light from the landing window, and even had to shut the lavatory door when using it.The whole evening was awkward and made him feel even more cut off from the world.

It was irritating, but the house seemed to come to life again and had a different feel until the friend had gone the next morning. Then the house was achingly lonely again, and he was relieved when he went to see Rose, and while sitting listening to her chattering away he recalled the evening, remembering sadly that the others had all been talking of family matters, grandchildren, dinners made by dutiful children, togetherness. Billy felt really low, lower than his now usual state of downness, in abject misery.

Later that day, back home after a good visit to Rose, his natural optimism drifted back over him. Sitting in his chair, he switched on the television and there were more crowds of together people. He looked, but he did not watch.His mind was busy thinking.

He had been lucky all his life. He'd had friends in the Caballeros, a good job, promotions, enough money, savings, good food and holidays. He had inherited money from his in-laws to allow him to buy a small house, he'd had illnesses but lucky enough to get good (and effective) treatment, and generally had good health.

Most of all, he had found Rose. And lucky enough to have her fall in love with him.

Yes, he'd been lucky. His current situation was just payback time.

He switched off the television and went to bed, leaving the bedroom door open and falling asleep the instant he turned off the light and sleeping restfully for almost seven and a half hours.It was a rare night of rest.

But there was always Peace Hall and his new "family" there.

He would just sit in Rose's room, watching her sleep or listening to her ramblings, although often she would just sit in her recliner chair staring blankly into space.

All the staff, from the manager to the lowliest cleaner, knew him by name and called their greetings when they walked past the room where he sat holding Rose's hand.

"We couldn't do without you," said home manager Becky. "Rose is always happy after you visit."

Billy blushed, feeling very pleased and proud.

She grinned and added, "In any case, you help us feed her."

Rose still slept through a lot of Billy's visits, and he was sitting beside her recliner watching the slow rise and fall of her breathing, his right hand resting lightly on her left arm when the home's visiting chaplain came into the room without knocking.

"If you want to talk," he said or rather, questioned. He stroked Rose's hair. "It's so fine, beautiful."

Billy felt the compassion in the simple gesture and had an urge to talk to this man and nodded. It was nothing religious, simply a need to speak to someone with genuine sympathy.

"I know you're Billy," said the chaplain in a soft southern Irish accent. "I'm Father Conor Bishop. Just waiting to become Bishop Bishop. But call me Terry if you want." His eyes twinkled. "First thing I have to ask though... do you believe in God?"

"Well... sort of."

Father Bishop pursed his lips.

An old lady patient wandered into the room, and the father stood and gently guided her out. "She's been stalking me," he said softly as he did. "Come on, Angie, back to your own room."

He helped the woman out, and a few moments later returned and sat on Rose's bed.

Billy continued more confidently. "I sort of believe, but I don't understand how he can allow things like... like Rose, and that..." he said, looking at the door to the corridor.

"I don't get it either, but you just have to believe there is some sort of plan."

Billy felt himself starting to feel angry about a god that allowed such a dreadful disease as Rose and the others were suffering. "But how can there be a, a, a plan that allows such suffering?" he asked. "This bloody disease.Sorry."

"This is where I'm supposed to say that old platitude about God working in mysterious ways, butI really don't know, Billy. I just believe, I have to believe, that he has it worked out."Terry smiled. "If I *could* work it out, I'd be a partner in God's business. Until then, I just let him get on with things in his own way, trusting, believing—perhaps just hoping—that he knows what he's doing. If I didn't, I'd be sitting in that chair instead of Rose."

Billy's growing anger faded and he took a deep breath."If you can't, how can *I* believe it's for good?"

"Don't ask me. I haven't got that second bishop to my name yet. I haven't been let into the secret."

Billy felt a surge of trust in this kindly man, smiling in front of him. He wore a natural smile, and his natural, friendly, calming air of serenity enveloped him.

"All I know is that I do believe there's some mysterious plan that's for our good. Eventually."

"Perhaps if I believed in religion..."

"Ah, that's another wee argument."

"I don't really see the point of organised religion," said Billy. "Surely it's much the same as Communism. Both want equality for all people, fair shares to be shared fairly for the good of everyone. The only difference I can see is that one has a political leader and the other a leader who claims he speaks for a god, the son of God. What's the difference?"

"It's a point of view, I suppose. But I don't know, son. All I can say is that you have to obey whatever your heart and head tell you. It's the belief itself that's so important, not what you actually believe. Does that make sense?"

"The rites and ceremonies are what put me off," said Billy seriously. "The rites have become more important than the meaning. People believe all the fancy dressings and actions of the ceremonies are what is important, but it should be their personal feelings that count."

Father Bishop was about to reply, but Billy continued. "If people can't cope... well, an organised religion can probably do it for them, I suppose. It's fine, but not for me." He was getting worked up again. "Why can't your God just go into the next room and talk to all the other religions' gods and sort out all the troubles and pain in the world?"

The chaplain nodded and smiled. "A good idea. I'll put it in my next sermon."

Billy realised he was gently being teased, and suddenly switched subjects and started recounting all his worries and anxieties to this stranger. It was the first time he had ever told anyone. And he felt better for it.

A carer came in to put a drink on Rose's chairside table. Billy said a polite thank you, and the chaplain noticed.

"Purely as a matter of interest, my own little information survey, does it worry you at all that so few of the staff are English?" he asked.

Billy laughed. "Hell no. Sorry. Why should it? They're all people and do a great job. I couldn't care less if they were red, green, indigo or violet. They're just human beings."

"Interesting," said the priest.

Billy was finding it stimulating to talk seriously and appreciated Father Bishop taking time with him.

"There has to be some power controlling things," he went on, returning to the subject. "If you go right back, you get the creation of Earth in a universe. What's outside that universe, and outside that over and over, all of it in an eternity that we small mortals can't possibly understand." He knew he sounded pompous.

"Something created it all. We call it, or him, God."

"But if there is a God, why did he invent disease, especially *this* terrible disease?"

"I can only answer in another cliche: it's in his grand scheme. And please, don't ask me what that is, I'm just a low-ranking cleric trying to make sense of it as best as my puny mind will allow."

"Sorry, but I just can't believe in God as a kindly old man sitting on a cloud and smiling benignly at the people St. Peter allows through the Pearly Gates."

"Don't tell my boss, but that's not exactly as I see him either. But I do believe and that gets me through the hard times."

"Sorry again that *I* can't believe..."

"Oh, but I think you do believe, in your own way," replied Father Bishop. "And that's what matters."

Beth came to the door with a message. "Terry, there's a phone call for you in the office," she told the priest. She bent and picked up a hair grip that had fallen on the floor and went out.

Father Bishop stood and put his hand on Billy's shoulder. "Well, I think I can honestly put a tick by your name and the archdeacon will pat me on my head and pay my expenses," he smiled. "But I'd better go and see what Big Beth wants."

He was the only other person Billy had ever heard call her that. He liked the chaplain, on top of the fact that he had given him the first real talk he'd had for some time.

"Just have some faith, Billy," said the chaplain, and followed the nurse out of the room.

And Rose slept on.

Three days later, Billy opened the door from the stairs to the corridor and the old grey-haired lady, Angelica, who had wandered into Rose's room—she was short and almost bent double as she walked, and it seemed far too grand a name for her—tried to walk past him balancing herself on a walking frame.

"I want to go home now," she shouted. "Robin will be waiting for his supper."

Billy blocked her way and pulled the door shut. "Come on, Angie, this way home," he said.

She turned and started to hobble away, then turned back. "I've lost my husband," she said. "I must look for him. Is he here?"

Billy smiled at her benignly. "No," he replied.

The little old lady turned and shuffled away, muttering to herself.

Billy watched her for a moment or two, then went to Rose's room.

His mind wandered, and as he sat beside her, he recalled the talk with Terry Bishop. God? Nature? Creation? It was all too vast for him, so slowly all those thoughts went and he just sat there holding Rose's hand with tears rolling down his cheeks again.But the talk and the two incidents with Angie simply made him more determined not to give up on Rose—he had lost her, but she was still physically with him and he clung to that ferociously.

After that, Billy continued with his routine-bound life, with visits to Rose hemmed in by outings for lunches and things (and days of acute loneliness when he didn't speak to anyone).

The regular visits would often upset him. He would usually get over the tears by the time he got back to the home's reception area for a chat with either of the receptionists, Jenny and Magda, but on other days, a depression sat inside him and the tears would roll unaccountably for the rest of the day.

The corridors and rooms of the home became as familiar to him as his house, as did his regular visits or check-up phone calls become familiar to the nurses and carers.But he could ignore all the human tragedies that existed all round him in the home and concentrate on that in Rose's room alone.

When he was not around the staff spoke of Billy's absolute devotion, but not to his face, because they knew he would tell them off and say he was simply doing what any caring husband would do. All of them were right. Some other husbands, wives or adult children did visit regularly (although perhaps not quite as often as Billy), but there were many patients who didn't have any visitors for months.

The home was full of widows and widowers, and the staff told Billy that Rose was the only one to get a regular near daily visitor. He was the only relative who visited regularly, going in at lunchtimes to feed her the pureed meat or fish, every time with potato, peas and carrots mashed up which she would usually eat happily (even when she was apparently asleep).

On the two or three occasions she refused the food Billy felt he'd failed Rose, but he was reasonably happy after most days seeing her, although there were still other times that made him sad.

One night, he was woken by the sound of rain lashing itself furiously against the windows of the bedroom. He propped himself on one arm and looked across at the illuminated numbers of the clock on the dressing table: 3:53.He curled himself into a tight ball, knees drawn up and arms round his shoulders, and tried to go back to sleep. His mind was wide awake.

A strong urge to hold Rose tight came over him, and he half turned under the duvet and reached across with his left arm. The other side of the bed was cold and there was nothing there. He ached inside, and once again he felt his eyes moisten.

The rain was still battering the windows, and Billy propped himself upright again to look at the clock: 3:55.

He sank back, still wanting to hold Rose. He felt that he needed to go to the loo, but suddenly it was five to eight, the rain had stopped, and a pale dawn was lighting the room through the curtains.He got up, washed and dressed in a daze, with his body still aching despite the hours in bed and even the thought that he was going to visit Rose later on couldn't stop the hurt of pure abject loneliness that filled his body. By the time he had driven to the home, his shoulders were particularly painful.

The nighttime rain had vanished and Billy walked from his car to the reception hall under a brilliant sun. The carpet was striped as light poured through the open doors of the rooms along the corridor, and Billy trod over the shimmering ribbons of light and dark until he came to Rose's room, the first on the right from the stairwell entrance door.

As he turned into the room, he was almost blinded by the glare shining through the window, and as he sat beside Rose, she clutched at his hand so tightly that the aches seemed to disappear. Without thinking, his mind concentrated on her.She was in a half world of her own—her mind in some place only she knew and her body in the present time—but that day Rose was lively and chatty.

Billy studied Rose's face intently. It was slightly more lined now, the face of an elderly woman, but with her high cheekbones Rose still had a unique beauty in his eye. *Not like the cut and paste blondes of today,* he thought.

He brushed the hair back from her forehead. It was white now, and a huge wave had fallen forwards and was almost covering her left eye, but it was still soft and luxuriant.

"You are so beautiful," he muttered in a very soft voice.

Some days were better than others, and Billy was able to get on and do things or meet people. Rose was always near the surface of his mind, but he was able to get by without consciously thinking of her.

Then there were the other days when he couldn't stop thinking of Rose. He had a constant picture of her sitting alone in her chair in her nether world, and his eyes would again fill with tears and his lips would tremble with a heartfelt sob.

And there were a few more days that were even worse, when he couldn't stop morbid scenes of Rose's funeral crowding his head. He tried his hardest to force those ideas away, but it was hard work.

When he was busy, things were bearable. It was when his mind was blank, in bed, alone or sitting pretending to watch television, that the slightest thing made him emotional, and he frequently found tears in his eyes and a lump in his throat for no reason.

It was always better on the days he saw Rose, although every visit was different in its own way.

More often than not she would forget who he was. But she still spoke about "we".

And there were other times when she seemed to know him or he hoped she did. She often said, "I love you," and called out "darling" during her ramblings and between the weird animal noises that made up her talk, and Billy cherished those times, and although he never knew who she was talking to he always liked to think it was him.

Once, Dipankar, the nurse, was talking randomly while feeding Rose. "She talks about you all the time. Billy this, Billy that. All the time."

As she spoke, Rose looked up with her eyes fixed on Billy. "I love you," she whispered then she was gone again.

Billy's eyes filled. "And I love you too, more than I can say," he said hoarsely, barely audible.

Dipankar watched, understanding.

Another time, Billy was in the room alone with Rose, holding her hand and looking unblinking at her face although her eyes were shut as usual. She was moving both her redundant legs more than usual, occasionally bouncing them in turn, and she had flopped sideways.

Billy started to reach round her shoulders. "Here, shall I sit you up?" he asked.

"No, Mummy," replied Rose, "I've already done it."

Rose chattered incessantly when she was awake, but her words and noises were spoken in a meaningless jumble, and usually bore no relation to anything that was going on around her. They were parts of conversations going on in her head.

"Oh, sorry. Thank you," she would say about nothing. A laugh.

When Billy was there, he would try to reply, to give her a reassuring voice to go with the words "No, thank you... for being you," he told her.

"I don't like that."

Like Dipankar, all the nurses and carers said Rose often spoke of "Billy", although when he visited her, she didn't often mention his name. There was the odd romantic word amongst the tangled torrent of words followed by her infectious laugh, and he was told that as well as chattering about him using his name, Rose frequently called him "silly boy". He didn't know where that came from. He couldn't recall her ever saying it before, although it was an expression she had often used in their early marriage to calm down their occasional minor tiffs and disagreements, but the nurses and carers teased him by giving him that name. They always smiled when they did.

Although he had always fed Rose her lunch, on the advice of the staff, he now let the carers take over because of fears that she might accidentally ingest the food into her lungs. They did sometimes let him feed her soup from a lipped plastic cup. The meals were served up pureed, mashed up into a more easily swallowable and digestible way, and it didn't make any difference to Rose.

No matter how he felt though, Billy knew he had to visit Rose. She had looked after him when he was quite sick, so he felt it right that he should try to look after her now she was ill. He knew he couldn't do much, but simply feeding her like a baby was something. All those years he had loved and, unconsciously, appreciated Rose, but now she was away from him, he realised just how much. No matter what, they were still two halves of a whole. He needed her.

Sometimes he wondered why he bothered visiting Rose. After all, she didn't really know he was there—not him, Billy, but possibly someone who seemed friendly and was no threat. He wondered if he could take much more. It was too emotional. But he knew he would be back. He loved her too much to abandon her.

Unstable though Rose was mentally, she was the only stable thing in Billy's life. He often went for whole days without meeting or speaking to anyone else. He was alone, but her presence was always with him, always tugging at his emotions.

Although he sometimes tried not to think of her, pictures of her would gather in his mind and she was still always a part of him. He loved her as much now as he had when they first discovered each other.

But it was physically and emotionally hard work. One day, he looked at his watch as she slept in her recliner chair. He had been there an hour and twelve minutes. He knew he was wasting his life sitting there beside her sleeping body, but he couldn't leave. He sat on until at an hour and thirty-seven minutes he stood without a thought, put on his coat, kissed Rose on the forehead three times and left the room.

After an exaggeratedly cheery goodbye to receptionist Magda, he walked to his car and drove back to the lonely house, on the point of depression.

The relentless agony went on. Rose was locked in his heart, and there was no way out. He knew she was there—he could feel her. But also knew she was not there. Not in mind. Not Rose.

"Keep fighting, Red," he would tell her. He didn't know why he used the old nickname.

After a long winter, when Rose had often needed a thick sweater over her loose T-shirt and vest despite the regulated heating in the home, and a bit of a dismal spring (even then Billy put an extra blanket round Rose's shoulders when she was cold), summer finally arrived. And Billy's visits continued.

Now, as he drove up the long approach avenue to Peace Hall, Billy couldn't help noticing the plethora of greens from the lining trees' super-abundance of leaves, the noon time sun shining through them in a spectacular dazzle. As he turned into the car park, he saw that the central garden was a riot of colour, yellow and red and blue flowers all reaching for the sun. The smell was intoxicating and drifted in through the open windows of the home itself.

Billy breathed it in and rejoiced at the living beauty of nature. Despite her very limited vision, Rose was also captured by the smell and feel of the beauty, and for a while, Billy forgot that it was that same "nature" that had made her ill. But awful reality did eventually sink in and he sat holding Rose's hand with a blank feeling.

Unaccountably, Rose suddenly lifted her arm and reached out to touch his face. She only kept her clenched palm there for a moment before letting it drop back to her lap, and it was lucky she did or she would have felt the habitual tears that yet again rolled down his cheeks.

Rose suddenly giggled at some unknown thought—she giggled a lot these days, she always seemed happy—and Billy hoped it showed she had been acting out some private joke.

Billy took her hand, and without opening her eyes or moving, Rose said, "I like that."

Billy hoped she meant it, and he took a deep breath and looked at her with adoring eyes. He would never know if it was genuine or coincidence, but he tried to convince himself that she meant it. That made him feel better.

He gripped her hand even tighter. "And I like you," he mumbled, but now Rose was asleep again, with a look of complete peaceful relaxation on her face, like a cat washing itself. The relentless agony went on.

Billy often wondered what was going on in Rose's mind. Was she still twenty-nine or thirty years old in her mind, or did she sometimes realise what was going on in the here and now? Was she there with him, or had her brain (or what was left of it after the disease had eaten most of it away) taken her to some mystery world far off in the vastness of space? He didn't know, just couldn't work it out.

Every one of the staff, nurses, carers, managers, cleaners and even the two gardeners and odd job man were so kind and thoughtful and considerate, but the visits were nevertheless becoming something of a recurring ordeal for Billy. He enjoyed the banter with the staff, really loved being with Rose and holding her lifeless hand for a couple of hours, but it was a nightmare leaving to be alone with his thoughts in an empty house. Billy's emotions were tugged both ways at once by the pleasures and heartbreaks of the visits.

But he still had the compulsion to be with her. His Rose.

As the year crawled on, Rose again began sleeping through most of his visits and they were becoming even more of an emotional torment for Billy. Even when awake, she kept her eyes shut most of the time, but that was mainly because she could not see properly and it was less bother not to open her eyes. *She had always been practical,* thought Billy. Even when she did open her eyes, there was absolutely nothing behind them—just a blank.

Rose still managed to surprise Billy and the staff though. One day, he was sitting with her and carer Chadani. Rose was asleep in her chair, but suddenly she woke up, opened her eyes, and smiled at the other two.

"Phillip William Saunders," she said.

He didn't remember her using his full name before, ever.

Chadani hid her surprise, simply stood up and walked across to Billy and put her arms round his shoulders in a caring, considerate semi-hug. It was a simple reassuring action, without the need for words, but so considerate and in keeping with the attitude of all the staff at Peace Hall.

They all seemed to love Rose and would often make complimentary comments to Billy on his visits. "Her hair looks nice today," he was often told, and they all told him that Rose had captivated their hearts.

"She lovely lady," said Big Beth, "We see why you fell for her."

"It's a pity she doesn't really know who I am," replied Billy.

"Oh, she know," said Beth. "Love may go from the brain, but it never leaves the heart."

Some of the carers told Billy about the other patients—how they screamed, scratched or even bit them. They loved Rose, not least because she was gentle and laughed a lot.

The carers and nurses worked hard and had to know every fancy and foible of every one of the patients. Billy hadn't really thought about it, but realised one day when he was talking to Ditya—the carer who was feeding Rose, who was still pouching her food—and he asked if many of the patient were like that.

"No, not really," Ditya answered. "They are all different. Some eat and drink quite happily. Others eat but won't drink, and some drink but won't eat. They are all different."

She diligently offered a spoonful of mashed-up food to Rose, who this time took it eagerly and chewed and swallowed it. Billy squeezed Rose's hand, and just admired the carer's patience.

"I think she is to enjoy this," said Ditya.

A voice came from somewhere down the corridor. "Help me," it called. "Help me! Help me!" It reminded them both of the reality of the situation.

Ditya turned. "I'd better go and see what Agnes wants," she said, "I'll be back to finish Rose's meal." She went out leaving Billy in a bit of a mental whirl.

Despite the bittersweet agony of each visit, Billy still felt a compulsion to continue seeing Rose. It was not so much a question of why he went to see her—simply that he couldn't not go. At first, he had cut something of a sad, lonely figure as he walked slowly to Rose's room, but now, after a few years, he had become, outwardly at least, the same

Billy that he always had been, covering his personal feelings in his old cheery manner. The staff liked the way he always tried to be optimistic and make them laugh, a slight break in what was a heart-wrenching job. He was very much part of the home's family, and they let him know it as well.

Things changed slightly after the surprise with Ditya though, and Billy began noticing the other residents. When he arrived at the home, he would always chat with whoever was at the reception desk, then climb the three flights of stairs to the first floor and use a security device to go through the entrance to Rose's ward. Immediately on the left of that door was a recreation room, and when he arrived, Billy would sometimes see patients sitting with their relatives in there. Walking down the corridor to speak to the nurse too, he would see other patients, all of them looking old and rather battered.

He began wondering what they had been like when they were younger, in their prime. Did their youthful passion still exist as his did? He found it difficult to imagine that everyone had once been a lover, a vibrant teenager, a person. Seeing the wasting human lives in so many people upset him.

That feeling was heightened a couple of weeks later when manager Becky invited him to a party to mark the anniversary of the home's original opening some ten years earlier and was held in the general lounge for patients and staff only. Billy was invited as one of the family.

"We couldn't do it without you," said Becky.

Billy blushed, feeling very pleased and proud.

She grinned and added, "In any case, we need the cheap help."

It turned out to be a joyous thing for many of the patients, those who stayed awake after their sausage rolls and mini sandwiches, but Billy had never seen anything quite as sad. All those old people with various stages of their dementia.

He looked at the faces of the residents, and again tried to imagine what they had looked like when they were young. He couldn't. He tried to figure out their attractions. He couldn't. People were so individual, until dementia dragged them down to a low communal level. All of them once vibrant young men or women with a whole exciting life ahead of them. And now... all of them living in a vacuum.

He turned back to Rose. He didn't think he was too biased, but he still saw her as a beautiful person, while all the other residents he saw were just old men and old women. Many of the carers agreed with him.

"She a lovely lady," carer Hanako had told him as he wheeled her into the lounge in her heavy recliner chair.

Billy sat beside Rose and looked around as the others gathered. All those people—once lively, spirited, contributing men and women—atrophying in front of his eyes. It was so sad. So vulnerable. So cruel. And he, like everyone else, so incapable of doing anything but provide love that they probably couldn't realise.

They were all existing in their own way. One woman was using a notebook to write messages to a man sitting next to her, and Billy watched them thinking that he was probably profoundly deaf and she was some sort of visiting relative. He saw the man read one of the notes, then scribble something back and hand it to the woman. She tore the page out of the book and reached down to put it in her handbag, but she missed and it fell to the floor. She didn't notice, so Billy jumped up to retrieve the slip of paper, and as he handed it over he read, "I lov eou."

Another woman sitting at right angles in the armchair alongside Billy and Rose was being awkward.

"Come on, Sylvia, it's a party and you have to get ready," said carer Kiara.

Sylvia growled and reached out to grab Kiara's arm fiercely, but the carer pulled away, then walked off, returning after a few moments to give Sylvia a small, white fluffy toy dog. Sylvia's face lit up as though she'd just won a million pounds, like a three-year-old getting her first ever Christmas present.

And that smile meant even more to the nurses and carers. They had provided a moment's happiness to one of "their family".

Billy watched it with the ever-ready tears in his eyes. How could these young members of staff live with this for hours every day?

He looked round the room. He saw all the old ladies and men seeing out their final weeks, months, years—possibly just days—of blank half living. He knew Rose was one of them and the emotion was too much.

Billy stood up, kissed Rose twice on the forehead and, without a word to anyone, fled from the room.

Chapter 14

It was the day of Billy's eighty-fifth birthday, and he celebrated when the carers let him feed Rose her mashed-up chicken lunch.

It was a special treat for him, because by now the nurses and carers always fed her due to her pouching and an increasing difficulty in swallowing. It was a slow affair, mouthful after slow mouthful watching anxiously to make sure she did not choke as she slowly chewed it.

Rose ate everything avidly, swallowing well most of the time but needing a bit of "persuasion" at times, and when the meal was over she closed her eyes and seemed to relax.

She seemed to be asleep, but she suddenly called out, "Billy..." She gripped the hand she was holding.

"I'm here."

Rose kept her eyes shut. "I love you."

A thrill ran through Billy—a special birthday surprise. He was ecstatically happy. Perhaps she recognised him.

"Yangs, abba da."

But the moment had been there, and Billy's mind grabbed it and held on to it.

It was a real highlight of his regular visits, which were becoming more and more awkward and draining now, and although he managed to get through them reasonably cheerfully (and still tearfully) he would get home after each one, sit down with a cup of tea, and involuntarily and unwillingly fall asleep for an hour or so exhausted. His age didn't help, and he knew that every visit could be the last time he would ever see Rose. It hurt him.

Billy was confused and helpless in his feelings over Rose's situation. He often wondered at the sheer terror she must have endured as the dementia grew, perhaps felt even now in the strange distant-but-living world of her own. He didn't want to think of it, didn't want to admit it, but it kept coming back to him and left him under a dark cloud.

Rose was slowly slipping even further away from him, but she was still a huge part of his life. For instance, everyone complimented him on his memory for birthdays, anniversaries and the like, and he didn't tell them he always checked with the book Rose had kept to note them. She was still helping him.

She was semi-somnolent most of the time now, sitting with eyes shut but occasionally muttering a few words or sounds. "A-bang, a-gig," she would say, often sounding cross, but then giggling.

There were still some words, and Billy listened for them avidly. She would talk about "Mummy" and "my baby", and fairly regularly looked sightlessly at him and say, "I love you." Billy smiled as always. But even when she put his name with it, he wondered who she was talking to.

He visited one Sunday, a rarity, and on the driveway to the car park, Billy passed three cars going out. It was nearly lunchtime, and they were going off for whatever. It made Billy mad, just as it had when he had taken Rose to the respite club. Why were they abandoning their relative or friend? He couldn't understand it, and this abandonment irritated. How could they just leave another human being in need? The patients were human beings in spite of having no (or fading) minds and conscious thought.

He tried to justify the actions of the leavers in his mind. Some couldn't cope, others were simply not bothered and saw it as a duty.

Many felt uneasy, even embarrassed, but fleeing (as he saw it) was putting themselves before the unfortunate with the dreadful disease.

He knew that he probably visited Rose more often than he needed, that to a large part it was to satisfy his own feelings, but he felt that though it might hurt him emotionally, even if it helped her for just one second in the hours he spent with her it was worth it. And he still felt the same about her as he had when they first started going out together.

He was with her one day watching carer Aabha feeding her some medicine with a small plastic spoon.

"Ahoy. Abash. Bam," said Rose between mouthfuls. "I love you. Hi. Boom."

"And we all love you," muttered Aabha.

Billy nodded. *Maybe*, he thought. *But not as much as I do.*

He wondered, *If Rose can't speak, does she know she can't speak? Does it affect her?* It was horrible, and Billy raged about it. But who or what was he angry about? He didn't know. Seeing her like that tore him apart daily, but he still had to visit her, touch her, hold her (even vaguely).

During visits, he would sit holding Rose's hand, occasionally brushing her still soft, luxurious hair back or stroking her forehead. Both of them were getting older now, and Billy noticed that her hands were slightly more gnarled and touched with arthritis, with her fingernails cut slightly shorter than fashionable so she wouldn't scratch herself.

Usually, one or more of the nurses or carers would drop in on the pair of them during visits, but Billy turned up one day when something was happening at the home and there was tension in the air. The staff were agitated, but he couldn't figure out why.

Nevertheless, when Big Beth looked in on him and noticed tears in his eyes and on his cheeks, she ignored the obvious crisis around the home and took time to help. "Sump'in' wrong?" she asked.

"No."

"Then why you cryin'?"

"I'm not, just got some dust in my eye."

"I can see, man. Don't worry. It good to cry."

"It's not very macho..."

"Phooey. Macho nothin', man," Beth interrupted. "You cry. Get it all outta you system."

There was a noise from the corridor, and Beth looked out of the door.

"OK, gotta go," she said. "You be all right then, pretty boy."

She left, and Billy and Rose were alone together again with the tears.

One day, he was sitting watching Rose's slow breathing as she slept, his mind wandering. Hanako, the pretty Japanese carer, came into the room and smiled at him in a friendly way, and he noticed the top button of her pale blue tunic had come undone. For a few seconds, his mind fantasised, and for a moment he fancied her and wondered what it would be like to have an affair with her.

He looked at her, trying not to see the hint of bare bosom behind the open button, and had a sudden, unexpected, ridiculous urge to grab her. He smiled to himself at the outlandish thought, then it reminded him of the one time he'd been unfaithful to Rose. He wondered, vaguely, what the girl in the stockroom many years ago was like now. Grizzled probably. He couldn't recall her face, think what she looked like, didn't remember her name. He turned back to Hanako, and the moment passed.

He hadn't thought of the stockroom incident for many years, the one indiscretion in their long relationship when he was much younger. It had been a one-time only, the only time, but he suddenly felt guilt again and quickly made himself wipe the memory away and concentrate on Rose instead. He knew she was still the only one for him.

She was still fast asleep, and after twenty minutes of stroking her arms, forehead and hair, he was desperate to hear her usual sounds and noises. But he didn't want to wake her, and in any case, there would only be the jumble of noises.

On another day, Rose sat in her chair with her mind as busy as always—with her mother teaching her all the things a girl should know about cooking, sewing and the like, playing with friends, talking of marriage and honeymooning with the young Billy.There was never a dull moment in her mind when she was awake.

On all of his visits to the home, despite his often desperate emotions, Billy still wore his automatic cheerfulness on the outside, as if to let the carers and nurses know that he didn't need assistance (although he, and they, knew he really did) because he could look after himself, and he had Rose to help him.

Not that Rose could do anything about it when he got a letter from his local county council asking for a back payment against the direct debit form he had filled in to cover a smallish contribution to the cost when Rose first went to Peace Hall. The letter demanded £12,000, which it claimed he had never paid.

He had filled in the form using Rose's own separate bank account and had never given it another thought, but now he contacted the home's accounts department to be told they were being fully paid and were satisfied. He delayed that day's visit to draft out a reply letter asking what was going on.

Everything seemed against him, then suddenly, days later, while waiting for a reply from the council, he got an invitation out of the blue to some sort of anniversary reunion of his old firm, and although by now he wasn't bothered he decided to go.

On the morning of the reunion, Billy was busy. A neighbour dropped in and accepted his reluctant invitation to have a coffee, and he had a telephone call giving him some bad news of a distant friend's baby needing a heart operation. He was distracted, but finally put on his old work suit (it was the first time he'd worn it for about ten years but it still fitted, although he wasn't at all happy to be wearing a tie) and got a train to London.

When he arrived at the reception, he was welcomed effusively as "an honoured guest" by a group of people he didn't know, and then ignored as another old man arrived to be greeted in the same way. He mooched around on his own for a while before he recognised another of the guests.He walked over purposefully.

"It's Ging, isn't it?" he called as he got close. "Ging Bennett."

The other man turned looking puzzled. Billy recognised the face, now without the acne, although the man was bald, stooped and wrinkled. He looked very old, although he was two years younger than Billy.

"Yes..." Recognition registered and he smiled. "Billy Saunders! Hi there, how's it going? Long time no see."

"What are you doing here? You didn't work for..."

"Oh no, I work for the PR agency that's organised this shindig."

He called a waitress over and got two glasses of some sort of cheap fizzy drink, then he led Billy over to one side and they started chattering about the old days, the Caballeros and Guiseppe's.

"I kept in touch with Jonno and Mary, lost track of the others," said Billy.

"Yah. I hung round with Frank for a time, saw Terry as well," said Ging. "We kept in touch for years."

They made small talk, then finally Ging suggested the bar.

"Come on, let's have a real drink before we attack the food. The booze is free," he said.

"No thanks, I don't drink all that much."

"Well, I can never eat on an empty stomach."

They had a whisky each—Billy with water—then, again on Ging's suggestion, they made their way to a well-stocked buffet table loaded with lots of bad-for-you food.

As they ate, they started nostalgically recalling the days of the Caballeros.

"Frank died a couple of years ago," said Ging. "I went to the funeral. It was like a reunion after the last time he'd been in nick."

"Prison?"

"Yes, something to do with racial activities. He was arrested at some sort of protest rally. Anti-blacks. He couldn't stand n—"

Billy interrupted quickly. "I didn't know he was like that."

"Oh yes. Hated 'em. Got two years for shouting things, punched a couple of coppers as well. It was good fun."

"Fun? Were you there?"

Ging nodded with a big grin, and Billy was disgusted.

"Two years, but he was OK with it. Well, he was given four but got time off for good behaviour. He always knew how to con the screws, made me laugh with his jokes about 'em."

"I never realised…"

"There was a lot you never knew about us. Frank, Terry and me," said Ging. "You and Jonno were never really part of the group. You were always up to your highfalutin ideas, and then those two birds…"

He noted Billy's sudden angry frown and paused. "Er, your girls… You didn't know half of what we got up to. We didn't only meet in the caff, we got up to all kinds of pranks, nicking cars and the like. Spraying paint over the outside of windows of the immigrants' council houses when the curtains were drawn, that kind of thing." He giggled. "There was one day we overturned every dustbin in a street into the front gardens. It was a right mess. Hilarious."

"I can't believe Terry was like that," said a slightly stunned Billy. "No, surely he was too superior for that."

"Oh, he was well dodgy. Thought himself intelligent, a great thinker, but he didn't know tuppence. He was another muddle-headed self-righteous ponce, but he loved a bit of fun. He was easily led and Frank led him."

Billy quickly found an excuse to move away, feeling as if his whole past was being swept away.His whole world seemed to have turned itself over. Rose was gone. He had no family. Now, after the meeting with Ging, his early youth seemed to have been taken from him as well, had somehow been destroyed. He felt he was alone in the world. Completely alone.

Then memories of Rose slipped to the front of his mind. He could picture her face, as she had been when they were young. Billy smiled to himself. No, he would never be alone. He had "his Rose" to help him along—as he always had.

It wasn't until he was getting ready for bed that night that it occurred to him that he had not called Peace Hall to check how Rose was that day. It was the first time since she had been in the home. Billy felt despondent and as if he had let Rose down, abandoned her. She wouldn't realise it, of course, but he worried about it until he fell asleep. It had been a bad day.

He felt much better the next morning until another letter arrived from the county council repeating the demand for £12,000, threatening legal action if he did not pay.

Several messages flowed between him and the council for a couple of weeks after that, then the council admitted that, after an internal investigation, it had discovered that despite two audits since he'd first sent the signed form to them, it had been filed in the wrong folder and had been forgotten. No cash had been taken as a result! Billy checked with a solicitor in the club opposite his house and was told that though they were "morally wrong" they were fully entitled under the law to demand back payment.

To save any more angst and because he appreciated that Rose had been given such excellent care and treatment by Peace Hall, he paid up using the money that had been saved in her account.

He was down, despondent, but things started to look better when he got another invitation—this time to Peace Hall's summer garden party, to be held in theenclosed garden below Rose's room.

It was a glorious summer day, with the sky beaming down from a rich azure blue sky, and Billy arrived in plenty of time, joining English nurse Diana when she took Rose down to the garden in her recliner chair, proudly walking round with them looking at all the stalls. It was not only the first time Rose had been outdoors for two years, it was also the first time they had been "out" together since she had collapsed and been taken to hospital.

It was a joyous day for many of the patients and the staff, acting almost like "normal" human beings, sitting or walking to lively piped music under brightly coloured paper bunting ropes, sipping tea or cold drinks, taking part in tombolas and raffles, playing hoopla and other traditional games, or just browsing or buying cuddly handmade toys from the various stalls being run by the carers or local volunteers.

It was a fun time, but Billy had never seen anything quite as sad. All those old diminished men and women with various stages of their dementia. What sort of life was it they were living? Life? Tears once more filled his eyes as he turned back to Rose.

After his experience at the indoor anniversary party, Billy had nerved himself to seeing so many of the patients in one go, and was determined not to run away again, but although he was steeled and prepared, he had never seen anything quite as sad.

He felt a duty to walk round, upsetting though it was to see the other patients as well as many relatives or friends completely baffled as to how to behave. As he did so on his own, he smiled automatically at everyone, offering no reaction to the way they either blanked him (literally) or half smiled back. He was unprepared when one smart, white-haired woman sitting with a young girl obviously her granddaughter reached out a hand and touched his sleeve as he passed her for a second time.

"Boris, I'm sorry," she said, and Billy noticed she had tears rolling down her cheeks.

He smiled, embarrassed, and hurried back to Rose and held her hand tightly.

They sat in the open air for about four hours, and although Rose babbled away unaware for most of the time, Billy was quietly happy watching her and the scene around them until it grew overcast and the staff began taking the patients back to their rooms.

Billy walked back to his car and sat there for a full five minutes feeling absolutely nothing. He thought he had never been so lonely, but he knew that really it was well worth the feeling because of the joy at sitting with an unknowingly happy Rose in a light-hearted, festive atmosphere.

Back at home, he slumped into his easy chair and looked into space. There was no noise, and he became keenly aware of it. *What do they call it?* he thought. *Oh yes, the sound of silence, that was it.* He could hear the actual deafening, penetrating sound of silence.

But life was proving to be a bit of a rollercoaster ride for Billy.

After the highs of some of his visits, the low of the home closure, up again for Rose's assertions of love, the lows of meeting Ging and the council payment debacle, there was the eventual high of the garden party.

The next step had to be down again. And it was.

It happened one Saturday lunchtime when his visit was, once again, against his normal routine and on a weekend. He had switched days as it was an early year bank holiday weekend, and he had reckoned the staff would be ultra busy with extra visitors, and he didn't want to add to their troubles.

He was sitting with carer Kiara feeding Rose, trying to help when she pouched the food.

"Open your mouth, *chew*," said the carer.

Rose did, but although for a time Billy hoped it was because she understood, he eventually reckoned it was a built-in reaction, rather like a dog being told to sit or beg.

He was quite happy, but almost three-quarters of an hour after finishing the meal, long after Kiara had left, Rose regurgitated it, spilling a pale yellow bile down her chin and onto her sweater. Billy, in a panic, rushed for help and called on the first carer he saw, Ditya, to come and see what had happened. Almost immediately, they got back to the room and nurse Ashish and three more carers arrived.

"Don't worry, it's not serious," said Ashish.

They calmed Rose, and soon the panic was over. Rose carried on chatting as if nothing had happened, but the incident shook Billy quite badly, and once again he realised how helpless he now was in looking after Rose.He went home and spent the evening just sitting staring at his TV set without seeing anything, and finally went to bed and fell into a troubled sleep.

He was woken early the next morning by a phone call from Ashish telling him that, although she was all right, Rose was not feeling too bright, but despite the assurance he cleared up at home quickly and rushed to Peace Hall as fast as he could.

When he got there, Rose was sitting in her chair looking sad and lost, but as soon as he arrived, a carer came in with a strawberry-tasting antibiotic that Rose always liked, and asked him if he would like to give it to her. He did so, and his mood brightened as she took the syrupy medicine.

It seemed to work too, and Rose was quickly babbling away happily, laughing and seemingly fine. Billy stayed with her for a couple of hours before going home, relieved that she seemed to be better.

That evening, Ashish phoned again to tell him Rose was in bed sleeping.

"Don't worry," she repeated.

Once again, Billy went to bed himself and fell asleep straight away, emotional exhaustion making it deep and untroubled.

Despite the long, resting sleep, Billy woke early next morning, and was at Peace Hall by 10. Rose was still in bed, with nurse Dipankar in her room, with various bits of medical test kit still on a chair beside her.

"She's fine," she told Billy. "Everything's as it should be, but her oxygen level is right down. I'm not happy, and I've been trying to get hold of a doctor, but it's bank holiday and I'm not getting any answer to my call. We'll just have to keep trying and monitor her."

Billy sat holding Rose's hand. She was breathing rapidly, her mouth slightly open and making wheezing sounds.

A carer looked in after a quarter of an hour or so, and Dipankar came back soon after to check. She clipped a device on Rose's left middle finger and bit her lip.

"The oxygen level has dropped even lower," she said after a pause. "I'll try the doctor again. I'm going to have to call for help," she said, shaking her head sadly.

She went away, then returned to tell Billy that as she had still been unable to get the bank holiday out-of-hours doctor, she had called the paramedics. "They can access a hospital doctor," she told him.

Feeling sad and listless, helpless, and certain in his own mind that he was about to lose Rose at last, Billy sat with his pre-emotive grieving holding Rose tight and listening to her slow rasping breathing until two paramedics appeared with Dipankar.

"We think that she may have swallowed some food the wrong way. Somehow, she may have got some into her lungs," said the nurse. "You see, she talks while eating, and as she pouches the food, it can go anywhere."

One of the paramedics sat on Rose's bed tapping into a laptop computer, while the other knelt on the floor beside Rose, using a stethoscope to listen to her lungs before taking her blood pressure and measuring her oxygen stats. He said that everything sounded well with her lungs.

"That's good," said Dipankar.

But the oxygen level was dangerously low. He suggested taking Rose to hospital for more detailed treatment.

The three medics discussed it for a few moments before one of the paramedics turned to Billy. "It's up to you," he said, "Do you want us to take her to hospital?"

Billy didn't know what to say. "If you think it best, then... well, yes," he replied, but there was something in Dipankar's look that made him pause.

"You did sign a form saying you didn't want her taken to hospital..." she said.

Billy nodded. "Can you deal with it here?" he asked.

The paramedic with the laptop looked up. "The hospital says that if we can get a steroid...." she muttered, and carried in tapping into the device. "There's one chemist open that might have it. Just one, but we can't go for it, it's outside our area…"

Dipankar's face was sad. "And we're short staffed because of the holiday," she added.

"I'll go," said Billy eagerly. "Just tell me what's wanted."

The paramedics printed out a prescription and gave it to Billy with details of the pharmacy. She and her partner started to pack up their equipment, and as Billy put on his coat, Dipankar said she would continue trying to get hold of an out-of-hours doctor.

Billy almost ran to his car and set off quickly, racing down the home's long driveway at a rather immodest speed. He was a man on a mission to help Rose.

The chemist was about twelve miles away, and Billy got there in what must have been record time, only to find a queue waiting to be served. He joined, hopping from foot to foot as he waited for almost forty minutes until his turn came.

The pharmacist looked at the prescription he gave her. "Oh, these have been on the long-term unavailable list for over a year," she said.

"Is there an alternative?"

"Yes," replied the pharmacist, "But I'll need another prescription before I can issue it."

Billy was in despair. He returned to Peace Hall with the news to find Rose sitting up in bed. She had perked up, her oxygen levels were almost back to normal, and she was happily eating her supper.

"I think the best thing is to let her go to sleep now," said Dipankar. "There's nothing more we can do at the moment, so I think it's best for you to go home and leave it to us till the morning. I'll keep an eye on her and let you know if anything nasty happens."

Billy left, hoping things would be better the next day, but instead they got worse again.

He got to the home early to find Rose still in bed, looking pale and wheezing badly. Diana was the nurse on duty, and she told Billy that Rose had slept well but had woken very early coughing a lot, with her oxygen levels again dangerously low.

Diana said Dipankar had spent over seven hours on the phone the day before trying to find a doctor to revise the prescription or a chemist which had the original in stock. She had finally tracked down three chemists that were possibles, and that morning Diana had got the new prescription and found a chemist close by that had it in stock, Billy again became the messenger and dashed off to pick up the new medicine.

This time he had to queue for almost forty-five minutes to get it, but when he did and returned it to the home, the steroid worked almost immediately. Rose perked up straight away, her breathing returned to normal and the crisis was over.

"It's a miracle," summed up Billy. "I really thought we had lost her this time."

Diana agreed. "It does seem to have been rather bad," she agreed, deliberately understating things. "But I think we must expect it to happen again."

For the time being though, things were back to "normal", and once the panic was over, the "excitement" faded and Billy quickly settled back into the routine of three visits a week. It suited him. He was happy seeing "his Rose", although fearful that there might be a recurrence of the crisis she had just survived. *It was*, he thought using a cliche, *a bittersweet practice.*

As he sat with Rose in the days that followed, he tried to remember their old lives together, but he couldn't. There were individual memories of events and places, but he couldn't really picture himself and

Rose as part of them. It was like having a huge jigsaw puzzle in pieces with no idea how to fit it all together.

The whole crisis episode affected Billy badly, and he felt sensitive about everything. It took Rose saying, "Ha ha, hee hee," one day to snap him out of his sombre mood and get back to his cheerful light-hearted ways.

It only lasted for two weeks though, because after a fairly eventless lunch, Billy went home in a fairly happy mood, only to receive a phone call from Beth telling him that Rose was sick again. This time, she said, the paramedics' tests showed she had ingested some food into her lungs, and it was giving her breathing difficulties. They were insisting that they needed to take her to hospital.

"They say you have to make the decision," Beth told him. "What do you think?"

"Whatever is best for Rose," replied Billy hesitantly.

"It has to be your decision."

"That's not fair. I haven't got any medical training..."

"But it has to be your choice."

"You can't expect me to decide, it's a matter of life or death. Should I let her die or not? It's like asking me to kill her."

"I'm sorry. But..."

"Well, OK, send her," mumbled Billy. He was dazed, shaken, confused, unable to think clearly.

Sitting at home, alone, he later tried to justify his decision. "I couldn't make myself lose her," he said to himself, "I know it's probably best to leave her in the home and not go through the business of a hospital, but if I'd done that, I'd always wonder if she could have been saved, could have had another month, even another day. Now, well, she could be with me for that day. Is that selfish? I just... just couldn't make myself say the words."

In his head, he knew what was sensible, what was really best for Rose, and he had made up his mind. But sitting in front of her, it had suddenly been a lot less clear. Could he chop even one hour away from her?

In the hospital Rose was diagnosed with pneumonia, but despite that the stay in the hospital was not a happy one for either Rose or Billy. He visited her every day, and the lack of the usual TLC that Rose received at Peace Hall was missing, and Billy fumed, worried and despaired over the treatment and lack of information about "his Rose".

It was, he felt, less than acceptable. And although he appreciated the extra stresses put on medical staff in the hospital, the complete lack of sympathetic care given to Rose and the other patients and visitors to the ward fell well short of suitable. There were none of the comforting words or actions essential for people in her condition.

There were six women in Rose's bay, and apart from her dementia, three of the other women were described as "confused". Within a quarter of an hour of Billy's first visit, one of them asked a nurse who was taking her blood pressure, "Am I a man or a woman?"

The nurse smiled. "You're a woman," she said.

"Can you look… you know, down there, between my legs?"

The nurse smiled, smoothed the sheets, put away her testing apparatus and left. Billy couldn't help thinking, *Was it tragic or funny?*

Events like that only added to Billy's melancholy, and that evening, he could not help thinking of the calamitous situation of Rose in that ward. A soul-aching sadness sat on him like a shroud, and he lay there alone in his double bed praying to his "dear God" that Rose would soon be released from the hospital, that she would be all right. It seemed like hours, slow hours, but was in reality no more than twenty-five minutes before he had to get up—his pillow was too wet from his emotional tears to rest his head on.

There were plenty of other examples of the offhand coverage in the ward, but possibly the worst was when anursing sister spent twenty-minutes talking to two visitors by the bedside of a patient (whom she ignored), and even when one of those visitors moved away to help the "confused" ninety-four-year-old woman in the next bed who was having difficulties standing up, did not go to help. In fact, the nurse left the ward minutes later without even looking at the second patient and helping visitor.

It was also noticeable that only rarely did any nurse or carer even look at the patients as they moved around the bay.

Rose developed at least five large scabs on her forearms as well as bad bruising on her arms and heels—the ward denied that they could be bed sores, but Billy was later told that was what they were, possibly because she was not turned in her bed often enough. On more than three occasions, Rose's food was left on a tray on her bedside table for over half an hour before it was fed to her cold.

Throughout the whole sixteen days of Rose's stay in the hospital, Billy was given contradictory replies to his queries. There was a complete lack of accurate information on her condition. He just wasn't told if she was getting better or not.

On the first day of her stay, a girl from the hospital's dementia unit gave him a form asking for full basic details about Rose's condition, asking what her hobbies were, what subjects she liked talking about and the like. A one or two second glance at Rose would have told her there was no need, and that considering she had been bedbound and in a care home with increasingly advancing Alzheimer's for many years, it was completely unnecessary and a waste of everyone's time, energy and money.

The same basic form was given to him to fill in three times and, incidentally, was then sent with Rose on her release so that Peace

Hall, who had been looking after her for so long, could find out all about her!

Words failed him when he visited the hospital's family support office to see if they could give information and advice and was spoken to outside the office in the busy reception area, with dozens of people walking past. And no details.

Rose eventually recovered from her original problem and everything righted itself when she was discharged and returned to Peace Hall—complete with the basic form telling the home all about her, despite their years of experience with her.

She got back to the home late on a Monday evening, and Billy rushed there the next morning. It was a delightful return for both him and Rose—the welcome was simply magnificent.

At least fifteen of the staff, from manager Becky Watts right through to handyman Kevin (Billy never did find out his surname), the nurses, carers and cleaners, all dropped in with laughs and chuckles to welcome the two of them "back home"! All either touched Rose on the shoulder, or straightened her hair with a stroke, or held her hand for a moment and Rose laughed and smiled with every one of them. The difference between that and the hospital was palpable. It made Billy very happy and even more emotional than usual.

It could not last, and Rose very quickly slipped back into her old vague ways. After the hospital, Rose had seemed fine for a couple of months, but her condition was worsening.

She was sitting in her chair staring blankly out of the window. Billy sat by her side, not speaking, just waiting.

"Oh, poor baby," said Rose suddenly, pointing to the floor with her left hand, the index finger extended. "Is he all right down there? We have to look after poor baby. He must have fallen."

Billy was amazed at the sudden use of all the words, in order, but he sat there powerless, knowing he was unable to do anything to help Rose when she needed him.

It was at times like that when, for the first time, he had regrets about their lost baby. He knew Rose had been devastated when it had happened, but he had managed to hold back his own disappointment. Now he wished he had a child, someone to share his loneliness.

But there was no baby, and the year ended as the previous year: Billy cut off from Rose.

Chapter 15

Rose was more or less sleeping through most of Billy's visits now, but he still visited her religiously three times a week. He sat by her chair, either holding her hand or resting it on her arm—she occasionally clutched at his hand and held it ferociously (a reflex action)—and with nothing else he could do, he let his mind wander.

All manner of memories came into his mind as he sat with her, trying to understand it all mixed with thoughts of what shopping he had to order, from whether he'd put out the dust bins to memories of their lives together.

As they did, Billy began to remember a lot more of the past. In fact, most of his thoughts when he was with Rose were of their earlier times together. Once the memories started coming, they kept repeating themselves whenever Billy visited Rose and when he was alone in bed, waking in the middle of the night.

He noticed things that others would not normally notice, like a slight smile that appeared on the corner of her mouth when he held her hand while she was asleep. Even if it faded after a moment, it gave him joy and he would drift off into his happy, vivid daydreaming thoughts.

The fanciful imaginings came at random and could be sparked by little incidents, such as when Ditya the carer came in with Rose's lunch, setting it on a mobile table and starting to mash gravy into the pureed meal to make it even softer to swallow.

Rose tried to lean forwards. "The baby, is he all right?"

Billy eased her back in the chair as a lock of white hair fell across her eyes, then he reached across to smooth it back into position. He sat back still stroking Rose's hair, and a big smile spread over her whole face. But Billy thought of their dead baby.

A high sun was shining through the window on one Friday visit, bright in her eyes and giving Rose's face a glow, and ashe sat holding her hand with damp eyes, Billy looked at her as Ditya began feeding her. His mind wandered.

They were sprawled across a sofa in their old house at Glebe Cottage in Avenue Road, Rose laying her head heavily on Billy's chest. He was stroking her hair, and she had her eyes closed and a gentle smile on her face. They lay there for what seemed a long time, then Rose pushed herself up.

"I've got to get on," she said. "I've got to tidy up and I've got to get supper ready."

"Do you have to?"

"Yes." She stood up firmly, then turned and threw a cushion over Billy's face.

He stayed, smiling, on the sofa for a while before he stood up too.

Rose was trying to tidy the dining room, an apron round her waist and a long-handled duster in her hand, but Billy walked in and tried standing in front of her to stop her from working.

"Oh, Billy," she said, exasperated. "Do be serious."

"I just want to talk."

"What about?"

"Oh, something sensible for a change. Politics, perhaps." Neither had any interest in politics.

"What do you know about politics?" asked Rose, resting the duster on the table.

"I know all politicians are the same. Once they can fake sincerity, they've cracked it."

"Oh, Billy, be sensible."

They kissed two or three times more, then Rose pulled away again. "If you're not going to let me clean the house, you do it," she said, pushing the duster into Billy's hand. "I'm going to the kitchen."

Billy flicked the duster round the walls and furniture desultorily, then followed Rose to the kitchen. She had a whisk in her hand and a beaming smile on her lips. Her eyes twinkled cheekily as she saw him.

"All right then, you win," she said, and they embraced.

As Ditya wiped Rose's mouth at the end of the meal, Rose opened her eyes and looked at the young girl. She had a cheeky grin again and had obviously been enjoying a happy dream. She looked straight at Ditya.

"Thank you," she said.

It was almost as if she really understood, and watching on Billy hoped she had. It was the little bits of "reality" like that he enjoyed and that he remembered for days. He sighed and squeezed his wife's arms.

"Rose, Rose," he muttered. "I wish I could talk to you."

That had been a happy daydream, but sometimes Billy's dreams were of what might—in his mind, should—have been.

Like the one day—just the one day—when for some reason, he woke up with an aching body and sore eyes and didn't really want to get out of bed, let alone visit Rose. But he made himself get ready, plodded to the car at his usual time and drove to Peace Hall.

It was a miserable drive, and when Billy got there, he didn't see anyone, and Rose was sleeping once more. He again had time to think and slowly a happy memory of their past together returned to his brain to cheer him up.

They were sitting side by side on a settee, Rose's arm draped carelessly round Billy's shoulders.

"Do you remember that film? Who was it... Fred and Eleanor Powell?" asked Billy. *"Dancing to Artie Shaw's 'Begin the Beguine'."*

"Wonderful dance."

"Oh yes, it was magic. I wish we could dance like that."

"I'd try, but you'd probably fall over in a heap..."

"And have the others do a grand jete over us."

They both giggled.

"It was a wonderful dance..."

Billy snapped his mind back to the present. He was still holding Rose's hand, and he looked down at her immobile legs. She hadn't walked for almost three years. He gulped and reality returned.

But he had enjoyed the dream. And being with Rose. He was very glad he had got out of bed and visited her because it was one of the very good days.

"I love you," he told her, and he made himself leave after nearly two hours but as he walked back to his car, the normal jaunty step was there again.

Two days later, Billy was back in his car, driving to Peace Hall. There was quite a heavy mist which reduced visibility—not that plenty of other drivers seemed to notice—and it was a very difficult and arduous drive.

When he got to the home and up the stairs to Rose's room, he was quite tired. Somewhat perversely, Rose was lively. She sat chattering away and waving her hands, getting quite animated but then breaking out into her typical laughing giggle.

It brightened Billy's sombre mood, so when, after forty minutes or so, she calmed down and seemed to go to sleep, he sat back relaxed and once again his daydreams took over.

He remembered the earlyish days when they couldn't afford a car but used buses to go everywhere (often canoodling in the back seat upstairs in the double deckers), then when they did eventually buy their own cheap second-hand car, how he had taught Rose to drive. She had been a nervous learner but turned into a very good driver and he was always relaxed in the passenger seat when she was behind the wheel.

He had mental pictures of the time he was looking after her at home and took her for daily drives—a hundred miles a trip most days—and how he missed her by his side as a passenger when she moved to the home.

Rose coughed in her sleep and jerked Billy back to awareness of where he was. He patted her hand, stroked her forehead, and smoothed her hair and she calmed down. Billy sank back to his fantasies, but woke as the carers came to put Rose to bed.

By the time he left, the mist had lifted slightly and the drive home was easier. But he was tired and muddled away the rest of the day doing nothing until he finally went to bed absolutely exhausted. He fell into a deep sleep almost immediately, yet despite the fatigue, he had a vivid dream.

Billy had always carried an impossible half-hoped desire that one day Rose might get better, although he really knew that was impossible. There was no cure for dementia. It was a killer.

Now, in his dream, he was sitting up in bed reading in the early morning pre-dawn half-light when the phone rang. It was a call from the home telling him that Rose was suddenly talking and acting normally.

"Come quick and see her," said Big Beth.

He literally leapt out of bed, dressed without washing and got to the home in just over half an hour, running through reception and up the stairs to Rose's room.

"Hello, Billy," she said, a huge smile on her face. "They said you were coming to take me home."

She was standing by her recliner chair, fully dressed, and he took her hand and led her out into the corridor.

Back at home, Billy unlocked the door and Rose swept past him and turned on the kettle to make him a cup of tea.

"Whatever happened to those biscuits I bought? Have you wolfed them all?" she asked brightly as she reached across and put tea bags into the red and yellow mugs.

Billy suddenly snapped back into full awareness. He was still in bed, wide awake now. Nothing had changed. He wanted to go to the loo, but he just pulled the duvet high up, almost covering his face and tried to go back to sleep. He managed it after more than half an hour of despair.

Billy was getting more and more maudlin, but amongst the many self-pitying thoughts, his mind often wandered happily over the past good times when he saw Rose.

On his next visit, he was back sitting in Rose's room and still tired after his nighttime shock two days earlier. She was sort of awake, her eyes shut but babbling her sounds and waving one or other of her arms in turn and occasionally jerking one leg up and down.

Billy was holding her left hand, letting her lift and lower it as she moved but trying to keep her still, and she gripped back tightly, and he couldn't pull away. She opened her mouth as if to speak, but instead looked as if she was feeling for a mug or a spoon. She was warm and thirsty and needed a drink.

The sun was shining through the bedroom window, angled across her body but with her face in shadow. Billy thought she looked beautiful.

He was thinking of a day when they had been on a coach trip and sat in the shade of a tree outside Ye Olde English Tea Shoppe on the edge of a small square in a village in Gloucestershire.

They had taken a day coach trip to the countryside because of the overly hot summer's day and during a short break, they were escaping the other passengers. Rose was dressed in a pretty dirndl cotton skirt which had billowed in a wide circle around her, while she had undone the top four buttons of her simple blouse to keep cool. Billy thought she looked the most beautiful girl in the world. He brushed her brunette fringe back from her face, and Rose took hold of his hand.

He was boastfully promising her an unlikely life of affluent luxury with tiaras, diamonds and bracelets and she was laughing at him. They were very much in love and in tune with each other.

A teenage waitress brought them tall glasses of cool, pink-looking strawberry milkshake, and they both stopped to drink them through long red, blue and white striped straws.

Rose went quiet and a smile slowly lit up her face with pleasure. "I'll always love you, Billy, even when you're a millionaire," she joked.

Chadani the carer came into the room, instantly noticing the smile on Rose's lips and the adoring look on Billy's face. Rose's white hair had flopped across her forehead and Chadani brushed it back with her free hand. "Here we are, Rose, a nice strawberry drink to cool you down," she said.

She put a bent straw to Rose's lips to start feeding the supplemented drink and Rose took a sip.

"Ajay, bij," she said.

That outing started Billy thinking of other trips they had made in the past. Neither he nor Rose had been able to go on holiday for several years, so mid-year breaks took centre stage, and as the year bloomed in its sun baked, flower heavy July, his daydreams inevitably moved with it to relaxed summer events.

Rose was stretched out on the fresh mowed back garden lawn of their new house, the evocative smell of new cut grass in her nostrils. Billy was beside her, propped up on his right elbow, and both were limp and very hot.

"It's such gorgeous weather. I wish we could go away somewhere to really enjoy the sunshine," sighed Rose.

Billy looked at her. "Why not?" he replied enthusiastically, a sudden smile on his lips and in his eyes. "We could go to the seaside for the weekend. Or Cornwall to sit on the beaches. Or we could even get the Eurotunnel to Paris."

"That would be lovely. Imagine walking down the Champs-Élysées in the sun."

"Glorious."

"We could have cakes at Ladurée."

"And eat at that bistro opposite the Gare du Nord."

"Oysters and crepes."

"Let's do it..."

"Yes, let's. It's a great idea. Thank you, Billy. I love you so much."

They kissed, then collapsed in the English sun.

Reality suddenly returned. Rose was still in her chair chattering nonsensibilities and Billy's eyes filled with tears again.

"Oh, Rose," he muttered, and it seemed that a passing cloud shielded her face from the sunlight pouring through the window.

He wanted to hug her, kiss her and tell her just how much he loved her. But he didn't have the right words—not now, now she could no longer understand.

He thought Rose might also be having nostalgic dreams and often tried to figure out what she was thinking. When she spoke her sounds, he tried to interpret what she was saying, and often invented his own ideas of what was, possibly, going through any of her mind that was left.

He was told Rose was going to have her hair trimmed on the following Monday morning, so that day, Billy left the house early so he could stop off at a barber on his way to Peace Hall.When he got to her room, she was sitting in her chair quietly.

"Your hair looks nice," he told her.

She smiled and opened her mouth, but no words (or sounds) came out.

I know there's someone there, someone different to usual, she was thinking. *It's a man, and although I can't see him or hear him, I feel that he's friendly. He's holding my hand, and I'm talking to him, but I don't know if he can hear me. Maybe he can, because sometimes he gives my hand a little extra squeeze after I've said I love him. It's nice. I love you, Billy."*

She blinked, looking at him carefully, studying. "Oh, Billy, Billy, what have you done to your hair?" she asked. "It's so short and I like it much longer. You know I've always loved your hair, so black and thick. And silky when I run my hand through it. But now you've had a haircut, silly boy. Perhaps it will grow again."

As she spoke, Billy ran his hand through his silvery white hair, receding slightly at the temples. He smiled, reached across and stroked Rose's newly cut hair.

The dreams continued to come fast and often, and they were not confined to his visits with Rose. Sometimes, protected in the snug, safe, womb-like cocoon of his bed, the duvet wrapped round him and only his nose exposed, Billy would often drift into a half-sleeping reverie.

Waking in the dark at half past three in the morning, he took a break from his own recollections and thought he could hear Rose and her frequent mentions of "Mummy" and occasional "Daddy".

She seemed to him to be having the same kind of memory dreams.

Billy came out of his reverie, and in the dark, he thought he could hear her calling, "Abba yig Daddy zing brave." She seemed a bit agitated, and he thought she must be thinking of something she had told him about her father.

He knew Rose's mental memories were vague and random, scattered recollections from various bits of her past, but odd words from their past came to him and helped him compile images.Billy drifted back to a half sleep.

The next day, a plump grey pigeon, having washed himself in the fountain outside Rose's room, was sitting on its low wall with his wings extended to let the sun dry them, and a couple more birds sat near it occasionally dipping their beaks in the water for a drink or waggling their tails in for a wash, but mainly doing little mating dances for each other. *Lovebirds,* thought Billy.

Rose noticed the movement and Billy thought she said, "Bird fly, Daddy," and began to wonder exactly what was going on in her mind.

He was sitting with his right hand on her arm as usual, and she was upright in her recliner, eyes staring blankly and a frown on her face.

A rare memory of her father was going through the recesses of Rose's brain. She was three years old, and he had taken her out one Sunday morning and they were sitting on a park bench with the sun occasionally peeping out from behind thick cumulus clouds. Paul was talking, realising that his little daughter would not understand but getting the memory off his mind, telling her about an experience he'd had towards the end of his war—the First World War.

"I remember creeping up to this huge concrete gun emplacement about a mile behind the German lines," he was saying. "I was with Hugo Cooke. He was a lieutenant, just twenty years old, and he'd led four of us on a raid to knock out this gun that was causing a lot of damage. The others were somewhere on the far side.

"I could see the muzzle of the gun sticking out—it was huge—and I heard this German talking, telling someone about his baby. She was one year old, apparently, and he'd only seen her the once on a weekend pass six months before.

"We blew the place up, but Hugo and the others were all killed by the explosion. All the Germans. I was the only one to get out. The gun had killed a lot of British soldiers, and it had been a necessary thing to do, but they said it was courageous and gave me a Military Cross. As they pinned it on, I thought of that German's baby."

Billy knew that Rose's father had never told anyone of the incident before and was the reason for his reticence and shyness in later life. Rose had been too young when he told her—but it must have stayed in the now lost recesses of her mind and she had told Billy the story one night after they had been married for a year.

Another time, she had a smile on her lips. She was sitting in her recliner but had flopped over to her right. Billy tried to straighten her, but he didn't have the strength.

"Abba ma jubble," she said at his attempt.

He had another try, again without much success, so he sat back and watched her.

"Mummy, look it," she said.

Billy's imagination erupted again. Her face relaxed and she slept, and Billy's recall was soon in action once more.

Rose was happily playing in the back garden of her childhood home, the sun shining in a blue, cloud-streaked sky.

"Rose, time for your juice," called her mother from the kitchen door.

Rose ignored the call.

"Rose," repeated Mavis, but the call was again ignored. "Rose!" The voice was stentorian, authoritative.

"No, Mummy, don't want juice."

"If you don't come in now..."

"No." Rose was determined. "Mummy, don't make me."

Billy was still holding Rose's shoulders when Kiara, one of the Nepalese carers, came into the room.

"Abba ma jubble," repeated Rose as the girl took over, heaving her back to a sitting position with one arm and pushing in a pillow from Rose's bed to wedge her upright.

Rose suddenly twitched, and Billy jerked attentively. She was asleep now, but suddenly laughed out loud as some other memory crossed her brain.

"Look at him," she said, looking down to the floor. "He's crawling all over now, never keeps still. He'll be walking soon." She had a benevolent motherly look on her face, smiling. "Careful, don't tread on him. My baby."

Billy remembered. There was another holiday: Positano.

They were sitting outside a small trattoria a little way along the Amalfi Coast from Positano, overlooking the ocean and at ease on home woven rattan chairs with tall glasses of cooling San Pellegrino Limonata drinks on a small table in front of them.

It was a perfect holiday day—the sun high and bright making glorious reflections on the Mediterranean waves below them. They were very relaxed, very young, very much in love and completely as one.

"It's gorgeous here," she said, taking a sip of the white opal liquid.

"Yep," replied Billy lazily. "Like last night, but I haven't got the peculiar feeling I got then after, you know."

"Yes, me too. I felt that too." Rose wrinkled her brow. "Do you think we actually managed...?"

"We'll soon find out."

"Oh, please let it happen. I so want to make us a family. You, me and it," she said, pointing to her stomach.

"Him," interrupted Billy.

"Yes, him, of course."

Thoughts morphed to home, and Rose was busily cooking in the kitchen.

"It's a new recipe: beef Wellington," she said. "It sounds good, and it'll be different from all the baby food we'll be eating when he's born. You'll like it, at least I think you will."

"Of course I'll love it. If not, I'll throw it at you," joked Billy.

"Not with the plate. You might hit baby..." She turned round to face him. "I can't tell you how much I love you. Particularly now you've made us a family."

The talk upset Billy, and he sat back in his chair. The dream now turned back to horrible reality.

Kiara came in with medicine, which Rose took in three small spoonfuls although still asleep, swallowing each until she was done. Kiara left and Billy stood up to leave. He walked back to the car sadly, thinking that Rose had never been able to be the mother she so desperately wanted to be. That he had also wanted. It was fate or something—something that was never destined to happen.

After more than a month of living with his fantasy memories, Billy realised that he had been ignoring Rose when he visited her. He made a conscious effort to stop the thoughts and to concentrate on Rose. At first, he did make a slight effort to try to bring them back, but in the end, he decided to simply do what little he could do to help make her happier.

Not that he could do much, although Big Beth insisted that his visits always seemed to cheer Rose up.

"She know you are there," said the nurse. "She always like it when you come. Talk about her silly boy."

The trouble was, as the daydreaming gradually disappeared, other memories started to cloud and disappear. Billy began to get forgetful.

He mostly kept to his routine and still visited Rose every other lunch-time, although his own appetite was less than it used to be. He was starting to feel vaguer and more insecure.

Chapter 16

Rose's stay at Peace Hall had passed through a second year then drifted past a third, and now it was moving fast towards a fourth although she had been admitted to the home with hospital doctors predicting a short three-month life expectancy.

By now, she had virtually lost the ability to use words completely—weird nonsensical sounds replacing them. She knew what she meant, but she couldn't enunciate the words.

She did sometimes use "real" words but was repeating some sounds constantly, and although he tried Billy just could not fit them against proper words. One repeated sound, "Raas", could have been Rose, but he couldn't be sure.As far as he was concerned, words had gone completely.

Amongst the few words that she did use, Rose often spoke of "Mummy" or "Billy", but Billy knew that she had long since stopped recognising him, and from many small instances both at home and at Peace Hall he knew that he was starting to get old and that the "young Billy" was still his rival, locked in the recesses of Rose's mind.

He would sit listening to her "talking", hearing only the sounds that she used over and over.

"A-jay. Abang. Doo doo de-g."

Billy repeated his nighttime prayer to himself. "Dear God, please look after Rose and keep her as happy and content and as healthy as she can be for as long as she can be."

Away from the home, Billy tried to figure out if there was any meaning to the sounds, if Rose was using them for particular words. At times she brought out the jumbled sounds in a rhythmic machine gun burst, bouncing her hands in her lap in complete synchronisation.But although several were often repeated, there didn't seem to be any pattern. They were just a jumble of random noises that were completely baffling like Morse or the wartime Enigma codes.

There was absolutely nothing Billy (or anyone else) could really do to help Rose except just be there, but a heavy loneliness sat on Billy and he felt so useless. After every visit, he would go home and fall asleep for an hour or so from the burden of his drained emotions.

There were a few other days when it was different. Days when little things pleased him, trivialities you wouldn't normally notice like a slight smile that appeared on the corner of Rose's mouth when he held her hand while she was asleep. Even if it faded after a moment, it gave him joy.

On one of those days, the sun was shining bright in a picture book brilliantly blue sky that was cloudless but with a white cross of jet vapour trails immediately overhead as he entered Peace Hall's reception area. As he walked the short distance from the car park to reception it occurred to him once again how cruel it was that Rose could never get out into that environment. She couldn't walk, couldn't even stand, could barely see or hear, and although she was occasionally wheeled in her recliner chair to sit on the balcony, it was just not the same.

The reception desk was empty and he was conscious that the large reception hall was quite gloomy, but as he knew all the door key codes by heart now, he let himself in to the stairwell and went through to Rose's room. Despite the ultra brightness of the day outside, tears came to his eyes as he climbed the three short flights of stairs to her room.

But as he got to Rose's room, carer Ditya was wiping her mouth after feeding her some medicine from a small plastic spoon, and as Billy entered, Rose opened her eyes and looked at the young girl.

"Thank you," she said, and it was almost as if she really understood and watching on, Billy hoped she had.

It was little bits of "reality" like that he enjoyed and that he remembered for days. He lived for such moments. Life had become like that for Billy—a series of incidents, pleasant for a few moments but with the reality of his continuing loneliness always nudging his mind. He knew Rose had no quality of life, but in his mind—and it was a big but—she *was* alive. And she laughed and usually seemed happy.

But there were still tears...

Billy didn't really know why he visited Rose so often and he still wondered while he was sitting there holding her hand as she slept whether it was for her sake or his own. He would let her grip his hand, trying to believe it was her way of showing her feelings, although he knew that it was really only the involuntarily twitching of her muscles. Despite her frailty, she had a very tight grip.

Rose's stomach was often bulging from constipation, almost as though she was pregnant, and when Billy looked at it his mind seemed to unlock some long-hidden memory, although he could not really remember what it was.

He often wondered why he put himself through the emotional agony of visiting her, but on another visit when he was allowed to feed her a mugful of hot soup he knew why. He got a physical pleasure out of helping Rose (even if it was just giving her a few sips of asparagus soup). She took it avidly and was not pouching and swallowed it well. Billy smiled, a huge smile of pleasure and thanks.

Billy was surprised when she looked at him and said, "Thank you."

"What for?" He held her hand. "No, thank you for being you. For being us," he said after a moment.

Times like that were not too uncommon but they were rare, so while Billy continued to suffer, Rose was never lonely. Although surrounded by loving carers and nurses, her world consisted of her mother and father, a young new and vibrant husband called Billy, and her particular friend Mary, a pretty young thing of eighteen.She talked to them all, often switching mid-conversation from one to another.

Luckily for Billy though, there was always the home: his new family.

Although they could see he was suffering, he was always, more or less, cheerful with them, always willing to help in any small way, and because of his outwardly stoic acceptance of Rose's condition he usually had a cheeky grin and told them how flattered he was by being looked after by "so many beautiful young ladies"!

He was very much part of the home's routine, and they let him know it as well. They always welcomed him as part of the family. He had become part of the fabric of the home, and everyone loved both him and Rose being part of things.

Visits were getting harder now with Rose's condition as it was, but on top of his feelings for her Billy still had the deep compulsion that he could not abandon her. She had devoted her whole life to him, and it was a conviction that was his main reason for being.

There were still days that made Billy feel it was all worth it.

It had been a torrid drive to Peace Hall and because of the driving rain, Billy had to constantly use his wipers at double speed to clear his front and rear windscreens. He drove slowly these days because he knew his reactions were slowing, and it was a terrible drive, not helped when a radio announcer told him it was the first official day of spring. *If only someone would tell the weather*, he thought.

Other drivers ignored the conditions, overtaking him and cutting in sharply, driving fullpelt through puddles that splashed up and momentarily blinded him, and he was glad as he eventually parked up at Peace Hall, although by the time he had walked from the car park to reception he was soaked and windswept, his hair dishevelled with the quiff hanging down over his brow and into his eyes.He was cold, wet and miserable, but things miraculously became better as Rose was burbling happily when he got to her room. She was lively and laughing, and she ate all her lunch with hungry glee.

He sat down and rested his hand on her forearm, his thumb gently rubbing her smooth skin. Her face looked older, her cheeks slightly sunken to highlight her high cheekbones even more and there were some new creases around the corners of her eyes, mouth and under her chin. But in Billy's eyes, she was still beautiful. Perhaps he was prejudiced.

He looked at her and her face looked young to his eyes and the skin on her cheeks and forehead was as smooth as it had been when she was a teenager. Her hair was silky soft and he brushed it back, and when it was smooth, he stroked her forehead.She smiled, and it was as joyful as ever.

She leant forwards so she was looking straight into his eyes, but there was nothing behind their opaque lenses. Rose neither saw nor recognised him.

"Oh, Rose, Rose..." he began, but he didn't know what to say.

She continued with her unblinking, unseeing, unrecognising look.

"Rose, I love you," he blurted out, quietly and hoarsely and with desperation and emotion mixed in his tone.

He was not the only one to think she was beautiful. When the nurses or carers mentioned it, he was delighted, although he would always pass it off with the deprecating comment of "I'm biased".

Visits like that only happened about half the time though. Rose was semi-somnolent most of the time now. On another visit, Billy had been sitting by her side for half an hour or more while she slept, leaning in towards her resting one elbow on the arm of her chair to get closer and stroking her hair. He could feel her breath on his resting hand a foot below her face. He smiled. At least she knew how to breathe on her own!

Rose's grip tightened, and her fingernails pressed into the back of Billy's hand.

"Oh, Rose, come back to me," he said to her blank face. He fought back the tears. "Come back."

Then she opened her eyes. "I think..." Her voiced tailed off and she was asleep again.

"If only you could think," muttered Billy to himself. Then, when he stood to go, he leant across to say goodbye and kissed her forehead.

"Good, good," Rose said, then she was asleep yet again.

More often than not, Rose would babble away—no words, just noises—and Billy couldn't decide if she was happy or angry. The noises were strident at times, but Rose interspersed them with joyful giggles. It was confusing, and Billy became even more than usually emotional.

He would sit beside Rose for over three-quarters of an hour before he felt an urge to run away. And on those days he would leave, giving her the customary kiss on the forehead and flee. Later, sitting at home, he would feel ashamed for abandoning Rose in that way.

Most times though, he would stay, holding her hand, not resisting when she jerked it up and banged it down on her lap to stop her putting her fingers in her mouth. His mind was generally blank as emotion took control, and sometimes he couldn't help thinking how much he missed her, or occasionally having thoughts about what it would be like if she was no longer there. He hated those thoughts.

It was the same most nights when he would wake up lying in bed growing maudlin, his mind vaguely full of thoughts of Rose as she had been when they were married but really quite vacuous. He wished he could somehow go back to another time, move in a parallel universe, perhaps, to a happier time. Not the first flush of youthful discovery, not the swirly mind time of early romance or newlywed honeymoon, not the lusty early physical years, nor even the middle part of a happy, contented marriage.

He wanted to be in a world where there was just Rose and him, together, knowing each other's thoughts, speaking them only when necessary but knowing. A time when a casual brushing of arms or shoulders or hands would excite feelings of love and togetherness. *A feeling of... what... a feeling of us.*

But Rose wasn't with him anymore, and surprisingly, it wasn't just that thought that upset him when he visited the home.

One day, he walked down the corridor on the way back from the nurses' room, pausing his step to look into all the other rooms. The semi-comatose half living patients—thirty or thirty-five dead people in living bodies. He still could not imagine them as lovers, cheerful happy friends, clowning about, laughing without a care.

In one of the rooms, he saw a man, his face and neck degraded and with red blotches, bending over an empty bed.

"Talk to me, lover," said the man in a pitiful croak.

Silly old fool, thought Billy as he moved on. *Lover? At his age?*

He heard the woman in another room scream. "You stupid idiot," she shrieked.

He got back to Rose's room and she gripped his hand, and then lifted it towards her mouth. She kissed it. "Silly boy," she echoed before falling asleep.

Silly boy... it was a phrase Rose had often used in their early and middle marriage (and sometimes during his earlier visits to the home), and it delighted him when she used it now.

He wondered how the nurses and carers coped.

Beth came into the room. Her eyes were hooded, and Billy thought she looked tired. "How you gettin' on?" she asked him.

"I'm OK. No need to worry about me."

"But we do, sweetie, although you gotta look after yourself. Do you get enough exercise?"

"Exercise? Sloth and greed have got me through so far, and I don't want to break the habits of a lifetime."

"You need a good woman to take you in hand."

"A bad woman would be better."

"Oh man, you gotta dirty mind. Jus' do as you told for once." She laughed, a loud pealing laugh, and left.

Billy felt better for the inconsequential banter. He still thought she looked tired.

Over the years, Billy's mind had wandered over a lot of things during his visits to Rose—jumbled, mixed-up thoughts at random, thoughts of the meaning of life, the meaning of love, if there was any meaning at all. He frequently tried to figure out what Rose was thinking, but that was as muddled as his own thoughts. The only constant was his quiet joy and happiness at being with her, just holding her hand despite the desperate feeling in his body and brain that she was not really there.

He had always lived in the present. He did not drool over past triumphs or complain about past failures, what was done was done, but nor did he try to predict the future. What would be would be. If life was boring for a spell, so be it. If it was exciting, so be it. He had always lived his life in the moment.

He had never wished for more of anything (he had been lucky enough not to have really worried about poverty) and had never been jealous of people who had more money or possessions. He had always accepted things as they were.

He had everything he needed. He had Rose.

She had always been quiet, but that had all changed now. She had virtually lost all proper language and was reduced to shouting seemingly meaningless sounds.

"Aja. Bebang. Bam. Oja. Abaj ajack."

Outwardly, she seemed to be in a world of silence and darkness, relieved only by touch and a feeling that someone or something was with her.

When there *were* words she rarely mentioned his name, although the staff said she often spoke about Billy when he was not there, he didn't hear it all that often. She used the word "love" frequently, but he didn't know who she was talking to.

It was all quite confusing, and Billy tried not to let himself sink into thoughts of how their lives together had changed so drastically since the dreadful illness had struck.

He knew that with dementia there was no going back. Death was inevitable, final, an end, a living death you know won't, can't, improve, that it's impossible. But now, at the back of the mind, there was always a faint, minuscule hope or plea that would bring the person back.

It was the hope that was the killer for Billy, the impossible hope. Every little apparent sign of normality—a sudden smile in answer to his comment or question, the infrequent and unexpected few words of love—all gave a desperate hope that there was still a spark of the old Rose lurking inside her.

Those occasions settled on Billy's raw emotions and gave him temporary hope. He knew that every time it was a false hope, but it was still hope.

Billy was crying less by now, but several happenings—a sound or action by Rose, a chance remark in a conversation, or even an episode on television—still triggered and tugged huge pangs of high emotion in his sensitive mind.

One of them in particular, when she pronounced "I love you", then after a beat called him (or someone in her distant mind) "darling" before bursting into her distinctive and lovely laugh had tears rolling down his cheeks or the side of his face.

He would always think, *If I could have just one more real talk with you—a real one like we used to have...* But he knew that was an impossible dream.

He sometimes wondered if Rose might be better off dead, but that morbid thought upset him and he couldn't bring himself to think about it. Even the vague non-living, non-seeing, non-hearing, half-life existence had to be better.

A half-life? Or a quarter? An eighth? Yes, it had to be better. Or was it? It had to be. Didn't it?

It was very sad, and Billy tried his hardest not to think about it when he was at Peace Hall.

There, neighbours and friends sometimes took over from the staff at the home trying to help him but too often going over the top. He appreciated it and knew they were all acting to be helpful. He tolerated it because he knew they felt (and were) doing the right things. In his muddled mind, they were the things Rose had always done for him, but he knew he could manage every little thing they did for himself. Or better still, if he had Rose back to do them for him.

Billy was fiercely independent, and if someone hinted that he was too old to manage he had to prove them wrong and perform a particular act with bravado.

He was being stifled by the offers of help. He found he could not even pick up a drink from the bar at the club and carry it across to a table without someone jumping out of a chair to offer to carry it for him.He appreciated the offers, but he was being stifled by them. He only really needed help when he asked for it.And he did ask, and soon found himself going out for regular lunches with the widow living opposite him. He had been quite close friends with her husband—had actually been for lunch with him as his last act before having a stroke and dying—and felt a certain responsibility to his wife Edith. For her part, she quickly used Billy as a companion at the same time as using him as a "stand in" for her husband—the male in her life.

There was nothing sexual or romantic in their friendship, but both enjoyed the company, often telling each other fairly intimate details of their former married lives.

They were due to meet one day between his visits to Peace Hall, and as Billy stood there shaving and getting ready he had a mental picture of a carer wheeling a bed-to-chair hoist along the corridor and it hit him. Rose had not walked, not even stood up, for something like four years. Four years. Imagine that! He gulped and nicked his chin. All thoughts disappeared as he stemmed the blood, then quickly dressed and prepared to go to lunch with Edith.

They usually went to the pub at the end of the road, Ye Olde Hayloft—it was convenient, and the food more or less edible—and had both become quite friendly with the girl serving food and drink there. Her name was Dawn, a tall, willowy dark-haired girl with a pretty face marred by a deep scar on her left cheek and a pert all-embracing grin. She had an easy, friendly way of dealing with customers and always made time to chat to them, and Billy—who still liked the look of a pretty girl—flirted with her platonically but outrageously despite Edith's presence.

It became a regular weekly interlude until after a couple of months when Dawn told them she was moving to a better paid job in another pub a few miles away. Without her, it was not the same, so for a while, Billy and Edith stopped going to the pub for lunch, Billy returning to his old routine of a snatched sandwich while watching game shows on TV.

But eventually, they decided to renew the weekly meetings and decided to go to the new pub to see Dawn. She recognised them immediately and crossed over to chat.

"How's the Hayloft?" she asked Billy as Edith took off her coat and hung it on a stand in a corner.

"Don't know. We stopped going when you left."

"Why on earth did you do that?"

"You know I only went to lust after you over the battered cod and mushy peas."

Dawn laughed. "Silly boy," she said and the words suddenly silenced Billy.

The weekly lunches were all right—sometimes a help against Billy's continuing loneliness, sometimes quite funny, sometimes a chore.

But it was still his visits to Rose that took up most of his life.

He was sitting with her, holding her hand as usual while she slept, and the radio was playing in the background—a programme of old pop songs. Billy wasn't really listening, but suddenly one song penetrated his head. He'd heard it before and it triggered a small spark.

What was it? It came to him. The old love song he'd crooned to Rose in Leicester Square after a night out many, many years ago. He remembered the record. He'd bought the ten-inch vinyl disc for himself and another copy for Rose.

Somehow the lyrics had stuck in the back recesses of his memory and now, ignoring the radio, he sung them to himself internally.

The song was about the dull ache of lost love—its words summed up how he felt perfectly, telling of "the girl who had left", a paean to a lost beloved, and its haunting arrangement with swirling violins and a swaying melody told a sorrowing narrative that summed up his feelings exactly. It was an anthem to lost romance, and in his mind it represented his past life with Rose, during which he had never lost his love for her and he was sure that somewhere deep in the recesses of her brain, she had never lost her love for him.

Back home later, he found a website that confirmed the lyrics and gave him a short video of the song. The picture instantly became part of his life.

The lyrics were now fixed firmly at the front of his memory, and at home he would frequently sing them silently to himself while waving his right hand in the air as the leaders conducting the big bands of his youth had done—leaving his left hand free as they had done, although they had always held an instrument there, a trumpet, trombone or clarinet.

On his next visit to the home two days later, he sang the words out loud to Rose in a soft cracked, off-key voice, his mouth very close to her left ear, and he thought she smiled. Rose had always loved the long-forgotten song.

For the next few weeks, months, the song seemed to take over a lot of Billy's thinking. Every morning, he would wake with part of the anthem playing in his mind, and his upper body would jerk with uncontrollable emotion before tears of sorrow rolled down his cheeks.

The dampness they left on the pillow under his head would bring him back to reality and he would get up with his brain in a temporary blank.

At that time he was most vulnerable emotionally. He would invariably have the desperately romantic words of his "anthem" song gyrating round in his mind, and he was always likely to play the short video he had of her on his phone's memory while trying to wake up in the morning.

He thought of all the cliches: a bank of violins honeying a song along, waves crashing silently on a shoreline, moonlight over a silent landscape. He felt them all, but it was a unique feeling like none he or anyone else had ever felt. He was still very much in love.

Rose felt the same emotion, but she dreamt of family homes, happy meals with children, helping Billy.

Billy would play the song over and over, and he once even thought of it playing at Rose's funeral. It was a maudlin thought and he knew it, but it was inexorably there tucked into his brain.He found it impossible to ignore the tune or phrases from it. They would repeatedly crop up in his brain and he would sort of sing it in his mind.

The thought of playing it at Rose's funeral began to repeat itself—too often—and he tried to make it go away.But it haunted him, taunted him, and he couldn't stop himself thinking about it. Yet, he still couldn't help singing the words in his mind.

No matter how hard he tried, Billy couldn't rid himself of the song, and it preyed on his mind and built up a growing sense of grief.

On visits to the home, he eventually forced himself to rid his brain of the morbid thoughts that now came with the anthem by actively recalling the Hollywood film stars of his and Rose's youth: Rita Hayworth, Elizabeth Taylor, the two Hepburns, Doris Day, Grace Kelly, Cyd Charisse, Eleanor Powell. He realised they were all dead. More maudlin thoughts.

He put his arm across Rose onto her right shoulder. "You're still the most beautiful," he said.

Rose's eyes fluttered but did not open.

"I love you," said Billy.

Billy's unhappy thoughts were growing, and he was getting ever more depressed. He was following his routine, still needing to visit Rose but with his mind blocking out emotions. It was hard work.

As he had been growing older, Billy had become ever more emotional. At first, he had thought it very unmacho. People put it down to old age, but they couldn't know how much the loss of Rose really affected him, nor about the residual sorrow over the unborn baby in their early marriage.

He couldn't mourn "his" Rose. She was still there physically and he could see her and hear her and touch her, yet to all real intents and purposes she had gone, left him, years before.

Everything seemed to be going against him, even a teabag split while he was brewing, leaving him with a cuppa that left unpleasant leaves in his mouth. When he mentioned it, friends simply told him to take a break.

"She won't know," they said.

But he knew that he had to keep visiting. It was a compulsion.

He knew that he had to be with her. After all, they had been together virtually every single day (apart from a couple when he was away on business) for almost seven decades, and he knew he wanted to be with her until the day he died.

Driving to Peace Hall was now an absent-minded routine, and Billy drove there one morning only noticing all the other travellers in their boxes speeding along at more than the legal limit. He automatically managed to give the impression of being the cheeky, cheerful chappy, but that was outwardly. Inwardly, he was grieving deeply.

He was still seeing Rose in the home regularly, but he desperately wanted her with him all the time. The way it used to be.

He slept badly, going to bed exhausted around 11 but reading until he couldn't focus properly and turned the lights out around midnight. Then most nights waking about three to four times in darkness, his mind awash with a whirlwind of absolutely nothing, and then dozing and waking every half hour until he got up around 8.

It got so he almost dreaded going to bed, hesitating before finally turning off his bedside lamp much later than usual to stare into an empty darkness before slipping into sleep, a little bit scared that he might not wake the next day to see or check on Rose.

He delayed getting out of bed in the mornings trying to shorten the day without her. It was making him almost permanently tired and fuzzy-brained, and during the day he felt he was never more than sixty per cent himself—he didn't have the incentive or motivation to do things. He was simply surviving and he needed Rose by his side to make him complete.

The passion was still there. It raged inside him.

The trouble was that Billy was not only getting confused and forgetful, but he was also getting very unsteady on his feet and had to take precautions. He still used a walking stick to help and it gave him confidence when he was out and about, but he left it propped by the door when he was at home, relying on the proximity of walls and stair bannisters to help.

Without the stick, he often banged into furniture or door frames, and was continually finding small bruises on his arms, legs and body.

He still managed to drive to see Rose, and one day when he was at the home two carers came into the room while he was sitting there, smoothing her hair and stroking her cheek in turn. Billy thought of the difference between them and the impersonal staff when she had been in hospital and was determined to write a letter of complaint to the head doctor.

When he got back to his car to drive home, he remembered that he had to write a letter, but he couldn't think who to.

Another day, he went up the stairs to Rose's ward, opened the door using the remembered code and stepped into the corridor. He started to walk, passing the first room on the right, looking for Rose's room. He could not remember the number.

Diana the nurse stopped him some way along the corridor. "Hi there. Where are you off to?" she asked.

"Just to see you."

"There's no one in the office, but I've got Rose's medicine and I'll try and answer any questions while I give it to her," she replied.

She led him back to Rose's room.

"I was only coming to say hello," lied Billy.

A couple of weeks later, he turned up at the home on Rose's birthday, a huge bunch of vivid red roses in his hand—Red Rose, her nickname with the Caballeros, somehow still in his memory.

He had been sitting with her and listening to her chattering away when almost all the nurses and carers crowded into the room carrying an iced birthday cake with a single candle burning in the middle of it. Rose laughed, and it showed Billy they were trying to treat her like a human being, like Rose, and not just another patient. She really was one of their family.

Billy was on the highest of highs when he left the home, and the feeling stayed with him for the rest of that day. But when he finally drew the curtains to shut the world away, the normal reality hit and he slumped back into his usual deep mood of loneliness. He went to the bedroom and lay on the bed, on top of the duvet but still wrapped in that feeling, sleepless in the dark until well into the middle of the night, alone with the empty shadow of the unused extra pillow in his and Rose's double bed.

But it was not only Rose who had a birthday. Billy also had one.

It was the morning of his eighty-eighth birthday and after bathing and dressing, he carefully went down the stairs, trying to work out how long he had known Rose. The dates were a bit vague in his mind.

They had been married for fifty-nine years. Or was it sixty? Or more? Or less? How old had he been when they married? Add on an extra three years from the first time he had met and dated her and the wedding. He got a piece of paper and wrote down eighty-eight, then twenty-six (was that how old he had been when they married?) underneath it. He looked at the two numbers, then crossed out the twenty-six and replaced it with twenty-seven, then crossed that out and put twenty-eight. He studied the numbers and added them up. A hundred and sixteen? No. He put a line through that.

He wrote eighty-eight and twenty-six again and instead of adding them, he tried subtracting. Sixty-two. He shook his head and tried again. Sixty-three.

He looked at the long list of numbers on the paper, studied them and frowned. What were they for?

He crumpled the paper and left the rolled mass on the table. He sat there for five minutes wondering how long he had known Rose before he stood up and went to make his morning cup of tea.

As he waited for the kettle to boil, he again wondered how long he had known Rose.Later on, he went to visit her.

He walked into her room and Rose was talking.

"Hush now, Billy. Baby's asleep..."

He looked very carefully, but he couldn't see a baby.

Chapter 17

Billy was starting to feel a bit old, but he mostly kept to his routine and still visited Rose every other lunchtime although his own appetite was less than it used to be.

He seemed to knock into people in the street simply because he didn't see them, and during his visits he bumped more of the other patients now, literally, as when he came through the door into the ward corridor and almost did a tango with an old man shuffling along using a rather posh walker, blue painted and with a seat rather peculiarly facing the walker. Billy wondered how he could sit in it and still move himself forward.

He extricated himself from the disabled man—who didn't seem to realise he was there—and entered Rose's room. Chadani was there in his seat quietly listening to Rose's breathing, and as he stood in the doorway unnoticed he heard a woman down the corridor calling out, "I want to go home. I want to see my husband."

Chadani didn't look up, but sensed Billy's unease. "Her husband died eight years ago," she said.

The carer stood and left, and Billy took over the chair—smiling as he noticed it was warm—and took Rose's hand. The movement woke her and she opened her eyes and started the usual nonsense noises and words. The sight and sound of her chattering away and suddenly laughing lifted his mood. He sat beside her and a metaphorical sigh and grin swept through him.She made his day.

But days like that were becoming a little bit of a rarity now. Rose spent a lot more time asleep, and even when she was awake she usually kept her eyes closed. Billy thought it was simply because she could hardly see and it was easier not to open them. When they were open, in any case, he could see nothing there, just a blank staring into space. He thought it was not worth opening them. She had always been practical like that.

Now there was no eye contact and she had lost the use of words Billy felt even more helpless. He wanted to do something for Rose, anything, but there was nothing at all that could be done except to hold her hand or arm to try to let her know there was someone there and she was not alone.

As far as Rose was concerned, it could have been anyone. It was a minute thing, but for Billy it at least gave him minuscule contact.

He would squeeze her hand but there was rarely any response (apart from an occasional involuntary tic), and as he looked at her it was Rose's face and body but it was not really Rose. He had never felt so completely alone. But he loved her still.

Although he tried to follow an orderly regime, Billy was starting to show his age, and he knew he was beginning to forget things.

"I'm nearly ninety bloody years old, dammit. I'm entitled to forget things," he would tell himself, often saying it out loud and with a vague smile as he thought Rose was a few years younger, a mere baby.

Billy realised things were not as they were and knew he was starting to feel a little frail. He had trouble walking, and his balance was not as steady as it used to be, so he made certain he always had something close to lean on—a wall, stair bannisters.

I always leant on Rose, he thought with a droll grin.

He was determined not to let his growing disability get the better of him, so he tried going for a few short tentative walks, but that came to an end when he got lost just a few hundred yards away from his own home. Luckily, he suddenly recalled a house from the vague recesses of his mind—it had been adorned with scaffolding during a drive with Rose—so he went to the front door and asked to be taken home.

"I can't remember where I live," he explained pitifully.

By chance, it was the same house where Rose had been found when she had lost her way. And the understanding owner drove him home.

Billy went indoors, made himself a cup of tea and took it to the living room. He sat down with it and tried to recall what he had done that afternoon. He'd come home in a car, so he must have been somewhere. Where? He couldn't remember, so he turned on the telly and watched a game show with little enjoyment.

That night he had a dream (at least, he thought it was a dream) that he was a contestant on a TV quiz, and he was giving all the right answers, even before the questions were put to him. It scared him at first, but after visiting Rose the next day and having the mickey taken out of him by Big Beth, he forgot about it.

While this was going on, Rose was, slowly but inexorably, getting worse. She was still having her "conversations" using sounds and was in a dark place, her mind and memory just a foggy blur, but although she could not see Billy when he visited, she could feel his friendly presence and knew she could relax with him holding her hand. His face was indistinct and she tried to picture it, but it was out of reach.

Billy was getting a bit fuzzy too. The first grey mists of his own dementia were starting to take over and, like Rose the white clouds of oblivion were beginning to cover his brain. But despite the muddled haze of his mind he nevertheless knew he loved this woman as he had never loved anyone else before. The love still enveloped him, engulfed him. He loved her with a deep, deep passion.

On visits, he would go into her room and whether she was in her recliner chair or in bed, he would sit holding her hand for hours, their eyes fixed not quite seeing each other clearly but both mentally walking in a beautiful spot hand in hand. It made both of them smile.

Sitting beside her in her room, Billy took her left hand and squeezed it as an unconscious sign of the way he felt, and she moved her right hand across to envelop his and pressed back.

"I love you—" he stopped. He couldn't remember her name.

But he ploughed on, disregarding the bodily aches he obviously felt and the frequent psychological void, but the nurses and carers at the home noticed how Billy was crumbling and recognised the symptoms—a lot of them the same symptoms that Rose had shown. When he twice more walked past Rose's room and once forgot to feed her and ate her meal himself they grew so concerned they got Big Beth to have a word with him.

"You slowin' down, man," she told him frankly. "Why don't you see our doctor to get a pill or a tonic or somet'ing?"

Billy listened, and before she left him, he told her that he would do so, but he never intended to do so... and didn't.

As far as he was concerned, he didn't think he needed to. He was all right and he knew there were days when he functioned almost normally, usually days when he visited Rose, but he ignored those other days when his increasing confusion suffocated him and things started to go wrong.

He didn't know it, but it was just the start of the disease, and he began to drift in and out of awareness, with no control of what was happening in his mind.

Physically, he knew he was not as he used to be. He realised he was walking with his legs wide apart for balance—a sign of his ageing—that his balance was a bit wonky and that he needed to sit down more frequently. He consciously moved his free left hand out of the way when he was pouring boiling water from a kettle in case his shaking right hand might splash it.

Going upstairs on his way up to bed one night, he tripped—on the tenth step.

Billy had become more than usually forgetful, so he started making short notes to himself to remind him of things he had to do for Rose, jotting her down simply as R—the nickname she'd had for a time with the Caballeros.

He tried to remember what Rose had been like in those days as a young girl, but his mind was clouded and all he could recollect was a whole lifetime of love and happiness and two-way devotion.

"I love you," he whispered.

Trying to behave normally as things got worse he went for short walks until one day he got in a panic as he couldn't remember where he was. He was actually in his own street, five houses down from his own, but as he twisted backwards and forwards trying to remember where he lived he got a sudden feeling that he was falling, sucked into a dark smoky vortex of blankness. He fell over on the road and woke up two hours later in hospital, dehydrated.

He was there for three days before he was sent home, told to see his GP, and was then referred to a mental health specialist to take a memory test at the local hospital.

It was just as Rose's test had been—a series of twenty-six formal questions, the date and some other routine things. Fairly early on, Billy was given an address to remember: 80 West Street, Guildford, Surrey. He was asked to count backwards from fifteen, and when he had done that (slowly and with much thought), he was asked what the address was that he had been given. He replied confidently that it was Maxwell

Gate, Rose's home before they were married, but couldn't remember the number or where that was.

The doctor asked a few more simple questions, and as with Rose, the appointment lasted just over twenty minutes, and Billy had totted up fifteen correct answers (Rose had only reached thirteen at her final test). He was told to go home and make an appointment to get the result a week later.

Before the next consultation, the clouds of doubt began to creep into Billy's mind until suddenly, they were all embracing. Then when he saw the doctor to get the prognosis he was given a fancy name for the condition, but luckily, the doctor broke the news gently, far more sympathetically than the specialist who had given Rose the news years before.

Soon after, it was Billy's ninetieth birthday. He had been receiving cards for days before—including one from an even older aunt of Rose's who he'd met only once but who had virtuously sent birthday and Christmas cards every year since—and on the day itself he received many messages and phone calls from friends, acquaintances and neighbours.

He got just one letter, from a grandson of Jonno and Mary and somehow that meant more than all the others. To his mind, it was well meant and somehow more genuine than all the other regulation cards—touching because he felt it a living continuation of a lasting friendship through the generations that showed he was not just some insignificant dot in the universe.

There was a kind of party when he visited Rose, and the staff brought a small iced cake to the room which he shared with them as they sang "Happy Birthday".

Billy was pleased, although he didn't like the fuss. Ninety? He didn't feel ninety, more like... what, seventy, fifty, fourteen? He didn't feel anything. It was just a number and he was just as he had been the day before and the day before that. No, ninety was just an excuse for other people to celebrate and marvel (and maybe feel in awe). To Billy, it was just another day, so he decided to ignore the fuss and concentrate on Rose. Now that was something he felt was precious.

Throughout the day, he had people coming up to him and he got dozens of phone calls and messages. It was nice to be remembered, but when he eventually went to bed and turned out the light, he was alone, by himself, lonely. Without his Rose.

All the staff knew what was happening—they had seen it often enough—and they knew what was going to happen, softening the fact by thinking that after all his hard years helping Rose at home and then the years visiting her at Peace Hall there would be no more memories of suffering, anxiety and worry.

Around that time, the ultra friendly Big Beth left the home for a job in a hospital's geriatric ward, and as Billy got worse she was replaced by new nurse Laura Border who Billy promptly dubbed Laura N'order.

She had only been in the job for two weeks when she got a call from the local hospital. She was asked what she knew about Billy's general health and mental condition. Billy had fallen in the street again while walking in heavy rain without a coat, and had been found, apparently after a couple of hours, slumped by the roadside soaking wet and unconscious. He had been ambulanced to the hospital, but they didn't know anything about him.

Laura, of course, had only a sparse knowledge of Billy and couldn't really help the hospital nurse she spoke to. Billy was put into a ward, on oxygen, and was treated for severe hypothermia. He was confused (even more than usual by the sound of things) and his speech was slurred.

It took three weeks before the doctors were satisfied that Billy had recovered enough to be released and he was sent home—to continue living on his own. He was not able to visit Rose and had two carers call on him daily to help him through the difficult moments of waking up and preparing for bed—one very pretty and the other rather elderly, stern and with a permanent scowl on her face. He preferred the older one, but they both looked after him dispassionately until they, after talking to the staff at Peace Hall, considered that his condition had deteriorated so fast that he too needed to be admitted to the home, where he was to have absolutely no recollection of either the hospital or the treatment they had given him.

The leaves were turning brown and falling from the trees as winter approached. Rose had been in Peace Hall for around four years (she was given a life expectancy of just three months when she was admitted) when it was decided, wisely, that Billy had to have full-time attention.

A place was found at the home, and within days, he moved in to be near Rose again. Nothing was done about Glebe Cottage in Avenue Road, which was left empty with its memories of Billy and Rose's happy times.Eventually, it was sold by auction and the money from its sale helped pay for both of them at Peace Hall.

Chapter 18

It was a sunny but cold early winter's Thursday morning when Billy Saunders was admitted to Peace Hall Care Home. He had been in a nearby hospital for three weeks before being put on a stretcher and moved on a fifteen-minute journey from there to the home in the back of an ambulance. He was then taken in a wheelchair into the home pushed by a Thai carer and with a nurse holding his hand. He sat in the chair looking blank and not really understanding what was going on.

Billy was suffering from advancing mid-term Alzheimer's, a form of dementia that was slowly eating away at his brain. Because of the disease, he did not know his wife was already a resident of Peace Hall and was living in the next room.

Although they were married, they were not given a single room for medical reasons—Rose was bedbound but put in a recliner chair most days as she could not walk—but he was put in a room next door to Rose so he could go and see her whenever he wanted.

He was to do so often and in fact, the first time was on his very first full day at the home. Billy decided to explore, and his first port of call was the room next door: Rose's room. Kiara was with Rose, generally soothing her and tidying up after giving her some medicine.

"Hello," said Billy brightly.

"Oh, Billy, have you come to see the lovely Rose?" asked Kiara, throwing the damp cloth she had been using to wipe Rose's face into the waste bin.

"Rose? That's a nice name."

Rose looked blank, and Billy looked around the room before taking a seat on a chair beside Rose. He studied her, interested, and he liked what he saw. She had high cheekbones and smooth skin, and there was something about her that made him feel she had a sense of fun. He noticed that Rose's pale facial skin was still generally as smooth as that of a teenager and her hair was still luxuriant, although a sharp white now.

He stroked her forearm and cheeks gently, almost mechanically, then compared them with his own, which were now wrinkled like the photos of desert sands. He did not see that her upper arm muscles and her legs were painfully wasted from lack of use. She seemed to be the most beautiful woman he had ever seen.

He reached across to shake her hand, and she gripped his fingers."Hello, I'm Billy. What's your name?" he asked.

"Abo-da-be-bang-roo," she replied, and somehow Billy knew she had said she was Rose.

He just knew he wanted to see this woman again.

Although neither could form any real logical cogent thought about it, there seemed to be an instant rapport between them. They were strangers, but as Billy left her, Rose was also trying to remember the boy who had been holding her hand. She couldn't quite manage it, but somehow thought that he had black hair. She couldn't focus, but she somehow knew he had laughing eyes and that she could relax when he was there.

She smiled at the vague thought, and her eyes closed as she tried to concentrate on his face.

"Gadoo," she said out loud. "Bejar. Boom."

They met again when Rose was wheeled into the communal lounge, somewhere she wasn't usually taken because her loud noises upset some of the other residents. Billy had wandered there about ten minutes earlier and was watching as the others tried to feed themselves, noticing one shrivelled lady as she put her fork down and lifted a shaking cup of water to her lips with wavering hands. He wanted to help but sensed that she wanted to be independent. She took two sips, then put the cup down, placing it with precision by the side of her plate, then he watched anxiously as she picked up her fork again, having difficulty placing it the right way round and into her hand. He noted the watch with a slim fading mock gold bracelet she had used for seven decades and more.

He turned away and was trying to figure out what he was meant to do when Rose arrived, and as soon as she was settled, he moved across to sit next to her.

"Hello again," he said. "I'm Billy, remember?"

Rose looked at him, a slight smile appearing on her lips.

"What's your name?" he asked.

"Roo-abang-ug."

"That's a pretty name," he replied, smiling at her although he didn't know what she had said.

They sat there "talking" monosyllabically for three-quarters of an hour before carers started clearing the patients back to their rooms or, those who were more or less able to look after themselves, to the central dining room for lunch.

Billy and Rose were both taken to their rooms, but after their meals had been served and eaten Billy got up and wandered next door again. He and Rose were already starting to build up a deep friendship, holding hands, talking, laughing a lot.

They saw each other several times every day in the following few weeks, and slowly the friendship developed and started to feel like something bigger—something neither could remember ever feeling before. Neither could tell what that emotion was, but both knew instinctively that there was someone they wanted to be with. They both felt right together—felt they could trust the other—and just wanted to be close.

Neither could really remember the other when they were apart, but both knew they wished the other "nice person" would appear again.

That wish was disrupted when Rose had a slight stomach disorder and the nurses decided to keep her in bed. They kept her door open as always but put a low barrier across it so neither Billy nor anyone else could interrupt her healing daytime sleep.

"I want to see her," Billy told Ditya the carer.

"Who?"

"The girl."

"What girl?"

"You know. The girl in the room."

"You mean, Rose. Why didn't you say her name?"

Billy started to answer, but before he could Ditya added, "You can't see her, Billy. She's ill."

Billy seemed to understand, and for the next four days he moped and fretted that he was not able to see his beautiful new friend. Some days, he played up, refusing to eat or take his medicine, but the staff were patient and kept him more or less compliant.

Then finally, Rose was better, and it was Ditya again who took him in to see her. She looked pale but was awake, and when she saw Billy she smiled a vague recognition.

"Hello, love," said Billy.

"Adgidg, adgadg," was the reply.

First thing the next morning, without knowing why, some unknown inner remembrance made Billy turn left out of his room rather than go right towards the communal lounge. It took him to Rose's room, where he sat beside her recliner as usual—all memory of her illness gone.

A week later, she was still in bed the morning Billy got to her room before breakfast and sat beside her, looking at her with half shut eyes. She was awake, and both were smiling and relaxed, and the now usual feeling grew inside both of them and he felt that he understood her.

Although he hadn't been able to understand the sounds, the grunts and weird noises that this beautiful woman was making, he had tried to make sense of them.

He had been convinced that "Ru" was her way of saying her name, Rose, but after the break in seeing her suddenly, inexplicably, it clicked and his garbled mind understood perfectly. The staff heard them both using animal noises, but Billy and Rose all at once began to understand each other perfectly and were able to converse in this strange animalistic language of their own.

"It's nice being here with you. I feel safe," Billy smiled. "I've been alone all my life, and this is much better. I'm not alone anymore."

He bent forwards and kissed Rose on the cheek. She turned her face towards him, and for a moment their eyes met, looking deep into each other. Then their lips touched by accident and they kissed. It was an instinct. Natural. With meaning. But accidental and unknowing. It was magic. Enchanting. Bewitching.

Billy drew back, and they looked at each other, neither consciously realising what they had just done. But although neither knew it, it was new love. True love.

They stayed, holding hands and looking into each other's eyes for a few moments.

"I had a baby when I was young, but I don't know where she is now," said Rose softy.

"Never mind, we'll have two more when we're married."

"Three."

"No, four!

They sat on, but had forgotten the kiss by the time Billy was led back to his own room for lunch although somehow the feeling and emotion of the moment lasted in both their jangled minds.

"I love you," said Billy when he returned after the meal. He didn't know her name, so he squeezed her hand.

A slight tear fell from Rose's right eye and rolled down her cheek. She wanted to say the same, but she couldn't remember his name either.

Although Rose could not see and could not hear, she kept the sense of touch and could sense people around her and could feel it when they touched her. She was still sensitive enough to differentiate between people, so she knew when certain carers were there (although she had no idea of who they were or what they looked like) and now she also had that special glow when Billy held her hand. She seemed to "see" him when he was with her. It was magic. Enchanting.

Although she couldn't really see or hear, Rose somehow knew when Billy was there on his visits, and the mysterious urges in them both deepened to complete relaxation, happiness and finally dependence. There was no deliberate or conscious thought from either, but that instinctive feeling that they wanted—and needed—to be together.

Like Billy, Rose had a strange, warm feeling at the idea of her beautiful new man, but she didn't know why. For both, it was the start of a deep, unexplainable love.

She was still smiling with her eyes shut when two carers brought in the hoist and Billy had to leave the room as they moved her from her recliner chair to her bed.

Another morning, Billy had been for a walk, ambling along the corridor slowly, and without realising, he turned into Rose's room. There was a beautiful girl in a recliner, with an armed low back chair beside her. He sat and reached for her hand.Rose felt her hand being taken, and knew she liked the contact. The two of them sat quietly to-gether, and in both, there once again surged a vague feeling that they had been there before.

They held hands for almost half an hour before carer Kamal brought in Rose's mid-morning hot chocolate drink.

"Ah, Billy, would you like a chocolate too?" he asked. "Or your usual tea?"

Billy nodded. "I prefer tea, but I'll have the same as her," he replied.

Kamal went out to his trolley and brought back a plastic mug of hot chocolate, and Billy sipped at it as the carer helped Rose with her drink.

When they had finished, Kamal wiped both their mouths, and left them holding hands again.

Billy spent almost two hours in Rose's room every time he went there, alternately holding her clenched right hand, smoothing her soft hair and talking to her over her own monosyllabic grunts, before a nurse or carer would gently, but inevitably, lead him back to his own room for some reason or other.

She would sit him in his chair, and he would have vague memories of having seen a beautiful girl. The most beautiful girl he had ever seen—prettier than any girl he had ever seen in his life. He had never known anyone like this lovely rose.

He smiled at the thought and tried to remember the girl's name and what she looked like, and was still smiling at the half memory when he fell asleep. Still in his chair.

He would always go back to see Rose when he woke up, usually the next morning.

One day, he walked in and Rose was sitting in her recliner as usual. Billy sat and rested his hand on her arm.

"What's your name?"

"Ya-bong-ru."

"That's a pretty name. I'm Billy."

Rose got a joyous feeling whenever this strange human appeared beside her, holding her hand, stroking her arm, muttering unintelligible words.

And Billy thought the woman in the next room was gorgeous. He liked being with her.

They both liked the feeling that took over whenever they were with each other—being with the other and sensing their presence started to be essential.

Billy wandered into Rose's room at around half past eight every morning shortly after breakfast. He sat by her side as usual, but nothing was said. As they looked at each other, both had a feeling they couldn't remember ever feeling before. A pang. A spark. An emotion.

Rose took Billy's hand. "I love you," she said boldly in her animal sounds, no emotion in her noise words.

"And I love you too..." Billy's voice tailed off as he couldn't remember Rose's name.

But from then on, without knowing how or why or what it meant, their love grew quickly. The nurses and carers thought of them as a couple, and everyone was happy.

Unlike most people of his age, Billy did not really live in the past—he concentrated on the now. Would Rose be awake or asleep? Would she be laughing, chatty or just silent? Would she have any lucid moments to share with him or would there just be the sheer utter void of her brain? He never knew what he was going to find, but he did know that he had to see her and be with her no matter what mood or condition she was in. That's why every morning he would wander into Rose's room next door to his own.

He would often go for a walk along the corridor first, and sometimes would go into her room by mistake, but eventually, he knew he liked being with her and as the unknown feelings grew between them, he did so deliberately, by instinct more than design. When he sat in the easy seat beside her, he would rest his hand on the arm of her chair and more often than not she would reach across and hold it in her tight claw-like grip. They would sit there for hours like that, just enjoying being with each other. In both their minds, there had grown a vague sort of emotion that neither could explain, that they could not do without the other. In thinking people, it was known as love.

A few months after he had moved into Peace Hall, Billy went to see Rose one afternoon after lunch. She seemed to be asleep, and Billy sat by her recliner with his right hand resting on her bare left arm.

A small smile appeared on her lips, and she opened her eyes. "I love you... darling," she said using proper words, then she giggled.

Billy also smiled. "And I love you," he said softly, despite a lump in his throat.

His words sounded so inadequate for the way he was feeling, but at the same time, he hoped that her using it meant there might still be a spark in her absent mind.

Although the nurses and carers heard Billy using words and Rose sounds, when they were talking the two of them understood each other perfectly. Surprisingly, almost bizarrely, Billy could understand Rose's noises and translated them into real words.

One day after breakfast, Billy went to see Rose as usual, but she was fast asleep so he went for a walk down the corridor until he got to the lounge. He went in and sat in the nearest armchair.A grey-haired woman with a lined face and bare, scraggy arms walked up to him about five minutes later.

"You're in my chair," she said.

Billy pointed to the chair next to the one he was sitting in. "That one's as good," he replied.

"You're in my chair." The woman raised her voice. "That's *my* chair."

Nurse Ashish rushed over. "Come on, Billy. Let Edith have her chair now," she said, and took Billy's arm to help him stand.

The woman darted in behind him to sit in the chair before he could do anything about it.

Billy shrugged off Ashish's arm and wandered back to the corridor, back to Rose's room. She was still half asleep but smiled when he got to there. Music was playing on a radio in the corner: a smooth romantic song. For some reason, Billy asked if she wanted to dance—he didn't remember that she couldn't walk—but she refused by shaking her head. In a way it was ironic, although neither knew—they had first met at a dance.

Rose drifted back to sleep, so Billy just sat there wondering why she had turned him down. He sat with her, his memory trying to remember things.

They were dancing at the Saturday night club. She loved to dance and was gliding, but he was plodding a little clumsily (he would have loved to be Fred Astaire but was nearer Fred Flintstone), but they were happy in each other's arms.

There was shouting outside in the corridor, and Billy snapped back to the present. Rose was still in a deep sleep, so he went back to his own room puzzled by something that had happened. He couldn't remember what.

Neither of them could, of course, remember much—the dementia was too deeply embedded in both. Although they liked being together, neither knew the other but they both felt an emotion without knowing what it was. It was simply that each had fallen in love with the other in their two separate and private worlds.

Although they were married neither realised it, but there were flashes, as when Rose opened her eyes one day, peering closely at Billy, trying to see his face.

"I had a husband... Billy," she said in her strange noise language. Billy somehow understood.

"He doesn't come now. I think he must have died."

"That's a coincidence. Same name as me. But I'm not married," replied Billy. "Never found the right girl before... although there was one lass, Rose..."

Nurse Diana stood in the doorway and listened to the pair of them, tears starting to form in her eyes. She was experienced, hardened to suffering and tragedy, but things like this conversation still moved her.

She went into the room. "Are you comfortable in that chair?" she asked Rose.

Rose didn't answer.

"She seems quite comfortable. You always seem to take care of that," said Billy on her behalf.

"It's nice of you to say that..."

"As long as we're together."

"Bedom. Bang. Hazee-bad Ah-jay-jay-jay."

"I think we're going to get married soon," said Billy.

The nurse smiled. They were both happy.

Diana told the other nurses about it, and a few more tears were shed amongst them all. By the end of the day Rose and Billy had forgotten the conversation.

Their mysterious life and love moved on, and weeks later, Billy was sitting on an upright-backed chair on the left of Rose's recliner, slouched over her and reaching across her to hold her right hand. She had an inscrutable smile on her lips and knew there was someone with her, someone different to the carers and nurses who usually looked after her. She felt comfortable and at ease with this person.

"What's your name?" asked the stranger.

"Rose."

"That's a nice name. I always liked Eliza before." The was Rose's first name. "But I think I like Rose more."

"Arf-I'm-boon."

On an impulse, he leant across and bent down, leaning heavily on his stick, and kissed her cheek. She reached up and put her hand on his shoulder. A physical touch. An emotional feeling ran through them both. For a few seconds, they clung to each other.

He had been sitting by her side for half an hour holding her elbow when he got an ache in his leg. "I need to stretch my legs," he told Rose. "Let's go for a walk."

"Ong nun a. Not now."

"OK, I'll go alone, but I'll be back soon."

Billy stood up and walked out of the room into the corridor. He took three steps, then stopped, turned, and went back to Rose's room.

"I hope I wasn't too long," he said as he sat down and took hold of her elbow.

They sat looking blankly into space.

"I love you," Billy said suddenly out of nowhere.

"Ay-yak-ya-ya-a," replied Rose, and Billy understood.

Their love for each other engulfed them—a feeling they could not understand but was strong and made them one. Neither could remember ever having that feeling before.

Chapter 19

It was 14 February, Valentine's Day. At seven o'clock in the morning the nurses and carers swept through the ward smiling at each of the residents in turn as they quickly and efficiently opened curtains, propped them up, gave them cups of tea and pills, checked dressings and incontinence pads, administered antiseptic creams and the like.

Bogdan helped Billy out of bed, took him into his en suite bathroom, washed and shaved him, combed his hair (and thinning quiff) before dressing him in tracksuit trousers, shirt and thick woolly sweater and giving him a mug of tea.

"There you are, Billy. All set to see Rose now," he said as he tidied up after his exertions.

His tasks completed, Bogdan left and as he went out of the door Billy picked up his mug and took it next door to see Rose. She was already in her recliner chair.

Twenty minutes later, Aabha brought in a tray of breakfast porridge for Rose.

"Ah, you are here," she told Billy. "I see you have found Rose."

She went out, returning a few moments later with another breakfast tray: cornflakes for Billy this time.

Another normal day had begun at Peace Hall, but it was a new beginning for Rose and Billy.

Hours late, they were still sitting with each other, side by side in Rose's room nearing the end of their supper. Although Billy had wandered out a few times during the day, he spent most of the day with

Rose, mostly chatting away in her sounds language and both laughing and smiling a lot.

Ditya was feeding Rose a few sips of a fortified drink from her plastic mug, but Billy was managing a cup of tea on his own. He finished the drink, but as he watched Rose drinking he tried to put the cup down on her moveable flat-topped table, but he missed the edge and it fell to the floor. The handle broke off. A clean break.

Ditya bent to pick up the two pieces, and as she did so, a flash from somewhere deep in Billy's addled brain shot through him.

"Can you stick it together again?" he asked without any real comprehension of what he was saying. "We liked that cup."

Ditya looked at the pieces. "No," she replied. "It's finished."

A tear fell from Billy's eye.

She tidied up, and after Rose had finished her drink the carer chivvied Billy back to his own room, letting Rose stay in her chair a little longer. When she had settled Billy, she returned to hoist Rose into her bed.

Billy waited until Ditya and all other nurses and carers had disappeared before returning to Rose's room, where he pulled the chair across to her bed and sat holding her arm. She quickly fell asleep, but he stayed hand in hand with her for some time until, with Rose looking completely relaxed and with a slight smile on her lips, he started to feel a little tired himself. He stood up to go back to his own room, bent forwards for a goodnight kiss on her forehead, and thought she felt a wee bit cold, so he adjusted the bright blue satiny blanket round her shoulders and pulled another blanket over her legs and lower body.

Rose opened her eyes briefly. "I love you," she said, then instantly went back to sleep.

Billy smiled, then turned to leave her to go back to his own room.

Kiara was walking past the room to go to the lavatory and saw him stagger slightly and bang into the door frame as he left Rose and she took him back to his own room again.

On the way back, she looked in on Rose, and something didn't seem right, so she hurried back to call Nurse Kuwarjeet before finally going to the loo.

Kuwarjeet was worried, and phoned the local surgery and called the doctor urgently. He was still busy at his open surgery, full with nine patients still waiting to see him, and didn't get to the home for over an hour, and when he did his examination it didn't seem to show anything drastic—Rose was still asleep, although her breathing was shallow.

"Let's see how she is in the morning," he told Kuwarjeet.

With all the other residents also apparently asleep, the home went silent—just a few shouts and moans breaking into the night's silence. The nighttime nurses and carers occasionally walked round to check that all was well, but they didn't see Billy leave his room in a darkness broken only by a few dimmed lights in the corridor to make his way back to Rose's room. They didn't see him drag a chair across so he could sit by her bed holding her hand while she slept.

He was still holding her hand at four o'clock, then finally feeling tired himself, he prised his hand free from her claw-like grip, kissed her on the forehead as usual, and went out into the corridor.

"Love you," he muttered as he left.

Billy shuffled back to his own room, dropping his walking stick in the corridor, and sat in his armchair until two carers came to put him to bed an hour later.

Rose never woke up, and eleven months, three weeks and five days after Billy had joined her in the home, she died in her sleep at 4:27 in the morning. After a minor stroke the previous evening, she had suffered a second massive stroke and died instantly.

It was getting on for twelve years after she had first been diagnosed with Alzheimer's and Billy had been forced to do everything for her. The last actual words she spoke to Billy were, "I love you," completely in keeping with her pre-dementia peronality.

Every single member of staff at Peace Hall was sad and lamented Rose's death, and all felt tragic pity for Billy, although they somehow managed to carry on looking after the other residents professionally.

Because of his own dementia though, Billy did not grieve. He had said his own goodbyes every single day during those twelve years. If he had been aware, he would have liked the fact that her last words to him were those three little meaningful words.

Chapter 20

Billy couldn't grasp what was happening. It was the news he had been dreading every single day for many years before he too fell victim of the dreadful dementia and now that it had come he didn't realise. He never did receive the phone call he had dreaded daily for so long. The God, or fate, or power he had railed at for years at least spared him that.

With Rose dead, the door to her room was shut and locked, and Billy could not figure out why he couldn't visit his love. He sat outside her sealed room on a chair he dragged into the corridor for most of the next three days.

Then the door was unlocked and the room was empty, with no sheets, blankets or pillows on the bed at one side.

Big Beth took a day's holiday from her hospital to return to Peace Hall to collect Billy and take him to Rose's funeral, driving him to the crematorium in her own car, a small SEAT Ibiza. Billy sat in the passenger seat enjoying the scenery as they drove through the countryside, but he was disappointed when they got to a building where there were several people looking sombre but none of the sandwiches or cakes he had been expecting.

Beth led Billy into the building. Despite the pale sun outside, it was cold indoors but the lights were overly bright, there was music playing softly, and there were more people sitting in rows: manager Becky, receptionist Jenny, several of the home's nurses and carers, and handyman Kevin. Beth saw Billy to a seat at the right side of the front row, and as he sat he looked round.

There was a big box sitting on a dais at the front, and he wondered what was in it. Raspberry trifles perhaps? He liked raspberry trifles.

Billy didn't realise what was happening. There were all these people, a lot of singing, a lot of talking, a lot of jumbled sights and sounds. And there was that big box at the front. He didn't understand it at all. All he wanted to do was go home to Rose. His Rose. His love.

They played his haunting "anthem" and when Billy heard it he thought it was a nice tune, and they also played a song about rainbows and some chirpy melodies that Rose had enjoyed in her younger years that he vaguely recollected. But he couldn't really grasp what was going on and why so many strange, unknown people came up to him after the service to hug him, squeeze his hand or kiss him on the cheek.

All he wanted to do was to get back to his home, to sit once more with the beautiful Rose he loved so much.

The day after the funeral Ashish took a breakfast tray into Billy, sitting alone on a chair in his own room.

"Wan' go Ro?" Billy asked.

9 781805 415374